NO CONSENT

A CONNER & HITCH THRILLER

L.J. SELLERS
TERESA BURRELL

SILENT THUNDER PUBLISHING

NO CONSENT
A Conner & Hitch Thriller
Copyright 2021 by
Teresa Burrell and L.J. Sellers
All rights reserved.
Cover Art by Madeline Settle

Library of Congress Number: 2021918999
ISBN: 978-1-938680-40-3
Silent Thunder Publishing
San Diego

Acknowledgments

Beth Agejew
Melissa Ammons
Vickie Barrier
Denise Bowman
Meli White Cardullo
Janie Greene-Livingston
Joan Huston
Crystal Kamada
Sheila Krueger
Gwen Rhoads
MaryAnn Schaefer
Colleen Scott
Uma Van Roosenbeek
Barry Young
Denise Zendel

CHAPTER 1

May 18, Tuesday morning

The back door of the central jail opened, and Nate Conner tasted freedom for the first time in nine months. He turned to the guard and grinned. "Adiós." He resisted the urge to add an expletive under his breath and bolted into the San Diego sunshine. The warm salty air felt better than any drug, and he was almost giddy when he reached the sidewalk.

The sight of a familiar red Jeep crushed his mood. Seth Atkins stepped out, blocking his way. "Get in, Conner. We have unfinished business." With a body like a steel cable and a pug-dog face, Seth was intimidating.

Conner swallowed hard. "I'm done with you and your scams." He spun to walk away, but a big man blocked his path. Seth's sidekick and enforcer. Heart pounding, Conner turned back. "What do you want?"

"You gave me up and screwed me over for nearly two grand." The ugly man's mouth tried to smile. "First, I want to hurt you. Then you're gonna earn the money you owe."

Fear squeezed Conner's already queasy stomach. Seth had

also been convicted of the theft charge, but he'd somehow gotten out early. Conner tried to reason with him. "I never gave your name to the cops. Ever. I swear."

"But you told the snitch. That was just as stupid!"

Conner was mad at himself too. How could he have known the sleazy guy who reeked of booze was an informant? Sitting in that holding pen surrounded by thugs, pimps, and drug addicts had been a very bad moment. The detainee, a guy his age named Troy, had been mysteriously released the next day, then reappeared in court six weeks later to testify against him.

"It's not my fault!" Conner shouted. Fear made him sound panicked, and he hated himself.

"Shut your trap and get in the Jeep!" Seth lunged toward him.

Conner felt the muscle guy moving in too. *Take the beating like a man or run?* Conner bolted into the street, nearly getting hit by an SUV. The old guy braked, honked, and swore at him. Conner paused in the center of the busy street just long enough to avoid getting slammed by another vehicle, then sprinted to the sidewalk on the other side.

Instinctively, he ran west toward the freeway. He rounded the corner and heard a familiar voice call out, "Hey, Nater!"

Nicole! Relief washed over him as he turned toward the sweet sound. His older sister, in her funky van, was keeping pace with him, holding up traffic. *God, he loved her.* Conner climbed in. "Boy, am I glad to see you. Now gas it and go."

Her green eyes flashed with anger, but she pressed the accelerator. A moment later, she reached over and punched his arm—a surprising blow from a skinny ginger.

"What was that for?" Conner resisted the urge to rub the sore spot.

"For committing theft. For not coming to me if you were that broke and desperate." Nicole had visited him in jail, but apparently she'd been saving that shot in the arm.

"You already know how sorry I am." Conner waited for her to look at him. "Thank you for picking me up. I love you." A lump filled his throat. His younger sisters had each come to see him once, but Nicole was like a mother and had shown up faithfully. He was lucky to have a supportive family—and ashamed of what he'd put them through.

"Sorry I was late," Nicole said. "But don't think I'll ever go soft on you just because you're blond and baby-faced." His sisters all had shades of red hair and their mother's delicate features, but he looked like their dad.

Nicole took the eastbound freeway onramp. Conner assumed they were headed to her place in Lakeside, a five-acre property called Nico's Parrot Rescue, where she took in abandoned birds and grew her own vegetables.

"What did Seth want?" Nicole asked, sounding worried.

"To give me a beatdown, then pressure me to pay back the money he thinks I owe him." Conner had known the shopping cart full of expensive tools was stolen when Seth asked him to return them to Lowe's—despite Seth's lame story about where he got them. But at the time, Conner had been jobless, broke, and desperate. Seth had promised him half the money, and the whole thing seemed harmless. Sort of. But the scheme had fallen apart when the store issued a credit instead of cash.

"The jackass." Nico's grip on the wheel tightened. "You need to report Seth to the police."

"Are you kidding?" Conner slumped in his seat. "That's never gonna be an option for me. Once you have a record, the police consider you a criminal and don't care what happens to you."

After a long moment, Nicole patted his sore arm. "You'll be safe if you stay with me. I could use some help with the parrots."

He cringed. Cleaning up bird poop again. Right back

where he'd started. But at least he had a place to stay. "I appreciate what you do for me."

His sister was quiet for a few minutes, which was totally unlike her. "What's wrong?" he finally asked. "Besides me?"

She glanced at him with watery eyes. "Kaylee's missing. No one has seen her in months."

Oh no. Their baby sister had left home with a boyfriend at age fifteen, then circled in and out of their lives—and in and out of trouble—for years. "You called everyone?"

Nicole nodded, her face grim. "Friends, hospitals, jails, ex-boyfriends. No one has even gotten a text."

"I'll look around. I know some of her old hangouts."

"Thanks, Nater. And you can stay with me as long as you need to."

"I appreciate that."

But Nicole's place was only a temporary solution. She lived too far out in the sticks to be convenient for him to drive back and forth. And he had a lot to do—check in with his probation officer, find a job, and restart his life. Plus look for Kaylee.

He also had a burning—and admittedly stupid—need to get even with Troy the Tattletale *and* the bastard ADA, Ramsden, who'd demanded more jail time when Conner refused to testify against Seth. A waste of loyalty that had been. They'd convicted Seth anyway, and now Conner would be looking over his shoulder for the rest of his life—all for a lousy thousand bucks he'd never gotten his hands on.

Conner had a wild thought. *What if he could fix this?*

He suspected the informant had been planted, and if he could prove it, he might get his and Seth's convictions overturned. But how? Who could he trust to help him?

CHAPTER 2

That same morning

Her office door banged open, and Deputy District Attorney T. Clara Hitchens looked up. A balding young man with a goatee burst in.

"Where have you been?" she shouted, as she stood. "We're due in court in twenty minutes!"

Troy Burton smirked and sat down. "So I'm a little early then."

Jerk! "I set aside two hours yesterday to prepare you for this trial and you didn't show. Now you waltz in here late, with an attitude."

"You don't need to *prepare* me," he said through bad teeth. "This ain't my first rodeo. And you need my testimony, so don't get huffy."

True. Her case was weak without his testimony. She knew Faber had robbed the 7-Eleven store, but she couldn't prove it. Two months ago, she'd told her supervisor, Martin Ramsden, that she couldn't win and they should drop the case. A couple days later, they'd caught a break when the defendant admitted the crime to his cellmate, Troy Burton. She didn't like using snitches to prove cases, but without Burton's testimony, Faber would walk.

Hitch sat back down, hesitant to wrinkle her black HUGO BOSS wool skirt and cream silk blouse. Along with her red high heels, the ensemble was her lucky outfit that she wore the first day of each trial. She wondered if she was getting too old to wear stilettos, but they made her feel tall. She liked being able to look other attorneys directly in the eyes.

Her hearing was scheduled for nine o'clock, and it was already a quarter till. Ignoring Burton for the moment, she contacted the bailiff in Department 32 and asked him to call her when they were ready to start. She knew it could be as late as ten or eleven before the judge took the bench, which would give her a little more time with the witness. It was only a five-minute walk to the San Diego Superior Court, so if they left as soon as the bailiff called, no one would be kept waiting.

She took a micro-recorder out of her purse and set it on her desk. It was one of the few pieces of technology she'd mastered, mostly because it had been around as long as she had. A few months earlier, on her forty-fifth birthday, she'd bought a smart phone, but it was so loaded with options and icons that she felt intimidated by it. Consequently, she didn't use it for anything except phone calls.

Hitch pushed the red button on the device. "This is a recording of a pre-trial prep session with witness Troy Benjamin Burton in the case of the State versus John Faber." She looked up at her witness. "You understand that I'm recording this session?"

"Sure. Why not?"

"There are a couple of things you need to keep in mind when you testify." Hitch had given this speech so many times she did it without thinking. "First, when you're on the stand, you must tell the truth, but only answer the questions you're asked. Do not volunteer any extra information. Do you understand?"

Troy nodded.

"You'll need to answer verbally. Otherwise, the court reporter won't be able to record your responses, and it will annoy the judge if they have to keep reminding you. That's why we're practicing."

"Yeah, that's the reason." He rolled his eyes.

"What do you mean by that?"

"Just tell me what you want me to say, and I'll say it."

Good grief! "I want you to tell the truth."

"Right."

Hitch raised her voice again. "You're starting to annoy *me*, and I don't think you want to do that. Let's get started." She paused. "Do you know the defendant, John Faber?"

"I shared a cell with him."

"That was a yes-or-no question. Just answer what I ask. If I want more, I'll let you know. That will be especially crucial when the defense attorney questions you. The more you say, the more they can trip you up or make you sound not credible."

"I'll be convincing, don't you worry."

"I am worried. We've been here ten minutes already, and you still aren't getting it. Another thing. Don't answer the defense questions too quickly. Pause for just a second or two before you answer to give me time to object if I need to."

"Look, lady, I know how it's done. You'll get the information you need to hang this guy."

"You're a cocky little jerk, aren't you?"

"And you're an uptight pain in the butt."

Hitch started to respond but thought better of it. They were too short on time. She took a breath and started over. "Do you know the defendant, John Faber?"

"We've met."

"Where did you meet?"

"In county jail."

"When?"

"Two months ago. They put me in Faber's cell to get him to confess."

"What?" *He'd been planted?*

"Oh, that's right. I'm only supposed to answer the question. Two months ago."

"Who put you in the cell to get Faber to confess?"

"Never mind."

"Why didn't you say anything about that in your first statement?" Hitch wondered what he was angling for.

"I knew I wasn't supposed to."

"And now you're saying someone told you to try to get a confession from Faber?"

"Yeah. They offered me a get-out-of-jail free card if I got him to talk."

"Who made you that offer?"

"I don't know his name. He said he was with the DA's office and had the authority to get me a deal. All I had to do was get the guy to confess. So I did."

"And your charges were dropped?"

"Yeah, for lack of evidence." The witness gave a sly smile. "Imagine that."

"You do understand that if you don't testify, they can re-file them."

"Oh, I'll testify. And I'll say all the right stuff. Don't worry. I'm just yanking your chain because you guys are all a bunch of criminals too, yet you act like you're better than the rest of us."

Hitch's pulse ticked up a notch. She couldn't use his testimony if he'd been planted to obtain information from someone who already had an attorney. It violated the defendant's Sixth Amendment rights. "You can't lie in court about why you were in Faber's jail cell."

"Sure I can."

"No. You cannot. Not on one of my cases. I can't put you on the stand knowing you're going to perjure yourself. I could be disbarred."

"Then I want a new attorney."

Oh boy. "I'm not your attorney. I work for the State of California. You are my witness, not my client."

"Whatever." Burton stood. "Where's the toilet?"

"It's down the hall to your right. And please don't dawdle. The bailiff could call us at any time."

Burton walked out.

Hitch paced her office, not knowing what to do with the information. Perhaps she could talk with someone before she went to court. The problem was who to trust. She considered telling Eric Hallaway, the head investigator for her department, but he was a gung-ho ex-cop who she suspected of overreaching to obtain the evidence he needed for trial. He could even be the one who'd set this all up. She didn't really know any of the other DDAs in the office that well. She avoided socializing with people at work because she hated the drama. As a result, she didn't have any coworker friends she could confide in.

Hitch rewound the tape to listen to what Burton had said. When she heard herself say, *"You're a cocky little jerk, aren't you?"* she thought she might need to work on her people skills. But she was frustrated with these two-bit criminals getting away with so many crimes. The only thing that bothered her more was corruption in the justice system. She believed in the U.S. Constitution and in the system. She knew it had flaws, but when everyone used it correctly, it worked—most of the time. Now she faced the very thing she detested. She hoped there was only one loose cannon in the department, or better yet, that Burton was grandstanding.

When she heard a knock, Hitch stopped the recording. "Come in."

Victoria Wu was one of the newer attorneys in the office and one of the few Hitch had made time for. Victoria was young, brilliant, and a hard worker who kept her personal life out of the office. "I'm sorry to bother you, Hitch, but I have a conflict on a case this morning, and I need someone to cover it. Are you, by any chance, available?"

"Sorry. I have a trial in Department 32 this morning. I wish I could help."

"That's okay. I'll find someone." Victoria turned to leave.

"Wait, I'd like to——" Hitch stopped midsentence. She'd considered bouncing her dilemma off Victoria, but the attorney was too inexperienced. "Never mind. It's not important."

As soon as Victoria left, Hitch checked her watch. The bailiff could call any moment. She thought about seeking advice from her supervisor but immediately dismissed the idea. Ramsden was a busy man who would tell her to just win the case. Her only options were to go forward with the trial and let Burton perjure himself, or to proceed without her star witness and hope to convince the jury with the slim circumstantial evidence she possessed. She could try again to get the defendant to plead, but his attorney had been very adamant that Faber wasn't inclined. Even so, Hitch didn't feel right using the illegally obtained confession as leverage for a plea bargain.

She checked the time again. Burton had been gone nearly seven minutes. She wondered if he'd skipped out on her, and she felt a flash of relief. That would save her from having to make a decision, at least for now. And she had another trial starting Friday that was far more important.

CHAPTER 3

Tuesday evening

Nicole pulled up in front of the Beachside Boogie and handed Conner forty dollars. "For an Uber ride home. This is a one-time favor," she warned. "To celebrate your release. After this, I'll only give you rides to work or to see your PO."

"I know. Thanks, sis." As he kissed her cheek, a horn honked behind them. Conner scurried out. "I'll be home before midnight." He hurried across the parking lot and into the bar. With any luck, he could find a ride home and pocket the cash for future use. The seventy-eight dollars in his savings account wouldn't last long—if it was even still there. The bank had probably confiscated it for fees or whatever. That's how this whole episode had played out. His car had been impounded, and his girlfriend had dumped him.

Inside the dark cavernous room, electronic dance music pulsed, and a crush of young people bounced to the beat. Joy filled his body, and he grinned at strangers as he grooved his way across the main lounge. In jail, he'd missed music even more than sex. Conner laughed. Only because music was more

11

accessible. At the bar counter, he wedged in between two lovely ladies, both focused on someone else, and tried to get the bartender's attention. One beer, he promised himself, and he would sip it all evening.

A few minutes later, he worked his way toward the walled-off back room where karaoke contests were held most nights. He didn't plan to get on stage, but it could happen. He cruised the room, checking out the women, hoping to spot Kaylee. His little sister changed her hair color and fashion style regularly, so she could be easy to miss. Especially in a dark crowded bar. She was still a minor, but she'd had a fake ID for years, and her older friends hung out here.

When he didn't spot her, disappointment and worry threatened to kill his music buzz. *She might show up later,* he coached himself. And his search had just started. Kaylee was a wild card, so this could be a long frustrating process. Too bad patience wasn't a mode he'd ever gotten friendly with.

Conner found a small table in the back where a woman sat by herself. He gestured at the second chair. "Mind if I sit here for a minute?"

She looked startled. "Uh, yeah. Go ahead."

"Thanks. I'm Conner." The only people who called him Nate were family members.

"I'm Karen." She laughed. "But I'm thinking of changing that."

Conner smiled. She looked older than the rest of the crowd, but he'd started to really like female faces with character and eyes that had depth and empathy. He hoped it wasn't a mommy issue. "Don't worry. It's a nice name, and the whole meme stuff will pass."

As Conner sipped his beer, a familiar voice singing a favorite Stevie Wonder song filled the room. He pivoted toward the stage.

Darius!

Running into his old friend was another good reason to be here this evening. Conner sat back and enjoyed the performance. Darius was not only an excellent running back, he could sing! Near the end, Conner hurried up to the stage. Around him, the crowd clapped wildly and called for more, but Darius put the mic back on the stand and started for the platform steps. Conner intercepted him. "Hey, Big D. When did you get out?"

"Conner!" Darius pulled him in for a one-armed hug. "Good to see you, man." He stepped back. "They cut me loose two weeks ago. Overcrowding."

"Cool. You hangin' for a while?"

"Of course. I'm goin' to round two. Come sit with me and some friends."

Conner followed him to a larger table where two attractive women sipped cocktails. Darius always had an entourage, but never a serious girlfriend. His friend zipped through introductions, and Conner tried to make the names stick. Rona was the compact blonde, and the tall dark-haired woman was Celeste or Selene.

He had other things on his mind. "Hey, have you seen Kaylee in here?"

Darius shook his head. "Not since I've been out."

Not good.

"She's disappeared again?"

"Yeah. But she'll turn up. She always does."

The blonde leaned toward him. "I heard she relapsed."

Conner's heart landed in his stomach.

"No." Darius reached over and squeezed the woman's arm. "Don't say shit like that." He looked at Conner. "Don't listen to Rona. She likes to stir shit up."

She got up and walked away, and the other woman followed her.

Conner didn't want to think about his sister possibly using

heroin. He had plenty of other problems to work through. Like getting a job. "Hey, know anyone who wants to hire an ex-con for the tax break?"

Darius laughed. "Actually, I do. The Roadhouse restaurant. The owner is my uncle, and he only hires ex-cons. But you have to go to rehab meetings."

"I can do that." Conner felt better already. "I'm glad I ran into you."

"Yeah. I was hoping to see you." Darius leaned in close. "I thought you would want to know that the last week I was inside a dude named Troy bragged about ratting you out to the DA."

"I knew it!" A rush of anger surged in his chest. "I mean, not at the time, or I wouldn't have told him anything."

"I'm sure he's a plant." Darius shrugged. "Not that it matters now."

"But it does." Conner sighed. "I owe two grand plus interest to a thug named Seth."

"Don't look at me. I'm broke." Darius reached for his wallet. "But I'll buy you a beer."

CHAPTER 4

Wednesday morning

Conner hustled into the SD probation department, worked up with sweat and irritation. The system gave newly released inmates only twenty-four hours to check in. He'd spent most of yesterday cleaning parrot cages to earn his keep, and this morning he'd indulged himself by sleeping in for the first time in a year. Waking up and realizing he wasn't in jail had nearly brought him to tears, then he'd bounced around Nicole's house like a kid waiting for his birthday party to start.

As he jogged up the stairs, reality set in. He would be on a tight leash for a while—but he would survive. He intended to get it right this time, and that meant cutting ties with old friends. That was how he'd always veered off the path— running into an old friend, smoking a little weed, and getting caught up in whatever dumb thing they were up to. Not this time.

Conner laughed out loud. He would try anyway.

He reached the landing and swung widely to round the corner up to the next flight of stairs. And collided face first with someone. She staggered back and landed on a step, her briefcase hitting the floor with a soft thud.

"What the hell?" the woman bellowed. A surprisingly loud sound from a rather petite person.

"I'm so sorry." Conner reached out to help her up. *Was she the DA who'd given him a break years ago?* She'd cut her long auburn hair off at the shoulders but still had the same pretty face. "Ms. Hitchens?"

"Yep." She eyed him curiously, then quickly got to her feet without his help. "I hope you're staying out of trouble." She grabbed her briefcase and started around him.

"You remember me?"

"Of course. Nate Conner, pot smoker and petty thief."

Conner laughed. She was crusty and direct, but years ago she'd given him a break and offered him a diversion program to keep him out of jail. But he'd missed too many rehab meetings and blown it. *When would he quit screwing up?* "Sorry for knocking you down. I'm late to see my PO."

"Then get moving!" She walked away.

Conner stood, watching her. She was the one person in the DA's office he might be able to trust. "Ms. Hitchens?"

She stopped, sighed loudly, and turned around. "Yes?"

"I need your help."

"That's not in my job description."

"I know. But I was set up." *Ugh!* He sounded like every other ex-con. "I mean, I think the DA who prosecuted me planted a snitch in the holding pen."

Her dark eyes tightened to a squint. "Why would he do that? Unless you've become a career criminal."

"No." Conner shook his head, hating the label. "I just made one costly mistake by helping a guy named Seth Atkins. A DDA was after him, and now Seth's after me."

She stared at him for a long moment. "Which DDA?"

"Ramsden."

"What snitch?"

"A guy named Troy."

"Burton?"

"That's the one."

She swore under her breath, then dug a business card out of her shoulder bag. "Go see your PO, then call me to set up a meeting in my office."

"Thanks."

She waved him off and headed down the stairs. Conner grinned and bolted to the next level, feeling upbeat. The PO's door was open, so he stepped in.

"You're late!" Ray Stratten barked from behind his desk.

"I'm sorry. I stopped to be polite to DDA Hitchens on my way up." He hoped her name would be a positive association.

"Don't bullshit me. Now sit down and listen up." Stratten's bald forehead was an unhealthy translucent pink, and his body barely fit in his swivel chair.

Conner eased onto the plastic guest chair, dreading every minute he would spend in this closet-sized room. "Yes, sir."

"The fact that you waltzed in here at the last minute doesn't bode well for your success. So I don't plan to invest much time in you." The PO handed Conner a printout. "And I won't tolerate any deviations from the rules."

The list was two pages long. *Dear God, he'd never survive this for six months.*

"Your priority is to find a job. Any job. Then call and let me know where you're working." Stratten stared at Conner's chest. "And don't wear smart-ass t-shirts to our appointments. Or to job interviews."

Conner glanced down. *Stupid!* He'd worn his *Rulebreaker* t-shirt. It had been on top of the tub of clothes his sister had stored for him. "I'm sorry. I wasn't thinking."

"And that in a nutshell is your problem. I suggest you start. Right now."

While he waited for the bus, Conner pulled out the card Hitchens had given him and called the number. His cell phone had a cracked case and a limited data plan, but he was grateful for it. Nicole had held onto it, then paid for a couple of months of service right before he got out. His sister understood how vital the phone was for him to find work and stay in touch with his PO. Many inmates leaving incarceration had nothing—no money, no identification, no support. Restarting his life would be challenging even with all that. The odds against those without help were like a monkey's chance of breaking into a safe. *Why did he always think in terms of criminal activity? What in the heck was wrong with him?* He had to stop.

The attorney finally picked up his call. "Hitch here. Who's this?"

The nickname fit her. "Nate Conner. You said we could meet and talk about Troy, the guy who repeated what I thought was a private conversation."

"Oh, right. I have time now. How soon can you get here?"

"I can be there in ten minutes."

"Don't keep me waiting. I have court again this afternoon." She hung up.

He slid his phone into his pocket, thinking he really needed a car.

CHAPTER 5

Wednesday afternoon

Hitch heard a knock on her office door. Most of the attorneys were in cubicles, but she had enough seniority to merit her own office. It only had enough room for a medium-sized desk, two chairs, and a credenza, but the window let her watch what was going in the rest of the office—while being out of the mainstream traffic.

"Come in," she said without getting up. Nate Conner walked in, and she checked her watch. He was only two minutes late. "Have a seat."

"Thanks for seeing me. And I'm sorry about crashing into you." He sat in one of the gray fabric-covered chairs across from her.

Hitch was still embarrassed about the fall and didn't want to discuss it. She also had to keep glancing away from his face. Gorgeous men were distracting and could not be trusted. "Tell me why you think you were set up."

"You always did get right to the point." Conner grinned.

The kid probably thought he was charming. "That's because I'm busy. Just tell me."

"Troy bragged to another inmate that he was just in jail to do a job for Ramsden."

A jolt of surprise. "Did Troy name him?" Hitch picked up a pencil, stuck it into a small battery-operated sharpener, then jotted a note on a legal pad. "Did he actually say 'Ramsden'?"

"I'm pretty sure he said 'the DA,' but that's gotta be who he was talking about."

"A lot of people don't distinguish between Deputy DAs and the district attorney himself. They call them all DAs." *Which drove her a little crazy.* "How can you be sure he was talking about Ramsden?"

"Because Ramsden is a piece of work." Conner leaned forward. "This isn't the first time. Others say the same thing."

"Be careful. That's my boss you're talking about." The warning was for herself too.

"You're okay if he gets away with it?" The kid looked upset.

"I didn't say that, but I'm not going to accuse anyone of anything without more evidence—especially the guy who signs my paychecks."

"There's no doubt in my mind that Troy was there just to get my confession. He was released the next day." He crossed his arms. "Can you do something about Troy? And the fact that I was set up?"

"Troy Burton is an idiot. He doesn't know when to keep his mouth shut."

"So you know him?"

"We've met." She sighed. Conner's whole account was hearsay unless they could track down the other inmate. "Who was Burton bragging to?"

"Darius Williams. I've known him since high school. We

both went to Mt. Helix and played football together. He was one heck of a running back."

That was more information than she needed. "And you remained friends?" Hitch sharpened her pencil again and jotted down the name.

"Yeah. And I saw him last night at a karaoke bar. He's an even better singer than he is a running back." Conner smiled again.

She tried not to be annoyed. "That's when Darius told you about the conversation with Troy Burton?"

"Yeah."

"You said 'inmate,' so Darius was in jail?"

"Of course."

"And Troy talked to Darius while they were both inside?"

He nodded. "They shared a cell."

"What was Darius in jail for?"

"Possession."

Good. A minor issue. "What about the others you say were set up by a prosecutor? Do you have names?"

"I can get them," Conner said, suddenly fidgety. "Does that mean you'll do something about it?"

"I'm in a bad position here, but I'll look into it. You just get me any names you can." She paused. "And one more thing."

"What's that?"

"The ideal situation would be to have Burton work with us."

"Why would he even consider it? He'd have to have a real incentive to turn on Ramsden."

"Then we'll have to come up with one. Any chance you could get through to him?" She raised her eyebrows. "Without violating your probation?"

"I can try. But I don't even know where he is."

"I may be able to help you with that." *What was she getting into?* Hitch put her pencil into the sharpener again, feeling unsettled.

Conner laughed. "You must go through a lot of pencils."

"I like them sharp."

"Whatever blows your skirt up." The kid stood to leave. "I appreciate your help, Ms. Hitchens."

She almost told him to call her Hitch, but decided she didn't really want to get that familiar with him. "I haven't done anything yet."

"You listened, and you took me seriously. That's something. I really want out of this mess I've gotten myself into." He started for the door.

"Conner." She had to try.

He stopped and turned. "Yeah?"

"Are you still smoking pot?"

"It's legal now, right?" The kid laughed. "If they'd just make stealing legal, I'd be in good shape."

"Look, if you want my help—"

"Don't get your panties in a bunch." He paused and locked eyes with her, his tone serious. "The truth is, I'm clean and sober and done with anything sketchy. I'm trying to live a decent life."

CHAPTER 6

Thursday morning

Conner woke to the ungodly racket of parrots squawking. The birds were in a separate building, but when they were hungry, they were louder than a three-alarm fire bell. He rolled out of bed and hustled into the kitchen, determined to be productive. Nicole, who was probably headed out to the cages, had left some cold coffee. Conner poured it into a tall glass, added generous doses of milk and sugar, then heated it in the microwave. He would have squeezed in some chocolate syrup or ice cream if he'd found any.

He gulped down half of the sweet caffeine, then pulled a bagel from the bread drawer. He started to spread butter on it, then heard his mother's voice in his head reminding him to eat protein in the morning so he would be "smart in school." He stuffed the bagel with leftover chicken and washed it down with the rest of his lukewarm latte.

After a shower and shave, he found Nicole waiting for him in the kitchen. "Is that what you're wearing for your job interview?"

He glanced at his chest. Plain black today. "What's wrong with this?"

"Jeans and a t-shirt? That says rather loudly that you made no effort. Put on slacks and a button-up shirt."

Conner groaned. "I don't even know what slacks are."

"I bought you some. They're on your bed." Nicole smiled sweetly.

The abrupt shift scared him. "What?"

"If you dress properly, I'll let you borrow the Mustang."

His heart pulsed. "You're serious?" The Mustang had been their dad's car, and he'd nearly wrecked it as a teenager. Nicole hadn't let him drive it since.

"For now. So don't blow it."

Conner jumped up and down, hugged her hard, then went back to the guest room to change. He'd wear a pink fluffy skirt if it meant having his own transportation.

On the drive into town, his phone rang, so he glanced at the screen. Conner pulled off into a horse stable parking area and quickly answered it. He would buy an earpiece as soon as he had a chance. "Good morning, Ms. Hitchens."

"If you say so." He could hear paper shuffling sounds in the background. "I got access to a police file and have a few possibilities for where you might find Troy Burton."

"Great. Where?"

"His mother has a house in Lakeside." She rattled off the address.

"Just text me that, please. Then my phone can map the location."

"Uh." A long pause. "Okay. I think I can do that."

She'd never sent a text? "Where else do I look?"

"Troy's last listed employment was a place called Party

Time on Main Street in El Cajon." She cleared her throat. "I think it's an adult retail shop."

It certainly was. "Text me that address too." He looked up to see a woman in jeans and boots headed his way. "Is that it? I have to get moving."

"Yep. Good luck." The DDA hung up. Conner waved at the cowgirl and zipped back onto the road. He had a job interview starting in twenty-seven minutes and couldn't afford to be late.

The restaurant smelled like smoked meat and fryer grease, and Conner's stomach growled. He churned through food like a Hummer burned gas, and he hoped the owner would offer him something. But Wally didn't. The big black man sat him down in a crowded little office and grilled him.

"How will you get to work?"

"Can you wait tables? If not, you start as a dishwasher."

"How many NA meetings do you attend every week?"

"Are you gonna quit the first time I yell at you? Because I yell at everybody who screws up. And I know you're a screwup because you're here."

Somehow, Conner made it through without walking out or saying the wrong thing.

Wally finally nodded and said, "All right. I've got an opening on the schedule I'm working on. Can you start next week?"

"Sure. Thanks." Conner offered his hand, and Wally shook it.

"Two main rules. If you can't make it to work, find someone to cover your shift. No exceptions. And no swearing. I can't abide it."

"No problem. I had my mouth washed with soap as a kid, so I never developed the habit. At least not out loud."

"I like your mother already."

"She's dead. But I liked her too." Conner stood. "What time next week?"

"Wednesday afternoon at two. I'll start you on dinner prep."

"See you then." Conner hurried out before the man changed his mind.

The lot at Party Time was full, so Conner parked next door. *How many people were shopping for sex toys at eleven in the morning?* As he crossed the parking lot, nervousness set in. Troy had no motive to work with him, and Conner had no leverage. This was probably a waste of time.

The store's dark interior offered some privacy to its customers, but not much. He passed the lingerie racks and tried not to think about his last girlfriend. Sasha had been a blast, but she'd been unpredictable (aka, crazy) and had dumped him as soon as she realized there were no conjugal visits in jail.

Standing between him and the counter, a couple blocked the aisle while discussing a purple device the woman held.

"Let's get the rechargeable one," she said, nodding her half-shaved head. "I hate running out of battery power right before I climax."

"But it's thirty dollars more!" the man argued. "And you won't remember to plug it in."

They finally noticed they were in his way. Conner grinned at the guy. "Get her what she wants and keep it fully charged." He winked at the woman and stepped past them to the counter.

The clerk was heavyset but pretty in a Goth way. "How can I help you?"

"I'm looking for Troy Burton. I heard he worked here."

"Not anymore. The owner fired him last month. He kept stealing the edible panties."

Conner tried not to laugh. "Do you know where I might find him?"

"Try the pet grooming place on East Madison. They called last week and asked for a reference for Troy."

"And what did you say?"

"That he was dependable, sort of, but too attached to the products." She smiled slyly.

Conner chuckled and headed out.

The Pet Palace was only a few blocks away, so Conner headed straight over. He couldn't picture Troy cheerfully scrubbing down a big unruly dog, but people sometimes surprised him. The fact that Troy was willing to work at crummy jobs meant he was probably on parole. The jerk's inability to stay employed was not surprising.

The blocky building had huge front windows and looked like it had once been a laundromat. The interior brightness was welcome after the cave he'd just been inside. He spotted Troy, a skinny guy with a goatee, at a station on the sidewall. He was picking snarls out of a longhaired, mixed breed that was part Afghan. The dog's owner, a middle-aged woman with a permanent scowl, hovered nearby. At a small counter across the room, an older woman in a green work apron watched the two out of the corner of her eye as she stocked the shelves.

Conner stepped behind a rack of dog shampoos. He would wait until Troy had a better moment to talk. And he didn't want Troy to spot him and scoot out the back.

A moment later, the dog whimpered, and the customer shrieked, "Stop! You're hurting her."

Conner peeked around the rack.

"No, I'm not. She's just restless," Troy countered, his tone meek. "I could get Dolly wet. That would help."

"Not until she's untangled." The woman crossed her arms. "You're obviously new at this."

"Actually, I've been grooming animals since I was a kid. And getting her wet and soapy will make this whole process easier." Troy sounded irritated now.

That was more like the know-it-all he remembered.

The older woman walked over. "Sheila, dear, I'd like you to let him do his job."

Troy smirked and reached for the hose. As he turned on the water and aimed the nozzle at the dog's back, Sheila grabbed for it. "No!"

For a moment, they struggled for control. The water volume increased, and the hose went wild, soaking the customer. She shrieked again.

Rattled, Troy reached for the faucet and let go of the dog. It bolted, shaking water on Conner as it ran past. Sheila shouted nasty things at everyone in sight, then ran after the dog.

Conner pinched the skin on the back of his hand to keep from laughing.

"You handled that badly," the older women chided, reaching for a stack of towels.

Troy yanked off his apron. "Your customers suck. I quit." He stepped from behind the table.

Conner moved toward him, afraid the guy might run. "Hey, Troy. Can I talk to you for a minute?"

The ugly man stared hard. "What are you doin' here, Conner?"

"I need your help."

"Hard no. Whatever it is." Troy tried to brush past him.

Conner stepped in his path and spoke softly. "Don't you want to help bring down a corrupt DA? The lawyer I'm working with might be able to get you released from parole." Probably not true, but he had to offer him something.

Troy stopped and thought for a moment, then shook his head. "No. I've got a good thing goin' with Ramsden." He scoffed and gestured at his surroundings. "I do these gigs for a few days at a time just to keep my PO happy. And I've only got a few months left in purgatory. So get out of my way."

Conner didn't budge. "This is your chance to do something decent. To be a hero." *Boy, he was selling it hard.*

Troy made a harsh sound, like a duck choking. "No thanks. I know who has the power in this town." He put his hands on Conner's chest and shoved. As Conner stumbled backward, Troy hustled toward the door.

"You'll regret that!" Conner shouted, letting testosterone get the better of him. He had no idea what he'd meant by that. But now, the shop owner was glaring at him, so he nodded and left. He and Hitch would have to find another way.

CHAPTER 7

Thursday afternoon

Conner bolted out of the DMV as though the place were
about to explode. But it was his head that was on the verge of
combustion. He'd forgotten to take his meds, and the sensory
overload of a hundred people in a small room, combined with
sitting for an hour, had almost snapped him. But he'd gone the
distance and successfully renewed his driver's license, giving the
cops one less opportunity to escort him back to jail.

Back in the Mustang, which sweetheart Nicole had let him
drive again, he popped an Adderall and said *adiós* to a good
night's sleep—the price he paid for taking it too late in the day.
What he really wanted was a cannabis gummy that would
smooth the edges and mute the noise. But that wasn't an
option, at least until he was off probation. So he settled for
tacos from his favorite vendor, then headed home to spend the
afternoon with the birds, or whatever Nico needed from him.

After dinner and an hour of news with Nicole, he headed back out to the club. The crowd at Beachside Boogie spilled onto the patio, and the music thundered into the parking lot. He hustled inside and vowed not to spend a dime or have more than one drink. Most important, he hoped to find Rona to see if she knew more about Kaylee. He'd tried to find her after she left Darius' table Tuesday night, but she'd disappeared.

After a slow walk around the karaoke room, he spotted Rona at a table in the middle with the same girl from last night. Conner walked past, stopped, then turned back, acting surprised. "Hey! Rona, right?"

"Yeah. Hello." Her casual tone radiated indifference.

A challenge! Conner gave her an eight-point smile on the sexy scale. "Can I sit here for a minute?"

"Sure." She'd already warmed to him.

He pulled up a chair and turned to the second woman, "Hello again."

She looked him over, seeming to judge his casual clothes. "Are you here to sing?"

"Maybe."

"You might wait to decide." The woman stood, showing off her body in a tight red dress. "I'm the competition to beat tonight." She walked toward the stage, as the crowd clapped for the previous contestant.

"Do you sing?" Conner asked, hoping to engage Rona. He tried not to stare, but she was so pretty. Big eyes, pouty lips, and really white teeth.

"No. But all my friends do. And I like the vibe here."

"Especially on the dance floor." Conner gestured toward the bigger room.

"No. I'm not dancing with you." She laughed softly. "Not until I've had another drink or two."

"Well, let's get you one." He looked around for the cocktail waitress, hoping Rona would offer to pay.

He'd intended to wait until later to ask about his sister, but the question just popped out of his mouth. "You mentioned Kaylee had relapsed. Have you seen her?"

"Not recently. I heard that rumor from someone else." Rona glanced away. "She texts me every once in a while, but you know Kaylee. She pops in and out of people's lives."

"I need to know what *recently* means. Three months, three weeks, three days?"

"Maybe a month." Rona's expression shifted. "Why do you want to know? So you can get all judgmental about her lifestyle?"

"What lifestyle? You mean the partying? She's my little sister—" Conner had to stop and get control of his emotions. "I just want to know that she's all right. Maybe buy her lunch."

Music suddenly filled the room, followed by a powerful female voice. Rona leaned in close to be heard. "After Selene's song, you can ask her. She's the one with the crush."

But Selene didn't come back to the table, and Rona soon went to the restroom, then disappeared. Conner headed back to the main room to dance for a few minutes before heading home. An hour later, sweaty but grinning, he headed for the door. Out of the corner of his eye, he spotted Troy by the main bar. Conner hurried over.

"Hey, Troy. Good to see you again."

The guy looked up and groaned. "I have nothing to say to you."

"Come on. Hitch and I need your help."

Troy started backing away, like a man about to run. "Leave me alone." He spun and hurried toward the side door.

Conner started to follow, but a stranger grabbed his arm. "Don't be that guy."

Conner laughed, then pulled free and headed out.

CHAPTER 8

Friday morning

Hitch squared her shoulders and walked into court, ready to begin a trial that could set a precedent for sexual assault cases. They had exhausted all chances at a settlement, unless the defendant had a last-minute change of heart. His attorney, Luis Arroyo, didn't exactly have a reputation for being a reasonable guy, but he couldn't be bluffed or bought either. This time, his client had decided to fight, so she would too.

Hitch spotted Arroyo—stocky and dark-haired—in the back of the room and headed over. "Good morning, Luis. Has your client changed his mind yet?"

"He's not likely to, unless you're prepared to dismiss the case." He gave her a charming smile. "He'll take that deal."

"Not a chance."

"My client isn't guilty, Hitch, and I can prove that to the jury."

"We'll see." Hitch walked away, wanting to appear confident, but she knew this trial would come down to jury perception.

She had all the evidence she needed to make a case for the burglary charge and the petty theft. A witness had seen a car in the driveway that matched the make and model of the defendant's vehicle, and the victim's computer had been found in Jason Evans' apartment. Knowing all that, the defendant now admitted to being there—and more.

Proving the sexual assault charge would be tougher. The victim had seen the perpetrator, but he'd worn a mask and used a condom, so there was no physical evidence for the rape. However, Hitch didn't want to settle for just the burglary, and she hoped to make her case with the victim's testimony. Hitch also had an informant who claimed the defendant talked about the rape while in custody. But she didn't plan to call him if she didn't need to. After learning that Troy Burton had been a plant, she was leery of using any snitches.

The judge entered, and they all stood and put on their game faces. Barenski, a big man with silver hair, was her least favorite jurist. She hoped he wouldn't let his conservative tendencies steer the trial.

After opening statements, Hitch put on her first two witnesses, presenting an ironclad case of circumstantial evidence for the burglary. Yet Arroyo didn't seem the least bit disturbed by the testimony. Hitch started to feel nervous.

Just after twelve, she wrapped up her second witness, the police officer who'd found the stolen laptop.

"Did you ask Evans where the laptop came from?" Hitch asked.

"Yes."

"What did he tell you?"

"He said he bought it from Heather."

Unbelievable! "What else did he say about that?"

"Nothing. He wouldn't elaborate. But he was adamant he wasn't a thief."

Hitch decided to let it go.

Arroyo did very little cross on the officer except to establish a timeline.

Hitch had only the victim left to question, which she estimated would take at least an hour. The judge didn't want to start another witness, so he dismissed the jury and set the trial over until Tuesday morning. Hitch gathered her files and left the courtroom. In the hall, her phone rang and she checked the ID. *Jake Nelson!* Her heart fluttered a little, then her brain kicked in. He was a cheat who'd broken her heart. And this was likely business related. "Hello, Nelson."

"Hitch. Thanks for answering."

"What do you want?"

"A second chance."

He wasn't giving up. "I'm in court. If this doesn't involve a case, I have to—"

"I'm at a homicide scene, and the victim has your business card in his pocket."

Conner? She was surprised by how much the thought bothered her. "Who's the victim?"

"Troy Burton."

Oh no. "Where's the scene?"

"In the alley behind Beachside Boogie. He was stabbed."

Was that the club Conner had mentioned? "I'm coming down." She hung up before he could say no.

She had to argue her way past a uniformed officer blocking the sidewalk, but she was a professional at the sport, and he quickly gave in. A minute later, she spotted Nelson with two other detectives in the middle of the block-long alley. They all turned at the sound of her footsteps.

35

Nelson hurried toward her, his emerald eyes lighting up. Hitch sucked in a breath. His face was a chiseled work of art, and that smile … *No!* He was an off-limits colleague now.

"I'm not sure you want to see this." *He stopped so close she could smell coffee on his breath.* "There's a lot of blood."

She stepped back from his physical presence. "I've been to a few crime scenes."

"Then let's do it. The technicians will be here soon, then we'll have to clear out."

He pulled paper booties from his satchel and handed them to her. Hitch pulled them on, glad she'd changed out of her heels in the car. "Any idea when he died?"

"He hasn't cooled much, so I'd say sometime after midnight. But the medical examiner will narrow that down."

"Who discovered the body?"

"A prep cook from a nearby restaurant." Nelson pointed at a green door farther along the alley. "Porky's. Have you eaten there? Amazing omelets."

Hitch fought the urge to roll her eyes. "Just show me."

Nelson led her past a dumpster next to a grungy back door. The body lay beyond, snugged up against the building's back wall, as though trying to get warm. Nelson hadn't exaggerated the amount of blood.

"Is there a weapon?"

"I pulled a knife from his chest. He was stabbed repeatedly by someone with a lot of strength."

"Maybe someone Burton had snitched on. Most criminals take that personally." *Oh hell.* That could include Conner. "Any leads?"

"Not yet." Nelson reached into his satchel again and held out a clear-plastic evidence bag. Inside was a bloody oversized pocketknife. "But see those initials?" He pointed to an ornate engraving she couldn't read. "There's also a partial fingerprint.

We plan to interview everyone Burton contacted in the last twenty-four hours. We'll find our killer shortly."

"Can you keep me informed?" Hitch asked, ready to leave.

"How about over drinks?"

A bad idea. But she wanted to keep it friendly, in case Nelson had information she needed. "We'll see."

CHAPTER 9

Friday evening

Excited, yet filled with dread, Conner drove into town. Wally had called earlier and asked him to come in for a shift at the restaurant. The dishwasher hadn't shown up, and the owner didn't feel like covering the position himself. So Conner was about to spend four hours in a small, humid room scraping food and running racks of plates through a noisy machine. But it was a paycheck, and now that he was working, his PO would chill and leave him alone.

He parked in a lot across the street, as Wally had instructed, and hurried in the back door. Another employee—a scary dude with neck tattoos—threw a rubber apron at him and pointed toward a narrow tile space along the back wall. "I'll get you clocked in. You start cranking loads. We're already slammed."

Across the kitchen, a swinging door opened, and the noise from the dining room overwhelmed him. Thankfully, he'd taken his meds.

"What are you waiting for?" Tattoo Guy snapped. "Wally said you had experience."

"Yeah. I got this." Conner put on the apron as he hustled to his work area. After stuffing in earplugs, he pulled on rubber gloves and reached for a scraper. He pushed aside his revulsion and shame and nodded to himself. His mother would have been pleased that he was once again a "productive member of society."

An hour later, he wanted to run from the building. But he wouldn't even get a break. Dinner shifts in restaurants were endurance contests.

"Conner!" someone yelled over the roar of the dishwasher.

He turned and saw the neck-tattoo guy standing nearby with a man in a gray suit. *Oh no.* Everything about the dude said *cop*. Conner took a deep breath and stepped away from the noisy machine.

"Let's go outside." Suit-guy gestured for him to follow.

Conner pulled off his apron and tried to tell himself it would be okay. He hadn't done anything wrong this time, but still, he was questioned by a cop during his first shift. He could kiss this job goodbye.

As they stepped out into the back parking lot, the sun was dropping in the sky, giving the horizon a pink glow. Conner had a bad moment, thinking it might be his last sunset.

"I'm Detective Nelson." The man didn't smile—but still looked like a movie star.

"Nate Conner."

"Yeah, I know. Where were you last night?"

A somersault in his gut. "At Beachside Boogie. Why?"

"What time did you leave?"

"Uh, around ten-thirty. I think."

"Did anyone see you leave?"

"I don't know. What's this about?"

"Troy Burton is dead. And I'd like to continue this conversation at the department."

An hour later, he sat at a small metal table in a windowless room. The detective had supposedly gone to get sodas, but Conner had been through this routine before. The point of leaving him alone was to make him anxious. And it was working. He rubbed his wrists. At least Nelson had taken off the cuffs.

Conner tried to swallow, but his throat was dry. If Troy was dead, this was a murder investigation. Maybe they were questioning anyone who'd talked to the victim in the last few days. Did he need a lawyer? Hitch was the only one he knew well enough to call, but she didn't seem to like him much. Besides, she was a prosecutor who played for the other team.

The detective stepped back into the room and sat down with two cans of Pepsi. "This interview is being recorded, so state your full name please."

Conner glanced at the tiny camera lens above the door. "Nathan Allan Conner."

"Detective Jake Nelson, San Diego Police Department." Nelson pushed a soda toward Conner. "Wet your throat. We'll be here a while."

"Why me? I barely knew Troy."

"But you threatened him at his place of employment yesterday."

"What? No, I didn't."

The detective glanced down at his notes. "According to the owner, you yelled, 'You'll regret that!'"

A chill in his armpits. "I didn't mean anything by it. Really."

Nelson leaned back, a man with all the time in the world.

"Tell me about the conversation. What would Troy Burton regret?"

Oh boy. Could he tell this cop about Troy being a snitch for Ramsden? About wanting to take the deputy district attorney down? Nelson might run straight to the top at the DA's office. Conner sipped the soda. He would play this down the middle. "Troy was in a holding cell with me last year, then worked with the prosecutors." *Crap on a stick! Why had he said that?* Criminals often killed those who ratted on them. "But it wasn't a big deal," Conner quickly added. "They would have convicted me anyway." *Time to throw someone else under the bus.* "But Troy probably gave up Seth Atkins, the guy who actually stole the tools. And Seth has a history of violence. I've never hurt anybody."

The detective leaned in now, his voice intimidating. "But you threatened Troy. Why?"

"Uh, I just wanted him to be honest with me about the whole thing." The scene at the pet wash came back to him, and Conner seized on an idea like a drowning man grabbing anything that floated. "Troy had just walked off his job. I meant he would regret that."

"Was that the last time you saw him?"

Conner really wished it was. "No. I spotted him at the Beachside Boogie club last night."

"Did you talk to him?"

"I said hello, but he was headed out."

"What time was that?" The detective seemed bored now, like none of it really mattered.

"Right before I left. So around ten-thirty."

"Did you follow him outside?"

He had stupidly tried to. "Nope. Troy went out a side door. I was parked across the street, so I left out the front."

"Then what?"

Had he done anything else? "I got in my car and went home."

"I think you went around to the back of the building and intercepted Troy."

"No. I did not." Panic filled his gut, but Conner tried to sound calm. "Look, Troy was a snitch. I'm sure a lot of people had grudges against him. Like Seth Atkins, the thief I mentioned earlier."

"But you confronted him twice on the day he died."

Such bad timing! "I wouldn't call either of those moments a confrontation. I'm not like that."

Nelson pulled a leather satchel up to the table, reached inside, and removed a plastic bag. Inside was a large pocketknife covered in dried blood. He recognized the engraved initials immediately.

Stomach acid rose into Conner's throat. When he'd been arrested a year ago, the jail attendant had taken his knife, along with all his other possessions. The morning of his release, the knife had not been inside the plastic bag with his wallet and phone.

"Is this yours?" The detective's voice was scary soft.

Conner started to shake. He was so screwed. "I'd like to call a lawyer."

"Do you know an attorney who will come down here right now?" Nelson openly mocked him. "At ten o'clock on a Friday night?"

"I think I might."

"Then you can call him from the jail."

CHAPTER 10

A few hours earlier

Hitch finished dinner, cleaned up the kitchen, and went out back to relax. She loved her oversized yard. When she'd bought the place ten years earlier, it had been mostly dirt with a huge magnolia tree in the middle, and every year since, she'd improved it. The first year, she'd put in grass, then added a pond with a little waterfall in the corner. Eventually, she'd surrounded the feature with palms, palmera plants, and solar lights.

She'd hired someone to pour an ornate sidewalk leading to the pond, but she'd planted everything herself. Bougainvilleas lined the wood fence, filling it with bright pink flowers. Over the years, she'd added fruit trees—apricot, tangerine, persimmon, lemon, lime, fig, and avocado. Once she'd filled the yard, she'd lined the deck around the firepit with potted geraniums, creeping Charlie, and birds of paradise. Across from the patio, a large bamboo overhang provided shade for her grill island. Now that she was done, she missed the projects. But the yard was her sanctuary, the place she went to think and unwind and listen to country music on the radio.

Hitch walked out to the pond, turned on the pump, and sat down on the white, wrought-iron bench. She loved the sound of the waterfall as it hit the rocks. She stared into the water that once held colorful koi—until the herons came and helped themselves. She missed the fish, but replacing them would just create another feeding frenzy. And she had bigger problems than koi right now. Someone in the DA's office was abusing its power, and she hated when the court system violated citizens' fundamental rights. She'd entered this profession to protect people, not hurt them. She'd seen her peers cut corners before, but nothing like this. Planting informants was an outright injustice, and she burned with outrage. But what to do about it? Was this guy, Conner, the one to help her dig out the rot? He was young and cocky, and she wasn't sure she could trust him, but what else did she have?

Ten minutes of solace in her backyard and she decided what she needed to do. She would work with Nate Conner, play it cautiously, and see where it led. Who was she kidding? There was no cautious way to play this. If she started the investigation, she had to be all in. But would Conner?

Hitch felt a chill, checked her watch, and was surprised at how late it was. As she headed inside, her phone rang. A robotic voice announced that the call was from the county jail. Her first reaction was to hang up, but then she heard Conner's name. "I'll accept the charges," she said, thinking she should've gone with her first instinct. Conner came on the line and tried to thank her, but she cut in. "Why are you in custody? And before you tell me anything, remember, I could be assigned your case."

"Then you'll have to recuse yourself," Conner said. "I need your help."

"What have you done this time?"

"Nothing."

"I've heard that before."

"Seriously. They're holding me on a bogus trespassing charge, which kicks in a probation violation."

"What did you do?"

"Why are you so quick to think I'm guilty of something?"

"Really?" Her sarcasm was evident.

"Okay. I've screwed up before, but not this time." A long pause. "They're trying to pin a murder rap on me."

She'd suspected this was coming, yet dread squeezed her jaded heart. "Troy Burton?"

"Yes. How did you know?"

"I saw the crime scene. Did you kill him?"

"No! I told you I didn't."

She believed him—even though she knew she shouldn't. And if Burton's death was connected to the corruption in the DA's office, she had to get involved. "You know you're stuck in jail until Monday morning. They won't arraign you over the weekend. I'll see what I can do for you then."

"I know the drill."

"And, Conner, don't talk to anyone, even someone in your cell—especially someone in your cell."

"Don't worry. I've learned that lesson."

CHAPTER 11

Sunday afternoon

Conner stood in line waiting to use the phone in the jail's common area. He'd earned the privilege by volunteering in the kitchen, his old turf. The chef—if you could call someone who served hamburger and potatoes in a dozen variations a chef—knew Conner and liked him. During his earlier stint, Conner had spent three hours a day baking industrial batches of muffins and cookies. He'd considered working at a bakery when he was released, but the shifts were insane. Starting work at four in the morning was just not compatible with his nature.

The dude ahead of him swore loudly at the woman he'd been talking to and slammed down the phone. Instinctively, Conner stepped back. He was arm's length away from an angry man. He'd learned that the hard way too. He picked up the scuffed and sticky wall phone and stared at it, dreading the conversation. He hadn't been home or talked to Nicole since Friday morning, and she was probably worried out of her mind. Hearing from him now wouldn't do much to improve her spirits. Conner took a deep breath and made the call.

Nicole picked up immediately. "Nate! Thank goodness you're okay." Her tone changed just as quickly. "Where the hell have you been?"

"In jail. But don't stress. I didn't violate my probation." He paused. "Or kill anybody."

"What?"

"The guy who ratted on me, Troy? Someone stabbed him. To death. So of course the cops questioned me." He wouldn't mention the knife yet.

"Please tell me you have an alibi."

"Not exactly. But I do have a lawyer on my side."

"Who? And what does that mean?"

"Clara Hitchens, a prosecutor, but we're working together to find out which DDA planted Troy next to me in jail."

"Are you crazy? You can't trust anyone connected to the police. Not with your criminal record.

"I can't afford a defense lawyer, and who knows who I'll get for a public defender. If I get a lousy one, he or she'll push me to plead."

"Oh, Nate." Nicole sighed, then burst into sobs. But she quickly got control. "Sorry. But I'd hoped your troubles were over." She shifted into taking-care-of-business mode. "We can sell the Mustang if you need a good attorney. That will cover a down payment anyway."

The thought devastated him. "It's all I have of Dad." His father had been wonderful ... until he wasn't.

"I know. But it's just a car. And I can't lose you to a long prison sentence. My heart can't take it."

"You won't. I didn't kill Troy, and Hitch and I plan to figure out who did."

"Be careful, please. I'm afraid you'll just get into deeper trouble."

"I'll be fine." *How many times had he told her that?* He didn't believe it anymore either.

"Keep me posted, please. And let me know if I can help."

"I have an arraignment in the morning if you want to be there to vouch for me."

"Of course I will."

"Thanks." Conner hung up before she started crying again. Or the guy behind him ripped the phone out of his hand.

Conner turned and ran into a dude he knew from his last stay. "Beaker! You're back."

"You too, man."

"Just a BS probation violation. I'll be out Monday." He hoped. "What about you?"

Beaker shrugged. "I relapsed and stole a lady's purse, and it had a little dog in it. The stupid thing bit me and drew blood, so they matched my DNA, and here I am."

"Bummer."

"Move along," a guard yelled.

On the way back to the dorm, Conner asked Beaker, without any expectation, "Do you know a girl named Kaylee Conner?"

"Your sister?"

"Yeah."

"No, but I've heard her name. Why you asking?"

"She's missing."

"Well, hell." Beaker stopped, as if he'd just remembered something. "My homie lived with her last year."

"Where?"

"Over on Spring Street." He rattled off an address.

Conner committed it to memory. He hated not having his phone. "What's his name?"

"Jay. Tell him I sent you. He'll hook you up with some kick-ass weed."

Conner laughed. "Thanks. I'll look him up."

CHAPTER 12

Monday morning

Hitch arrived at court and went directly to Department 30 where they held felony arraignments. The hall was already starting to fill with people waiting to get inside. Once they opened the doors, the room would be packed.

"Good morning, Steve," Hitch said to the bailiff.

"You're looking lovely today, Hitch." He pushed open a door and let her inside.

Near the front of the courtroom, seven attorneys milled around, six of them male. Law was still a man's world, but she liked that she helped shift the balance a little. Hitch searched the group for Jerry Leahy, a defense attorney. He'd represented Conner previously and had been frustrated when he lost the case. Hitch didn't blame him. After reading through the old file, she was convinced Leahy had done all he could. If it hadn't have been for Troy Burton's testimony, Leahy would have likely won the case. She didn't know the attorney that well, but his reputation was hardcore defense. When a case was a slam dunk for the prosecutor, many defense lawyers just wanted to make a deal, get paid, and go home—so they talked their clients into taking whatever the prosecutor offered. Leahy was different. He would tell his clients what he thought about the offer, but he never tried to convince them to enter a plea. Hitch once heard him say, *"I'm going home to my family no matter the outcome. The decision to fight or not has to be yours."*

Still, he was easy to work with, even though he was on the other side. She believed she could trust him with her suspicions about the corruption in the DA's office. He would do what was best for his client, and he would fight hard.

When she didn't see Leahy, Hitch left the courtroom and headed down the hall toward the escalator. He would eventually show up. She had checked the court calendar, and he had two arraignments this morning. As she stepped off the escalator, she noticed a young woman staring at her.

"Are you Ms. Hitchens?" The redhead moved toward her.

"Yes. And you are?"

"I'm Nicole, Conner's sister."

They had the same stunning green eyes, but that was the only resemblance. Hitch led her to a bench near a window, and they sat down. "I'm glad you're here. It will help get Conner released if he has a place to live. You are willing to take him back, right?"

"Of course. But what is going on?"

"He's charged with trespassing and violating his probation, but I think they're after him for something else."

"What exactly?"

"Your brother can tell you. It's not really my place."

Nicole suddenly scowled. "I don't understand. You're with the DA's office. Why do you want to help my brother?"

"Because I believe him, and I think he's getting railroaded."

"You're going to represent him?"

"I can't do that. In fact, I have to be careful not to get too involved."

"But he can't afford an attorney."

Hitch looked up and got a glimpse of Jerry Leahy stepping off the elevator. "I have an idea," Hitch said. "I see someone who might be able to help. He's the best around. Wait here."

Hitch stood and walked toward the elevator that had just unloaded half a dozen people.

"Mr. Leahy," Hitch said, "may I talk to you a minute?"

"Sure. But call me Jerry." Thin, with dark hair, he had a pleasant Irish face and a sweet smile.

Hitch briefly explained the situation, including her belief that the informant in Conner's earlier case had been planted and that they were now trying to railroad him for Burton's death.

"How well do you know Conner?" He seemed a little skeptical.

"Not well."

"But you believe him?"

"I believe there's corruption in our office. This isn't the only case with a last-minute jailhouse confession that benefits my supervisor."

"That's quite a limb you're going out on."

"I know." Hitch paused. "Can I count on your help?"

Leahy nodded. They walked to where Nicole was waiting, and Hitch introduced them.

"I'm going inside," Leahy said. "I'll let the court know I'm willing to take Conner's case and see if I can get appointed."

"Will the judge appoint you?" Nicole looked hopeful.

"Your brother doesn't have any money, so she'll have to appoint someone. It's likely to be me since I already have a relationship with him."

Hitch patted Leahy's arm. "We need Conner on the outside if we hope to prove any of this."

"That shouldn't be a problem with these charges. They don't really have much on him, and the jails are overcrowded."

After he left, Hitch turned to Nicole. "Go ahead without me. I can't be seen with you or thought to be connected to your brother. Nothing personal."

Hitch waited until the courtroom filled, then went inside. She didn't want to talk to any attorneys who might question why she was there, so she stood in the back. Her eyes were immediately drawn to a broad-shouldered man standing with the prosecutor. *Why was Jake Nelson here?* Detectives rarely attended hearings. She scanned the rest of the room. To the left, six prisoners sat on a bench behind a plexiglass partition, all chained together. Conner was on the end. A moment later, she spotted Leahy chatting with the public defender, who looked happy to get a case off her load.

When Conner's case was called, Leahy asked to be appointed, and the judge, a reasonable woman named Helen Mayfield, granted the request.

Leahy stepped up to the podium. "Your Honor, my client has been charged with a minor offense, and had it not been for his probation, he wouldn't be here. I ask that you release him on his own recognizance. Nate Conner works part time for his sister at her parrot sanctuary to pay for his room and board, and he has already procured a second job at a restaurant. In fact, he was working when he was arrested. His sister is here in the courtroom and ready to take him home with her."

At the other podium, Nelson tapped the young DDA on the shoulder. Fisher quickly spoke and ineptly argued, "We're concerned about the company Mr. Conner is keeping and his involvement in other crimes."

Leahy looked like he was about to speak, then stopped, apparently reading the judge far better than the prosecutor had.

"Do you have other charges to file?" Mayfield asked.

"Not at this time, Your Honor, but he is a person of interest."

"I suggest you either file the charges or deal with the case before us, Counselor." She looked over her glasses. "Do you have a *good* reason why this young man should not be released on his own recognizance?"

"He's only been out of custody for less than a week, and he's already having trouble with the law." The DDA's voice lacked confidence. "He's a flight risk, and he shouldn't be released without bail. He's been hanging out at a karaoke bar."

"A karaoke bar?" The judge's sarcasm was apparent. "Is that in and of itself a violation of his probation?"

"No, Your Honor, but ... "

"Mr. Conner," the judge said, turning to Nate. "I assume your employer wasn't happy when you were arrested. Do you think you can get your job back?"

Conner, who'd remained standing throughout his arraignment, said, "I'll sure try, Your Honor."

"Mr. Conner is released on his own recognizance." Mayfield ordered him not to violate his probation conditions, set a hearing date, and moved on to the next case.

Hitch watched Nelson get up and hurry toward the exit. He apparently had only been there for Conner's arraignment. *Either this case was important to Nelson or to someone who was pressuring him to keep an eye on it.* Hitch held her breath for a second, hoping he wouldn't see her, then realized how foolish that was. When Nelson was almost to the door, he caught her eye, smiled, and winked.

CHAPTER 13

An hour later

Hitch got out of her dark-green Mazda Miata. She'd only had the car for a few months, and she already hated it. It was so small. *What had she been thinking, getting a sports car?* She had decided when her two-year lease was up, the car would be history.

She walked up to the gate at Nico's Parrot Sanctuary. She'd never been there and didn't even know it existed until Conner told her about it. She didn't want to meet him in public and thought she could get a better feel for him as a person if she met him on his turf. But the noise made her question her judgment. The sound of a hundred squawking birds overwhelmed her, and the cacophony emanated from a zoo-like exhibit to the left. The ventilated building was connected to a large outdoor wire enclosure, and a few colorful birds roosted in the trees. But the rest were obviously inside, most likely in cages. Hitch didn't want to find out. With the exception of hummingbirds, she wasn't crazy about the creatures. She loved to watch them soar through the sky, but up close and personal, she could do without.

A ranch-style home sat a hundred yards to the right—not far enough to escape the noise. Between the buildings, a flagstone path was bordered by white gravel and ceramic pots planted with a variety of cactus. Loathsome landscaping! But cheap and drought-resistant.

Hitch reached for her phone to call Conner and instruct him to meet her elsewhere, but he stepped out of the parrot enclosure and headed toward her. Looking around, she called, "Maybe it would be better if we go to the cafe up the road."

"I know it seems noisy, but you get used to it." He gestured at her. "Come with me."

Hitch's phone rang. She knew by the tone it was Nelson. She needed to change that, but she didn't know how. Nelson had set it up so when he called, she heard George Strait claim his unconditional love for her. *If only.* She declined the call.

Conner led her between the house and the aviary, then up a small grassy hill to a big rock that formed a natural bench. On the walk up, she wished she'd changed her shoes, but the partial view of the valley pushed the thought out of her mind.

"This is nice," she said, surprised. "How did Nicole come by this sanctuary? It seems like an odd thing to have here in Lakeside."

"My mother started it." Grief washed over Conner's face for a moment. "I did actually. When I was ten, I found an injured cockatoo that someone had abandoned and brought it home. Mom and I nursed it back to health, then decided little Petey needed a companion." Conner smiled at the memory. "My sisters got jealous and wanted birds too, so Mom converted the back porch into an enclosed room, and we ended up with some parrots and macaws. I lost interest, but Mom and Nicole went all in. They joined online groups and learned everything they could about feeding and rehabilitating tropical birds. Soon people started bringing us wounded and unwanted birds to take care of, and Mom formed a nonprofit. Then she applied for some kind of grant and built the sanctuary. Now Nicole runs it."

"What happened to your mom?" Hitch asked, then wished she hadn't.

"I can't talk about it." Conner looked away. "Let's discuss my case."

"We should wait until your attorney gets here. And before you say too much, I want you to know that I don't believe you killed Troy Burton. But if I discover you did, I will not protect you. I will not help a murderer, and I'm not putting my license on the line for one."

"I didn't kill anyone," Conner pleaded.

"I believe that or I wouldn't be here. I want justice, and I want the corruption in the DA's office stopped."

"I don't know why you believe me. I'm not sure I would if I were in your shoes, but I appreciate your trust."

Hitch glanced at her dusty black pumps. "Don't ever violate it."

"There's my lawyer now." Conner stood and waved, directing him up the hill.

When Leahy reached them, Hitch shifted closer to Conner, making room for Leahy to sit down, but he remained on his feet.

"Thanks, but it feels good to stand. Although it's a bit warm out here."

She missed the ocean breeze too. "I was just telling Conner that I believe he's innocent—or at least that he didn't kill Troy Burton."

"How do we prove it?" Conner asked.

"We don't have to prove it," Leahy said. "The prosecution has to prove you did."

"They can't, because I didn't."

"You're right. All they really have to do is convince twelve jurors that you did."

"Enough of that," Hitch said. "We know you're a suspect in Burton's murder because he snitched on you, but what else do they have?"

"A detective named Nelson questioned me. Do you know him?"

"Oh yeah, I know him."

Leahy gave her a look.

"You said that like it's a problem." Conner looked worried. "Is he sketchy?"

"Nothing like that. He's a little gung ho, but he's a straight shooter."

"But you don't like him?"

"Let's just say we've been on better terms." Hitch took a breath and moved on. "You're stalling, Conner. Just tell me what evidence they have or think they have."

"I talked to Troy twice the day he died. Once at the Pet Palace where he worked and again that night at the club. Nelson claims a witness heard me threaten Troy, but I didn't actually." Conner shifted nervously beside her. "He had shoved me, and I told him he'd regret it."

"What else?"

"The knife used to kill him is probably mine. I had it on me when I was arrested, along with my wallet and phone. When I was released, the knife wasn't in the plastic bag."

This was a problem. "Did you ask for it?"

"Of course, it was my grandfather's. But they denied any record of it." Conner paused. "That's pretty damaging, isn't it?" He looked up at Leahy.

"It certainly doesn't look good, but if they had a fingerprint match from it, the DA would've already charged you with murder." Leahy sighed. "That doesn't mean you're out of the woods. They'll run a DNA analysis, and more than likely they'll find yours."

"That's not good."

"Don't worry. Your attorney is clever." Hitch patted Conner's leg, then snatched her hand back. She turned and faced Leahy. "I suppose you'll stipulate up front that the knife is Conner's. That gets ahead of it and keeps the prosecution from putting on a big, dog-and-pony show. Am I right?"

"For the moment," Leahy said. He caught Conner's eye. "She's right. It's best if we can get out in front of it, so that's the plan unless we can track what happened to the knife."

"We need to find proof they took the knife at the jail," Hitch said.

"How?" Conner asked. "They'll claim I didn't have it when I was booked in. No one will believe me over the cops. And the receipt they gave me doesn't show a knife."

"They have to match the property list from when they arrested you," Leahy said.

"That's just it. They gave me a copy of the list. It's not on there."

Both attorneys were quiet. This was even worse than Hitch had thought. "They planned from the beginning to keep that knife," Hitch said. She locked eyes with Leahy. "Do you think someone planned to set him up way back then?"

"Not necessarily for this crime. The DA's office may have wanted the weapon in case they needed a plant later." He shook his head. "Or maybe a deputy liked the knife and kept it. Or someone adjusted the paperwork later, maybe just prior to his release."

"The jail should have a video of the booking," Hitch said. "That would show the exchange of the knife."

"I'll subpoena the video." Leahy didn't sound optimistic.

"That'll prove they took my knife," Conner said. "That's probably enough, right?"

"Probably."

Conner glanced between them. "So why don't either of you look pleased? You think I'm lying about not having it?"

"No." Hitch shook her head. "I think if someone went to that much trouble to cover taking your knife, they've also done something with the video."

Conner sighed.

"Hey, it's worth a shot. Maybe they didn't think of it." Leahy turned to Conner. "Did they take all your possessions at once?"

"Yeah."

"That's good, because the video might be too risky to tamper with. I'm slammed this afternoon, but I can get the paperwork done first thing in the morning."

"I can do it for you," Hitch offered. "I'll also prepare subpoenas for the club videos."

"Thanks," Leahy said. "I'll walk them into the courthouse this afternoon."

"Great. I need to keep a low profile if I want a chance to see what's going on with this case. One wrong move, and I'll be watched like a hawk." Hitch grimaced. "Not to mention risking my job."

"Don't do anything that puts you in that position," Leahy said. "I can do all the heavy lifting."

Conner looked surprised. "You both actually believe me."

"Of course we believe you, or we wouldn't be doing this," Hitch said. "Well, Jerry would do it anyway. He's getting paid to represent you, but I sure as heck wouldn't."

"I resent that," Leahy teased. "But Hitch is right. I would represent you whether or not I believed you. You still deserve a good defense." His tone was somber. "I would, however, be taking a different direction right now. If what we suspect is going on, this is bigger than all of us and needs to be stopped."

Conner looked worried. "This is serious stuff."

Hitch couldn't argue. "It's important that you don't get into any more trouble."

Conner's expression shifted to determination. "I know what I have to do."

"What are you planning?"

"I need to figure out who killed Burton. That's the only way they can't pin it on me."

CHAPTER 14

After the NA meeting concluded, Conner handed the host his attendance card and waited for him to sign. He felt like a grade-school kid who couldn't be trusted to walk down a hall unsupervised. And why had his PO mandated he attend these snoozefests? He wasn't an addict. An adrenaline junkie, yes. Lack of impulse control and poor-decision making? Check. But listening to addicts yammer about their sad lives wasn't helping him. In fact, it had the opposite effect and made him want to run outside and stir up something. Or get high to feel better. But he couldn't afford to take chances.

"See you next week?" The host beamed, as though he'd invited Conner to a rave party.

"Probably." *If he wasn't in jail.* Conner hurried toward the door, torn between his need to get out and his curiosity about the woman named Eve who'd winked at him in the meeting. But he couldn't think about hooking up with anyone right now. He'd gone nearly a year without sex. Another couple of weeks wouldn't kill him.

Conner headed for the freeway, savoring the pleasure of driving the Mustang. If he couldn't get his job back, Nicole might sell the car and get him a cheap motorized scooter instead. Yeah, that would help get him laid. He laughed out loud, but it felt hollow. He would stop at the restaurant later and talk to Wally. First, he had to check out his only lead on Kaylee. Finding her felt more urgent every day.

The small house on Spring Street had been neglected for decades, but someone was taking care of the potted begonias. Conner stepped out of the car, and the pungent aroma of marijuana plants rolled over him like a warm ocean wave. *Oh man.* This would test his resolve for sure. As he walked up the cracked concrete path, sound filled the air. Electronic dance music (EDM), his favorite. Maybe he should hide out here until his troubles blew over.

Three minutes of pounding on the door and shouting "Hey!" finally got a response. The dude who opened it looked dressed for a day at the office. Not what he'd expected.

"What's up?" the guy shouted over the music.

"I'm Nate Conner. And I'm looking for my sister, Kaylee," Conner shouted back.

A long blank stare. Then the guy waved him in and turned down the volume. "I'm Ryan." He gestured at a cat-covered couch. "Have a seat, Nate."

"I go by Conner."

"Whatever."

Conner sat on the arm of the couch, and Ryan plopped into an oversized bean bag chair on the floor. He reached for a bottle of coconut water. "Kaylee hasn't lived here in a long time. In fact, Jay hasn't been here in a while either."

"Do you know where either of them is? Especially Kaylee."

"Jay talked about moving to LA. But I don't know."

The budding-pot smell from deep in the house was making Conner a little nauseated. "Do you have Jay's phone number?"

"Not anymore. But I doubt he's in touch with Kaylee. He got aggressive with her, and she dumped him. Then Jay got all pissy and mean. I was glad he moved."

Conner hoped they weren't back together. "What about Kaylee?"

A long pause. Ryan reached for a vape pipe and sucked in some cannabis. "I heard Kaylee was living in a content house and making videos, if you know what I mean."

"What?"

"Nothing hardcore."

Conner didn't want to know details. Not now. "Where is the house?"

"I don't know. The locations are kept very private."

"Do you know how to contact her?"

"Look up her OnlyFans profile and message her."

Dread pooled into his belly. He'd heard the site mentioned in jail and not in a good way.

"What's her ID?"

"Special K."

The nickname Dad had given her. "I have to find the house. Who else lives there? Do you know?"

Ryan sucked in another hit, savored it for a moment, then shouted, "Matt!"

Conner wanted to snatch the vape pipe out of Ryan's hand. He hadn't been high in almost a year. It wasn't mentally healthy to be this sober all the time. How did people do it?

A dude with grimy dreadlocks and surfer shorts wandered into the living room. "What's up?"

"This guy's trying to find Kaylee. Can you help him out?"

"Special K?" Matt grinned like a pedophile in a daycare center. "We all want her, man. She's so freaking hot. I'd nail her anytime, anywhere."

Conner was on his feet and in the man's face before he caught himself. "She's my sister. Have some respect."

"Sorry, dude. I didn't know."

Conner took a deep breath. "I need to find her. Can you help me or not?"

"How?"

Ryan had stood too and moved toward Matt. "You know the profile names of the girls in her content house, right?"

"Oh sure." Matt looked relieved. "Baby Jennie, Candy Corn, and Aloha. They have a video of themselves dancing to the YMCA song wearing only body oil and flip-flops. It's so hot, I swear it makes me want to throw Kaylee down and—"

Conner grabbed him by the throat.

Matt held up his hands and grunted. "Sorry! I wasn't thinking."

Conner stepped back. *Dang.* He'd never hurt anyone before. The stress of everything was pushing him to his limit. And Kaylee would always be his baby sister who needed protecting. Dad had drilled that into him. "Do you know anything about these women? Any idea where they live?"

"No. Just their profile names."

Ryan patted Conner's shoulder. "Good luck to you, man. I admire your family loyalty. But you need to chill." Ryan pressed something into his hand. It felt like a tiny vape cartridge. Conner didn't look at it. "Thanks." He bolted from the house.

CHAPTER 15

Hitch arrived at the Firehouse Lounge in Pacific Beach a few minutes before six. She knew Nelson would already be there and waiting upstairs. He was never late for anything. His attitude was that if you arrived on time, you were late. Hitch headed up the stairs, admiring the ocean view as she climbed. She spotted him sitting at the bar where he'd always sat when they'd met here in the past, a bottle of Bud Light in front of him. He was such a creature of habit.

Nelson stood when she approached. "I'm so glad you finally accepted my invitation."

"You called on Friday, again on Saturday, three times on Sunday, and twice today. It's the only way I could get you to stop."

He flashed his most charming smile.

"You said you had new information about the Troy Burton murder." Hitch got right to the point. "That's the *only* reason I'm here."

"Whatever works." Nelson got the bartender's attention and ordered Hitch a margarita. "Right?" he asked, catching her eye.

"Sure." She eased onto the barstool next to him. "What have you got?"

"How about we enjoy the sunset before we talk shop?" Nelson nodded at the gorgeous view. Hitch wondered if he actually had anything new about the case, and if he did, whether he would share it. She was tired, and he knew she had a weakness for watching the sun set over the water. The bartender brought her drink, and she finally sat back and relaxed. She knew Nelson well enough to know he would tell her something—because that was the only chance he had of luring her back again. But not until he was ready. She might as well enjoy the scenery.

They caught each other up on friends and family, then Hitch inquired about his blond lab, Austin. The puppy had captured her heart, but she wasn't the one who'd had to take him out all hours of the night.

"He's still eating bark and chewing on everything he can get his mouth around. I started taking him to obedience school, but he's still pretty young and is far more interested in playing than learning." Nelson grinned like a proud daddy. "He's no dummy though. He figured out how to take the carabiner off his cage and get out. Actually, I think he chews on it until it breaks, then escapes."

When the sun started to set, he reached his arm around her shoulders, giving her a quick squeeze. Then he pulled back before she could object.

Still, his touch had been electrifying, and she needed to get this meeting back on track. "Do you have any suspects for the Burton murder?"

"A few. I didn't realize how many people he had testified against. I guess he had a way of persuading people to talk and figured out he could use it to help himself."

"Yeah, I'm sure that's the way it worked." She didn't hold back on the sarcastic tone.

"What are you saying?"

"Nothing. What else do you have?"

"Not a lot."

She didn't believe him and knew he planned to make her work for every tidbit. She decided to call him out on his court appearance. "What were you doing at the arraignment this morning?"

"I go to court a lot."

"You were there specifically for Nate Conner's piddly case. Why?"

"We like him for the Burton murder."

"Who is *we*?"

"The taskforce. Our investigation is pointing right at him."

Oh no. "Did you get Burton's phone records?"

"Yes."

"Can I see them?"

Nelson scowled. "You know I can't share them. If you're so interested, why don't you see if you can be assigned the case? You have seniority over most of the DDAs."

"I can't. There's a conflict."

His tone softened. "Hitch, if this guy is a friend of yours, you need to be careful. I couldn't stand it if anything happened to you."

"He's not a murderer."

"You know Conner that well?"

"No. But I believe him."

Nelson took a deep breath and locked eyes with her. "Are you in love with him?"

"No!" Hitch sat up straight.

"But you're dating him." It was more of a statement than a question.

"Don't be ridiculous. It's nothing like that. He's just a kid." She hesitated, unsure if she should mention her concerns. "I believe there is far more going on in this case than is evident right now."

"Like what?"

"I can't tell you." She shook her head. "You used the word *we*. Who else thinks Conner killed Burton?"

"The DDA on the case."

"Fisher? That twelve-year-old? Of course he does. But who's pulling the strings?"

Nelson sighed. "Ramsden."

CHAPTER 16

"Hey, Hitch," a voice called. She turned toward the sound and saw Ramsden waving at her from a dark booth in the corner. "Come talk to me," he slurred. "I'm lonely."

And drunk! The last thing she needed. She'd stopped in the restroom on her way out of the Firehouse and now regretted it. But he was her supervisor, and she couldn't be rude. Reluctantly, she headed over, telling herself *five minutes.*

"Have a seat." He gestured at the other side of the table. "Let me buy you a nightcap." Other than the expensive suit he wore, the man was average and forgettable.

Hitch knew better than to argue with a drunk. It would just delay whatever it was he needed to get off his chest. Hitch sat on the edge of the padded seat, one leg outside the booth, ready to bolt.

An unexpected thought hit her. What if he had guilt about his corruption and wanted to get it off his chest? It couldn't hurt to ease him in that direction. He might not even remember this conversation. She slipped a hand into her jacket pocket and snuck her phone into her lap. On the slight chance he started talking about informants, she would record him.

"You're here by yourself?" she asked. People from the DA's office usually came in pairs or small groups.

"Yup. My divorce is final today, and I'm alone. Aria is gone. Gone for good."

He was barely comprehensible, and his tone melodramatic. *Jerk,* Hitch thought. "I'm sorry to hear that." But she was mostly sorry for his wife.

"Kicked me out of my own house." Ramsden made a snatching gesture. "Then her lawyer took it."

And now self-pity, a staple of alcoholic emotion. "That's rough." She wanted to steer the conversation anywhere else. "So how's work going for you?"

"Not good." He shook his head, an exaggerated motion that made his jowls flap. "My main campaign contri"—he stopped and tried again more slowly—"con-tri-bu-tor pulled out. How am I gonna run for DA without any money?" Ramsden slumped back against the booth seat. "I messed up."

"How so?" Hitch leaned in, hoping for real information. Her five minutes, and patience, were about expired.

He stared at her, his eyes barely able to focus.

"At work?" Hitch prodded. "Maybe I can help you fix it."

"No. I ruined everything." A beat. "Almost." Ramsden gulped the last of his drink, set it down, then laid his head on the table.

Time to go. Hitch got up, took two steps, and stopped. Was he passed out? She had a flash of guilt about leaving him like that. Someone could take his wallet and phone. But who would she call to help him? No idea.

His phone. Did he have incriminating texts or phone numbers she should get a look at?

Hitch turned back and scooted in next to him. Ramsden made a moaning noise but didn't lift his head. She glanced around, then slipped her hand into his jacket pocket. A set of keys, but no phone. She stepped out of the booth, wondering if she had the nerve to scoot around the seat to check his other side.

"Hey, Hitch." The young DDA from Conner's arraignment walked toward her.

"Hey, Fisher." She moved away from the booth, feeling her face flush. Had he seen her stick her hand into Ramsden's pocket?

Fisher peered around her at their boss. "What's up with him?"

"He's drunk. He called me over to chat, then passed out. Can you check on him? I have to go." She didn't wait for a response before bolting for the door.

Hitch walked through the alley to the small parking lot behind the Firehouse Lounge. When she heard footsteps behind her, she automatically slipped her hand around the pepper-spray canister she carried on her keychain. For a second, she wished she'd taken Nelson up on his offer to walk her out. But she'd been afraid he might try to kiss her. He'd had just enough alcohol to put him in an amorous mood. She didn't want to have to shut him down, nor was she sure she would have stopped him. The man was so darn attractive.

The footsteps behind her got closer. Hitch turned and saw a man staggering toward her. He was either drunk or pretending to be. She walked between two parked cars, keeping an eye on him. He turned toward the beach and disappeared out of sight.

Hitch climbed into her car and started toward home, still on edge. As she drove, memories of a year earlier came flooding back to her. She took a deep breath and tried to shake them off, but they kept surfacing. Just as she pulled into her driveway, her cell phone rang, bringing her out of the past. She glanced at the ID. Not a number she recognized. But as a prosecutor, it was common to get calls from victim's families. "Hello."

"If you know what's good for you, you need to be a team player," said a male voice, deep and threatening, but with an odd cadence.

"Who is this?"

"Just lay off the informants. They're doing a much-needed job."

"You can't intimidate——"

The phone went dead.

CHAPTER 17

The same evening

After dinner with Nicole and her sort-of boyfriend, Conner went to his old bedroom. He'd spent much of his childhood in the small space, but at least he'd had some privacy. His sisters had all shared a room and often picked on him because they'd thought he was spoiled. And he had been. His mother had overlooked his misbehavior and given him almost everything he wanted—that they could afford. They'd loved each other fiercely, and for a few minutes, he fought the overwhelming grief of her absence.

He forced himself to refocus. Grief led to cravings that led to trouble. Conner opened his ancient laptop. One day, he'd have the money to buy a computer made in this decade. The OnlyFans website automatically reloaded, being the last place he'd visited, searching for *Special K*. If Kaylee was still active on the site, why didn't her profile name load? Had she changed it? Or moved on?

But he now had the profile names of three women who might know where to find Kaylee. He searched for *Aloha* on the site and her page loaded quickly revealing a stunning Hawaiian girl in a white-crochet bikini. His body responded to her sexuality, and for a moment, he drifted into a sex-on-the-beach fantasy. Conner forced himself to click her contact icon and make her image disappear. He keyed in a short message, then expanded it. His wordcraft skills were only average, but he could spell anything.

Dear Miss Aloha: This is Nate Conner, and I'm trying to find my sister, Kaylee. We have a family emergency, and she needs to contact me right away. Can you please get this message to her or tell me how I can reach her? Thanks much. NC.

It wasn't even a lie, he told himself. He was facing possible murder charges, and Kaylee was missing and had likely relapsed. They were both emergencies. He copied the message and sent it, then searched for *Candy Corn*. He found himself staring at another beautiful woman. This one tall, blonde, and lightly freckled. She wore a white see-through tank top with an orange-and-yellow mini skirt, and had the sweetest cleavage he'd ever stared into. *So hot!* And so much better than porn. But not now. He moved to the message app, thinking he would watch some of Candy's videos later. Or maybe not. What if the first one he loaded featured Kaylee? He couldn't take that risk.

He sent Candy the same message, then keyed *Baby Jennie* into the search bar. Several profiles loaded, but he eventually focused on a girl with pink-tinted hair who looked fifteen. One of her videos was labeled, Sexy YMCA/pay-per-view only. It had been viewed thousands of times at fifty bucks each. These girls were making impressive bank. He hoped they were using it for college tuition or funding a retirement account. Conner laughed at the thought. Nobody that young and hot was thinking about retiring.

What was Kaylee doing with her share of the cash? Years ago, she'd wanted to become a veterinarian, but he feared the worst. That kind of money could buy a lot of pure heroin, her drug of choice. At only twelve, their parents' deaths—murders —had hit Kaylee the hardest. She'd become quiet and depressed, and three years later had dropped out of school. Then she'd started partying nonstop. Nate had never judged her. He'd spent most of that post-horror year stoned and/or drunk and had been lucky to eventually graduate. Gina had gained a lot of weight, then moved to Seattle to get away. Only Nicole had handled it well. But she'd broken off her engagement and stepped into their mother's role as "parrot woman," choices that might not have been mentally healthy. They were all messed up.

A new thought slammed him, and his brain plunged into dark places. Kaylee could overdose and die. Or be murdered by a drug dealer. And he was about to go to prison for twenty years for a crime he didn't commit. Nicole would likely punish herself for both by living alone with her noisy birds.

Conner reached into his jeans pocket for the tiny cartridge, then grabbed his backpack. He'd stopped on the way home and bought a vape pen to use it with. He loaded the cannabis oil into the vape pen and stared at it for a long moment. He really needed to get out of his anxious head, otherwise, he wouldn't sleep well. But what if the cops picked him up again? And gave him a UA? He was on probation. And Hitch was counting on him to stay clean and help her bring down a corrupt prosecutor. He also needed to keep his job. Conner had stopped at the Roadhouse, and Wally had said he could come back to work once he'd been cleared. But the restaurant owner gave random drug tests.

Conner hid the vape in his bottom drawer under sweatshirts he never wore and went out for a run. Maybe he could exhaust himself into a stupor.

CHAPTER 18

Tuesday morning

"Call your next witness, please." Judge Barenski, sounding grumpier than usual, nodded at Hitch.

"I call Heather Davis to the stand." Hitch had hoped the victim wouldn't have to testify. The poor woman didn't need the added humiliation. But it was either her or the informant, and Hitch didn't want to call him. At this point, she was skeptical about using any *confessional witnesses*. Besides, sometimes it was good for victims to face the perpetrators. At least that's what Hitch told herself. Heather, a pre-med student at UCSD with excellent grades, seemed like she would be a strong, confident witness. Hitch hoped the jury wouldn't be distracted by Heather's cheerleader good looks and obvious sexual appeal.

Hitch questioned her about her background and established that Heather had no criminal record or history of legal trouble. Then she moved on to the night of the attack and burglary.

"Where were you?"

"I was home, in my little guest house rental, studying at my desk. In fact, I was listening to an anatomy lecture so I didn't hear him come in. The next thing I knew, someone grabbed me from behind."

"What happened after that?"

"He spun me around and yanked me out of my chair. I tried to pull away, but he was too strong." Heather paused, her distress obvious. "He pushed me onto the desk. When I tried to get up, he pulled out a switchblade and flipped it open. All I could see for a moment was that knife."

Hitch glanced at the defendant and thought she saw a slight smile cross the defendant's face. *Vile man!* "Did your attacker say anything?"

"Not then. He just grabbed my hands and bound them together."

"In front or in back?"

"In front."

"What did he use?"

"A zip tie. He must have pulled it out of his pocket because I didn't see it until then."

"Do you remember what he was wearing?"

"Dark clothes. A black t-shirt, jeans, and a black ski mask. His shirt had writing on it, but I don't know what it said." She pressed her lips together. "I was too terrified."

"Can you give us a description of his body size and build?" Hitch continued.

"He was about five-eight and pudgy."

The defendant, sandy-haired with a square jaw, squirmed in his chair.

"What happened next?"

"I pleaded with him to stop." Heather's voice trembled. "But the more I begged, the more excited he seemed to get."

"What do you mean?"

"I could feel his penis against my leg, and it got harder the

more I pleaded. So I stopped pleading and just went limp."
She glanced down. "And so did he."

A few muted chuckles from jurors. Hitch glanced at the defendant. His face was flushed, and he looked furious.

"What did he do then?"

"He put the knife to my throat, leaned in close to my ear, and whispered 'Beg.'"

"Did you?"

"Not at first. But then he pushed the knife tight against my skin, and I felt a trickle of blood. I didn't know what to do. I wasn't sure if he wanted me to beg him to rape me or beg him to stop."

"What did you do?"

"I begged him to stop. I couldn't make myself say anything else. I was so scared."

Again, the defendant shifted in his seat. His attorney placed a calming hand on his arm. Hitch hoped the guy would testify so the jury could see his physical reactions. He'd make a lousy poker player. "Did you get a look at his face?"

Heather shook her head.

"You need to answer the question out loud," the judge said.

"No. He never took off his mask. But I could see his eyes."

"Did you get a good look at them?" Hitch knew how Heather would respond to each question because they'd gone over them many times.

"He was staring at me the entire time."

"Can you estimate how long?"

"It seemed like an hour, but it was probably more likely ten or fifteen minutes." She glanced over at the defendant. "All I could see were his strange eyes."

"What do you mean by *strange*?"

"They're an unusual color, kind of a light, greenish-brown, with a dark brown fleck in his right eye." The jurors all turned to stare at the defendant.

"Did he penetrate you?"

"Yes. With the knife still in his hand, he pushed that arm against my throat, then used his other hand to drop his pants." She closed her eyes for a moment. "Then he seemed to be fumbling to put on a condom. I tried to get away, but he pushed harder against my throat, and I had trouble breathing. All of a sudden, he was inside me."

"I'm sorry, Heather." Hitch softened her voice. "I know this is difficult. Just a few more questions."

The victim took a deep breath and nodded.

"What happened next?"

"When he was done, he pulled up his pants and waved his knife as if to threaten me again. With his other hand, he grabbed my laptop and shoved it under his arm. Then he reached into his pocket, pulled out some cash, and threw it at me. Then he smiled, told me thank you, and walked out."

"What did you do after he left?"

"I called the police."

"Immediately?"

"Yes. I had just been raped."

"What did you do with the money he left behind?"

"Nothing. I didn't touch it. The police bagged it as evidence and took it. I later learned it was three hundred dollars."

"I have no further questions at this time, Your Honor." Hitch pivoted and took her seat. She noticed her phone had lit up with missed messages. She glanced at it. She had both voice and text messages, all from Nelson. She shook her head. *What did he want now?*

CHAPTER 19

Barenski glanced at this watch. "Would you like to cross examine the witness, Mr. Arroyo?"

"Thank you, Your Honor."

The defense attorney walked slowly to stand directly in front of the witness. He paused, then asked in a soft voice, "Ms. Davis, do you know my client, Jason Evans?"

"No." Heather responded cautiously.

"You've never met?"

"No."

"You said your attacker spoke a few words. Is that correct?"

"Only a few."

"Did you recognize the voice?"

"I don't think so."

"Did it sound familiar to you?"

"A little, but he didn't say much."

"You're an undergrad student at UCSD, correct?"

"That's right."

"Do you also work, Ms. Davis?"

"I'm not employed by anyone at this time." Heather chose her words carefully.

Hitch suddenly felt nervous.

"How do you pay for school?"

"Objection." Hitch spoke as she stood. "Relevance."

"If the court will allow, a couple more questions will reveal the relevance," Arroyo said with confidence.

"Overruled." The judge turned to the witness. "You may answer the question."

"I have my own online business." Heather squirmed, obviously uncomfortable.

Where was Arroyo going with this? Hitch was afraid she'd missed something.

"What kind of business?"

"Objection." Hitch was more forceful this time. "Relevance. This witness is the victim. What she does or does not do for work has nothing to do with her attack."

"Will the attorneys please approach the bench," the judge said. "We're off the record."

Hitch was out of her seat and in front of the judge before Arroyo. Barenski covered his mic and asked Arroyo to explain the relevance of his questions.

"If the court will give me another minute, I'll show that the witness knows my client through her business."

"That doesn't make it relevant," Hitch argued.

"I think the court will see otherwise."

"Okay, Counselor, but tie it up quickly," the judge instructed. "We're back on the record. The objection is overruled. Please answer the question."

Heather was silent.

"Do you remember the question?" the judge prodded.

"I'll ask again." Arroyo raised his voice a notch. "What does your online business consist of?"

Heather sucked in a breath. "It's a content subscription service."

Oh no! The jury had heard it, and they could never put it back in the bottle.

"What exactly does that mean?"

Hitch leaped to her feet again. "Objection! Unfair and prejudicial, relevance, and lack of foundation."

"I'm creating the foundation," Arroyo countered. "The relevance will be obvious shortly, and it's necessary to explain what really happened in this situation. Mr. Evans deserves to have the facts before the court."

"Your Honor, the probative value is substantially outweighed by the danger of unfair prejudice and confusing the jury." Hitch wished she knew what she was dealing with. *What had Heather been up to?*

"Overruled." The judge turned to Heather. "You may answer the question."

"I don't remember what it was."

Barenski started to ask the court reporter to read it back, but Arroyo was happy to ask again. "What exactly is a content subscription service?"

"I create live videos for subscriptions on a monthly basis."

"Your Honor, may we approach the bench?" Hitch desperately wanted to shut this down.

"No."

Hitch was shocked. Though she shouldn't have been. Any other judge would have been more sensitive to these types of issues, but this was Barenski she was dealing with.

"I'll see you both in my chambers." The judge stood. "The jury will remain in the courtroom."

Hitch and Arroyo followed the judge, who didn't sit down in the side room. That meant he planned to deal with this quickly and get back to the trial.

"Where are you going with this, Counselor?" he asked Arroyo.

"Ms. Davis' occupation is the center of what happened in this case."

Before he could say anything more, Hitch cut it in. "It's obvious he's trying to make the victim look like she was *asking for it*. No matter what her occupation, she didn't want this to happen." Hitch turned to her colleague. "I'm disappointed in you, Luis. It's not like you to blame the victim."

"That's not what I'm doing." His eyes flashed with anger, then he took a deep breath and went on. "I'm merely trying to show that this was a consensual act. That my client had every reason to believe Heather was a willing participant. This testimony is paramount to my defense."

When the judge hesitated, Hitch felt a sense of dread. *He was actually considering it.* Hitch made one last attempt, but the judge turned to the defense attorney. "Mr. Arroyo, I'll give you a little more leeway, but you'd better show me something soon or I'm ending this. Go back to court. I'll be right there."

"Your Honor," Hitch said, "I'd like a short recess."

Arroyo cut in. "I only have about fifteen more minutes of questioning. I'd like to finish up before lunch."

"Me too." Barenski turned to Hitch. "You can do your redirect this afternoon."

Hitch hurried out, with Arroyo following, and they started down the hall. Hitch knew he wouldn't tell her what to expect, so she didn't bother to ask. *Maybe he had nothing, and his plan was to make the jury think he did. If that was the case, his bluff had just been called.*

"You have the jury thinking Heather has some deep, dark secret," Hitch said. "So what's your plan now? To move on to something else, making it look like the judge ended that line of questioning? Barenski won't like being played like that."

Arroyo stopped, pivoted, and looked directly into Hitch's eyes. "You really don't know, do you?" He started walking again. "You're always so on top of your cases. It's kind of fun to catch you on an off day."

Hitch felt her face burn. *What had she missed?* She checked her phone before she went back into the courtroom. Three more texts from Nelson, all telling her to call him, followed by an indication of urgency.

CHAPTER 20

The same morning

"Leftover pizza for breakfast?" Nicole smiled as she came into the kitchen.

"It's the American way." Conner gulped the last of his sweetened coffee, feeling good about himself. Nutrition wasn't high on his self-improvement list right now.

"Will you clean the cages?" Nicole asked. "I have to teach an online class."

"That's new. Is it about taking care of birds?"

"Yes. Why?"

"I just wonder sometimes what else your life could be. You know, if Mom had lived, and you'd gotten married. You wanted to be a flight attendant. Remember?"

"Not anymore. People are crazy, and I have no desire to be trapped on a plane with any of them." Nicole kissed his forehead. "Don't worry about me, Naters. I have a good life here."

That wasn't the same as being happy. "But are you—"

"Just stop. I'm fine." She laughed. "You're the one who needs to get his act together." She started to leave, then turned back. "Are you seeing your PO on schedule? Does he know about the arrest?"

"I'll call him this morning."

"Go see him in person."

"Do you ever get tired of bossing me around?"

"Nope."

After an hour in the parrot sanctuary, he took a shower, then called Stratten. The PO didn't answer, no surprise, so he left a message. "It's Nate Conner. You probably already know, but I was arrested Friday night. They charged me with a probation violation, but it's ridiculous. I was working at the restaurant when they decided to harass me. But good news, I still have a job. And I have a lawyer, two lawyers in fact, who are helping me. So I'm still on track. Cheers."

Too casual? Maybe he should have mentioned Troy's murder. *No.* Why cause his PO unnecessary alarm?

Conner opened his laptop to check his messages. *Holy pancakes!* Aloha had responded:

Hey Nate. Kaylee moved out more than a month ago. Truth? We had to boot her. She was fluffed up all the time and dating someone who became a problem for us. Sorry, but we're running a business here.

That seemed to be a pattern for Kaylee. Conner checked the time on Aloha's message. Only a few minutes ago. Maybe she was still online. He texted back: *Thanks for letting me know. Any idea where she is now? Or a phone number?*

He resisted the urge to watch any of Aloha's videos while he waited. But he didn't know what else to do. He was supposed to be figuring out who killed Troy Burton, but he felt clueless about where to start. Troy probably didn't have any real friends. Narcs rarely did. Except maybe their mothers. Conner would track Mrs. Burton down this afternoon, if he could.

His laptop pinged, and he opened the new message from Aloha: *I think she's staying at the Marigold Motel downtown. This is the only number I have for her. Good luck.* The message was followed by a number he thought was outdated.

But he had a location. *Progress!* Conner's heart felt lighter in his chest for the first time in a week. But as he googled the address for the motel, he realized what he was up against. If Kaylee was strung out, she would resist any help and not likely want to go anywhere with him. Maybe he could abduct her and take her home to Nicole's to get clean. They could confiscate her phone, and Kaylee would be too far out of town to consider walking anywhere.

Or... he could just be her friend and slowly influence her to want a better life. Many different methods could be successful. And all of them could fail. He would assess the situation when he saw her. He bolted out of his chair, grabbed his keys, and headed out, waving at Nicole on his way. Mid-Zoom lecture, she nodded and kept talking to her students. He wouldn't mention finding Kaylee until he actually did. No point in getting her hopes up.

A half hour later, Conner parked in the nearly empty lot and climbed out. The Marigold Motel wasn't as sleazy as he'd expected. Still, it wasn't a place anyone wanted to end up, and the paint was a dirty, eye-popping mango. An older woman sat in a lawn chair on the upper balcony, smoking and looking like she had nowhere to go. Not located near the beach or a freeway, most of the motel's business probably came from longer-term rentals. And for some people, it was home. The potted plants, lawn chair, and other personal items lining the slatted railing indicated so.

In the tiny front office, a dark-skinned man with an Indian accent flashed him a bright smile. The clerk's welcoming expression disappeared as soon as Conner mentioned his quest.

"No Kaylee here. Sorry."

He'd expected that. Conner held out his phone and showed the clerk Kaylee's photo, taken on her last birthday, the last time they'd all been together. Even Gina had participated briefly through FaceTime.

"Maybe. She's very pretty."

"You have a sister, don't you? Wouldn't you want me to help you find her if I could? Please tell me what room she's in."

A long moment. Finally, the clerk said, "Two zero six. Top floor in the back."

"Thanks." Conner hustled out, his pulse racing. Had he taken his meds? *Nope. Oh well.* He really only needed them for work.

He jogged to the back of the building and took the stairs two at a time. He hadn't called the number Aloha had given him for fear of scaring off Kaylee before he had a chance to see her in person. She'd been out of contact with the family for her own reasons.

Conner knocked on the door. "UPS delivery."

No response.

He knocked again. "Ms. Conner. Are you in there? I need you to sign for this." *Stupid!* She would either recognize his voice or think he had some kind of legal papers. But maybe she'd be happy to see him. Addicts were unpredictable, depending on their needs in the moment.

The sliding window was open a few inches, which told him the building was older than he was. Conner stepped over and put his face next to the opening, intending to call out again.

What was that smell?

He pulled back. So dank. Was it just sweaty-people funk? Maybe combined with spilled ... what? *Oh no.* It smelled like piss. And blood. He pounded again. "Kaylee! It's Nate. We have a family emergency."

A nearby door opened, and a big shirtless man stuck his head out. "She's not in there, so you can stop pounding."

"Where did she go?"

"How the hell should I know? We're not besties." The fat man stepped back inside and slammed his door.

Conner hustled downstairs to the front office. The clerk took a moment to appear again. "Did you find her?"

"I need you to unlock the room."

"Oh no. I can't do that. Our guests deserve privacy."

"Something is wrong. I can tell. Please help me."

Conner had never hesitated to ask, or even beg, for whatever he needed. Unasked questions/favors were doors not opened. He pulled out his wallet and extracted a twenty. He'd sold his guitar to Darius, who often functioned like a pawnshop for him. Conner made a mental note to buy his friend a drink, or something, as soon as he could. He pushed the cash across the counter.

"Please. I really think she needs help. My other option is to call the police."

The clerk picked up the twenty, tucked it into his sleeve, then walked around the end of the counter. "Only because you say her safety is involved."

A few minutes later, he slid the master key into the lock and called out "Management" before pushing open the door.

They both gasped in shock. A naked, bloody man lay on the bed. And Kaylee was nowhere in sight.

CHAPTER 21

They were all back in the courtroom with Heather on the stand, and Arroyo asked, "What kind of content is on the videos you sell?"

His confidence unnerved Hitch.

"Different things," Heather said. "Cooking demonstrations, exercise, do-it-yourself projects, and crafts. I give some dance lessons too. That sort of thing."

"You are naked during these demonstrations or lessons, correct?"

Naked? Oh hell! "Objection, relevance," Hitch interjected.

"Overruled. You may answer the question."

"Sometimes," Heather said.

"Other times, you are scantily dressed, correct?"

"Sometimes."

"Ms. Davis, you work with a company called OnlyFans, is that correct?"

"Objection." Hitch would continue to say it for the record, but there was no stopping this.

"Overruled." The judge stared at the victim.

"Yes," Heather said.

"Is it correct to say that you sell your content through the website so you can reach a larger audience?"

"Yes. But also so I can remain anonymous. I don't use my own name."

"What name do you use?"

"Heaven."

"And you have videos titled *Cooking in Heaven*, *Yoga in Heaven*, *Dancing in Heaven*, right?"

"That's right." Heather looked uncomfortable. Hitch wanted to object, but had no legal grounds.

"But your online name is Heaven, not In Heaven, right?"

"Yes."

"So why do your titles say *in* Heaven and not *with* Heaven?"

Hitch couldn't let it go on any longer. "Objection." The judge glanced at her, waiting. She needed to give a basis for the objection. She couldn't say *relevance*. That would give Arroyo a chance to explain the relevance—exactly what she was trying to avoid.

"Your basis for the objection, Counselor?" Barenski asked impatiently.

"I'll withdraw the question," Arroyo said.

Dang! He'd gotten exactly what he wanted. She'd fallen into his trap. The objection itself gave the jury reason to believe exactly what Arroyo wanted them to.

"But your face is shown during the videos, correct?" Arroyo continued to cement his position.

"Most of them."

"And most of your content is sexual in nature, correct?"

Heather looked upset. "That didn't give him"—she pointed at the defendant—"the right to attack me in my home."

"Is that a yes?" Arroyo asked.

"Objection. Relevance, prejudicial," Hitch said again.

"Overruled." Now the judge glared at Arroyo. "You'd better make a connection soon, Counselor."

"I'm about to do that, Your Honor." Arroyo turned back to the witness. "You create role-playing videos for some of your clients, correct?"

"Yes."

"How do you determine what roles you play?"

"I do what is trending."

"And sometimes clients make requests and you act out those roles, correct?"

"When I can."

"You have a monthly subscription from someone who calls himself *TheDominator,* correct?"

"Yes."

Really? Hitch despaired. *Heather, what have you done?*

"Good tipper, right?"

Another objection denied.

"Yes."

"And you're aware that my client uses that identity on the website?"

"Not until right now. I didn't know his real name."

"But he did tell you his first name was Jason, right?"

"Yes. But I didn't know if he was telling the truth, and I didn't know his last name."

"You did a lot of role-playing with Jason in which you were being surprised by a rapist, correct?"

Oh dang. Hitch wanted to cry.

"That seemed to be his favorite kind of video." Heather's lips trembled.

"You weren't ever afraid Jason would come to your house and attack you?"

"He wasn't supposed to know who I was or where I lived."

"But you knew he was local, correct?"

"He may have mentioned that in a message. I don't remember."

"Isn't it true that Jason paid you generously for the rape-role-play videos and offered you a hefty sum to act out the whole scene in person?"

"Lots of clients do that. I don't take them seriously. It's part of the job."

"Part of the job is to offer in-person services?" Arroyo pressured.

"No!" A tear rolled down Heather's cheek. "Part of the job is putting up with harassment. I felt safe because subscribers are not supposed to know who I am or where I live."

"No further questions," Arroyo said.

When Heather left the witness stand, Hitch stepped over to her and whispered, "Meet me in my office. We need to talk."

"Now?"

"Now."

The judge set the case for the afternoon and dismissed the jury. Hitch and Arroyo left their tables at the same time. He opened the gate on the bar for her. "Sorry, Hitch. You win some, you lose some." He didn't sound the least bit sympathetic.

"It's not over yet," Hitch snapped.

"What were you thinking?" Hitch asked, trying to control her frustration. She wasn't nearly as angry as she had been earlier. The walk to her office had given her time to calm down. But she still couldn't sit. She might end up breaking a few pencils. "Why didn't you tell me you had videos on OnlyFans?"

"I didn't think it was important." Heather sank into a guest chair. "And I made a massive effort to keep that part of my life private."

"It didn't occur to you that it might come up in court?"

"I didn't think it would. I don't want everyone knowing what I do." She covered her face. "But I'm already compromised. The jury members and everyone in court will probably go home tonight and look me up. That's what I didn't want to happen."

"Did it ever occur to you that it might be one of your *fans* who found you and attacked you?"

"No. I thought it was random. I had no idea he was a subscriber. I don't see any of them, and I had no idea they could find me."

"Well, Jason did. Any idea how that happened?"

"No. I really thought I was anonymous."

"You keep saying that, but you show your face in the videos, right?"

"Yes. But there are millions of people in this area. What are the chances someone would live or work close enough to recognize me in public?"

A pretty good chance, apparently. Hitch wanted to shake her and wake her up to the risks, but it was too late. She only hoped Heather had learned her lesson. But what about all the other naive girls out there engaging in this kind of behavior?

A loose thread finally made sense to Hitch. "That's why Evans took your laptop. For the videos."

"Yeah. And I don't know what I'll do now," Heather lamented. "I need to make money to pay my tuition, but I can't continue what I'm doing. Too many people know now. I should've never come forward about the rape."

"That's the one thing you did right. You can't let him get away with it."

"But he will if the jury thinks I agreed to it."

"We'll just have to show them you didn't. We'll present everything to the jury on redirect."

"What if they don't believe me? The defense attorney

made me look like a prostitute. And I know it didn't help that I hid the information about my work. They probably think I'm a liar too."

"Don't worry. I have another witness who could make all the difference." *She would have to call the informant after all.*

CHAPTER 22

Hitch's stomach growled as she walked back to the courtroom. With the time she'd spent talking to Heather and the quick research she'd done on OnlyFans, she hadn't had time to eat. Nor did she have time to call Nelson and find out what was so important. She checked her phone as she walked. Conner had called but hadn't left a message. She listened to the other messages, all from Nelson. She called Conner back, but it went to voicemail. She decided she'd better call Nelson in case it had something to do with Conner. No answer there either. She left a message. "I'm in the middle of a trial. Going back in now. I'll call you when I'm done."

Hitch shut off her phone and walked into the courtroom. She would do her best to make Heather look … more whole-some? Meaning less slutty. Hitch hated society's double standards.

Once Heather was on the stand again, Hitch asked, "How long have you posted on OnlyFans?"

"About a year."

"How did you get started?"

"I was working as a caregiver in an assisted living facility, but I wasn't earning enough to pay my tuition. I got another part-time job at a gym teaching yoga, but I still wasn't earning enough, and I didn't have enough time to study. I'm a pre-med student, and I have a lot of science classes with labs. There just weren't enough hours in the day to do it all. My grades were dropping, and I was still just barely making enough money to keep going." She took a breath and went on. "One of my friends told me about OnlyFans. She'd been posting videos there for a few months and was making good money, so I decided to try it out."

"And did it work for you financially?"

"Yes. The first month I gained twenty new subscriptions and made more in tips than I was earning at the gym. So I quit that job. I kept the caregiver job for another month, then quit that too. My subscriptions had tripled, and so had my tips."

"What kind of content did you have on OnlyFans?"

"I started out teaching yoga. It was well received, but right after I quit my caregiver job I realized my numbers were dropping."

"What did you do about it?"

"I talked to the friend who had introduced me to the site, and she told me she was doing sexual dances and nude shots and that it paid very well. I didn't want to do that, but I was getting into a real financial bind. I decided to try dressing more provocatively for my yoga classes, and my numbers started to increase. I soon discovered I could dance and do naked yoga because there was a big demand for it."

"Have you ever met any of your clients?"

"No, never."

"Have you spoken to any on the phone?"

"No."

"Have you messaged any of your clients?"

"A few. There is a system set up so we can communicate, but it goes through the website, so there is no direct contact."

"Can fans make requests for certain videos?"

"Yes. They often do, and I try to accommodate."

"Do you remember getting requests from *TheDominator* about doing a rape scene?"

"I don't remember specifically one from him, but I get a lot of requests for that kind of content." Heather paused, shifting in her seat. "A lot of men seem to be turned on by a woman being scared or forced to do something."

Arroyo started to object, then changed his mind.

Hitch continued. "Have you ever agreed to meet with a client?"

"No."

"Have you ever encouraged a client to find you?"

"Never."

"Do you know how the defendant found you?"

"No idea."

"No further questions," Hitch said.

Judge Barenski checked his watch, then said to Arroyo, "Cross, Counselor?"

"Yes, Your Honor. Just a few questions."

Arroyo took a couple of steps toward the witness stand. He kept an appropriate distance but stood directly in front of Heather and spoke in a gentle tone. "You went from regular yoga exercise videos to scantily dressed yoga videos, correct?"

"Yes."

"And that increased your revenue, right?"

"Right."

"Then you started doing nudity and sexually provocative videos, correct?"

"Yes."

"And you made more money with that, correct?"

"Yes."

"You gradually increased your level of sexual exposure until meeting in person was the next step, isn't that right?"

"No. I never met anyone or encouraged anyone to meet me."

"But you told my client where you lived, right?"

"No! I did not."

"You said you felt safe with your anonymity on OnlyFans, correct?"

"Yeah. They seemed to have a lot of safeguards."

"So how do you explain my client knowing your address?"

"I don't know."

"You said many men requested rape scenes?"

"Yes."

"Did you think it might encourage men to act out their fantasies?"

Heather shook her head. "I thought it would do the opposite. If they could relieve their tensions through watching, they wouldn't need to act on their fantasies."

"So you were doing a service to the community and other women?"

Hitch jumped up. "Objection, argumentative!"

CHAPTER 23

Conner's impulse was to run. He'd never seen a dead body before, and all the blood and naked flesh was freaking him out. But he couldn't move. A dozen thoughts flashed through his rattled brain. He was already in serious trouble, and another dead body in his proximity would land him back in jail with no hope of bail.

Had Kaylee done this? Or was she hurt too? Maybe she was in there somewhere. Fearing for her, he finally stepped forward.

But the clerk grabbed his arm. "No! This is a crime scene."

"But my sister might be wounded. She could be in the bathroom or on the floor on the other side of the bed."

The clerk glared at him. "My father will be so angry."

What? Conner scowled.

"No. Wait." The clerk pulled out his phone. "Twitter will love this. It could be good for business if I handle it correctly." He rushed inside and snapped several photos of the dead man.

Conner reluctantly called 911 and reported the incident. The dispatcher tried to keep him on the line, but he was too upset to deal with her, so he hung up.

The motel clerk stepped back out and announced that the

bathroom was empty. "Your sister is not here. But I'm sure the police will find her now."

Great. They could have a family arraignment day.

If Kaylee was even alive. Maybe she'd been kidnapped. *Was this a drug deal gone bad?* And who was the dead man? Hating himself, he asked, "Do you the know the guy? Is he a guest?"

"No. But I think I've seen his photo on the news." The clerk turned his phone and held it out.

Conner instinctively glanced at it.

Oh, for freak's sake. Even with a slack, pale face, Ramsden was easily recognizable. Conner swore so many times, the clerk grabbed his arm and squeezed. "Get a grip." Then his eyes widened. "You know him, don't you? Who is he?"

"I think he works in the prosecutor's office." That was an understatement. And a pointless evasion. Conner stared at his own phone. He had to make some phone calls before the cops arrived. Hitch first. His hands shook as he pressed her number. She didn't pick up. Conner left her a message, realizing how rattled he sounded, but unable to catch his breath. "Ramsden is dead. In Kaylee's motel room. But she's not here, and I'm worried she's in trouble. But I could be too. I don't trust the police. What if they plant evidence at this scene too? I need your help. Someone has to watch them search the room. Please." He hung up, feeling hopeless.

Sirens wailed in the distance. He would be in the back of a patrol car in a matter of minutes. Unless he bolted. He'd already called in the crime. Was he legally obligated to stay?

"You're very pale." The motel clerk stared, open-mouthed. "Are you okay?"

"Actually, I'm not." He felt like he was having a heart attack. "I think I'll go home and lie down." *Or get on a bus headed out of town.*

"No!" The clerk grabbed his arm again. "You must stay and tell them this was your idea."

"What?"

"I mean to check on your sister."

What if this wasn't Kaylee's room? Maybe the clerk was wrong about matching her photo. "I have to check something." Conner rushed into the dark space, holding his breath. He glanced around, looking for something to identify the occupants. Women's clothes spilled out of a suitcase on the floor. He didn't recognize any. But Kaylee changed clothes constantly. Second-hand stores were her favorite hangouts. What else might be in the luggage? He squatted and riffled through the pockets, finding hair-ties, flip-flops, and deodorant. And a package of peanut M&Ms. Kaylee's favorite. *Damn.*

Conner hurried into the bathroom, a small messy space that smelled like pineapple shampoo. Another Kaylee favorite. Some things in her life apparently didn't change. Cosmetics and jewelry littered the small counter, but he didn't see anything particularly personal, so he started to turn around. Then he spotted the curved end of a phone sticking out from under a makeup bag. He grabbed the cell, noting it was small, cheap, and damaged. But the pink-nail-polish dot indicated that the phone was his sister's. Kaylee had started marking her belongings as soon as she'd started grade school, mostly to keep her older siblings from appropriating them.

He stared at the device, trying to make up his mind. The phone could lead him to Kaylee. At this point, it was the only lead he had. And if she'd killed Ramsden, the jackass somehow deserved it. Conner had to protect her if he could. Find her and get her into rehab under a new name. Maybe send her to Gina in Seattle.

Conner stuffed the phone into his pocket and hurried back out to the balcony, where the motel clerk paced nervously.

"I don't think this is my sister's room," Conner said. "That was an old photo I showed you."

"I have to return to the office and notify my family. Please stay here." The young man pivoted and jogged toward the stairs.

The sirens grew louder, and the phone weighed heavily in his front pocket. A pocket the police would search. He had to stash it somewhere. Or give the phone to someone to hold for him.

Still shaking, Conner called Jerry Leahy. He really needed a lawyer. Or a journalist with an on-air camera crew to record the police. Thankfully, Leahy picked up. "Hey, Conner. Anything new?"

"You could say that."

CHAPTER 24

He ended up in the back of a cop car, as predicted, but at least he wasn't cuffed. The female officer who'd questioned him briefly wanted to keep him at the scene, but she wasn't treating him like a criminal—yet. He suspected the poor woman didn't know what to think. Neither did he. How in Holy Mordor was Kaylee connected to Ramsden? Conner groaned. The prosecutor's interest in his sister was obvious from the motel room. But how had they met? Had Kaylee gotten into legal trouble? If so, then Ramsden had leverage over her. Or he'd *had* leverage.

And where the heck was his sister? How had everything gotten so messed up?

Two more patrol cars screamed into the lot and parked in front of the motel's office. One officer headed upstairs, and another jogged into the office. A few minutes later, the female officer came back down and headed Conner's way. Officer Pratt, he remembered. He tried to pay attention to such things, but he was rattled.

Two more vehicles pulled in. A dark sedan—likely a police detective—and a white Prius. *Leahy!* Thank goodness. His attorney jumped out and intercepted Pratt to ask her something. Conner couldn't hear because the patrol car's engine and air conditioning were both running. Still, a stink of sweat permeated the interior.

Leahy turned to the cop car and motioned for Conner to get out.

The officer put up her hand, gesturing that he should stay.

Conner reached for the handle, realizing he wasn't locked in. He opened the door, and climbed out. "I need some fresh air."

They both ignored him, too engaged in their rather heated exchange.

"A detective will need to question him, and they won't want to wait," the officer insisted.

"But I need to be present, and I don't have time right now." Leahy sounded calm and intense at the same time. "I'll bring Conner into the department this afternoon. You have my word."

"I trust you, but not him." Pratt glanced over at Conner, glared, then turned back to Leahy. "I ran a background, and he's already facing a probation violation charge. I can't release him."

"You have no legal reason to detain him."

"He's a suspect in a homicide!" Pratt was losing her cool.

"So is everyone in this building." Leahy gestured at the motel. "My client called in the crime. The room was locked when he arrived in the presence of another witness." Now Leahy pointed at Conner. "And there's not a single drop of blood on his white t-shirt."

Conner grinned, unable to control himself. He'd briefly described the circumstances when he'd called his attorney. Conner hadn't mentioned Kaylee's phone, which he'd stashed behind two potted plants near the top of the stairs. A good move, because Pratt had patted him down before putting him into her patrol unit. She'd taken his own cell phone and still had it. He didn't think that was legal.

Conner stepped toward the two. "Hey, I need my phone back, please. My boss might call me to come in for a shift at the restaurant."

Leahy shook his head at the officer. "You can't seize his phone without probable cause, and you can't search it without a warrant. You obviously have neither."

Pratt pulled it from her shirt pocket and handed it to Leahy. "I didn't want him making any calls without my knowledge. Supervisor's orders."

Across the parking lot, Conner spotted Detective Nelson climbing out of the dark sedan.

"Can we go?" Conner desperately wanted to leave before the detective saw him. That jerk would cuff him and ignore his attorney.

"Have him at the downtown headquarters in two hours," Pratt said.

Leahy's office near the courthouse was larger and plusher than Hitch's. Conner had noticed the lack of knickknacks in her minimal space, but Leahy made up for it with little ceramic animals, tiny cactus plants, and bright abstract paintings. It was almost too much. But Conner plopped into a chair, happy to be here instead of in a holding cell at a police station. He was starting to think he might avoid that altogether.

Leahy, who'd just ordered a pizza, put down his phone. "I figured you'd better eat before you get questioned. They might detain you, and I would have to file motions to get you released."

His hope of staying free evaporated. "Thank you so much

for coming down to the motel. I know you're busy, and I must be a huge pain."

"You are." Leahy laughed. "And I had to cancel something else. But Ramsden's death is so unexpected and bizarre, I have to assume he had a lot more going on than anyone realized." The attorney shuddered slightly. "And considering his position in the legal system, I expect an effort to cover it up. And I can't let that happen."

"Thank you. They're already trying to frame me for Troy's death, and I know this looks bad."

"Indeed it does." The attorney stared into his eyes. "Why were you there? Do not lie to me or I can't help you."

"Looking for Kaylee, my youngest sister. A friend thought she might be staying at the Marigold."

"But why were you looking for her?"

"My family is worried about her. She's been out of touch for months."

"A homicide detective will ask you those questions and many more. If I'm not present, don't answer anything. Just tell them you want your attorney present."

"But then they'll arrest me."

"If they have grounds to arrest you, they will anyway. Don't give them any extra ammunition. But for now, I need to know everything. Even the details you shouldn't share with them." Leahy gave him a knowing look. "We'll go through your statement step by step. I'll be there to stop you if I don't want a question answered. If you're ever in doubt, say nothing."

Conner sighed. He wanted to tell Leahy about Kaylee's phone, but his attorney might make him turn it over to the police. Conner needed to retrieve it first, to make sure it was still there. And to search it for anything that could help him find poor Kaylee.

CHAPTER 25

At the police department, Conner and Leahy sat at a hard table in a small windowless room. Across from them, Nelson sat next to another detective named Drummond, who was so pale, he could have been albino. They took turns asking questions, bouncing from one subject to another like a pinball. The repetition and chaos made Conner's head hurt. That was probably the point.

"Why did you hate Ramsden?" Nelson sounded sure of himself, just like last time.

"I didn't. I barely knew him."

"But you blamed him for your incarceration?"

"Well, yeah. He prosecuted me."

"You blamed Troy Burton too, didn't you?"

"Of course. He ratted on me."

Leahy cleared his throat. "We've been over this. And my client's feelings about the dead men are irrelevant. If you don't have any incriminating evidence or pertinent questions, we're done."

"He's not done until I let him go." Nelson leaned back. "Your client was in the proximity of the murders of two men responsible for his incarceration."

Detective Drummond cut in. "Besides his own criminal behavior."

Nelson picked back up. "That makes Conner our primary suspect."

Leahy shook his head. "The system is loaded with inmates and ex-inmates who hated Ramsden. And my understanding is that Troy Burton helped put a few others away. You have plenty of suspects."

"None of which were present."

"Which is why they're all better suspects," Leahy countered. "Why would a guilty person hang around and call the police?"

"You can argue his case in court. Right now, you need to let us question him." The detective locked eyes with Conner again. "The motel clerk says you went into the room. Why?"

Conner had expected the question. "Did he tell you he went inside too? To take photos to post online?"

Nelson's eyes flashed with anger. "Answer my question."

"I wanted to check on Kaylee. I thought she might be injured or dead in the bathroom." *True.*

A moment of silence.

Conner started to speak, but his attorney nudged him. *Oh right.* Do not elaborate.

"Did you touch the dead body?"

"No." Conner shuddered.

"Did you touch anything? We're fingerprinting everywhere."

"I looked at some things in the suitcase—because I didn't think it was really Kaylee's room." *Also true.*

"Are they her clothes?"

"I don't know."

"How did your sister know Martin Ramsden?"

"No clue."

"Where would Kaylee go to hide?"

"I have no idea. I haven't seen her in over a year." Conner dreaded the next few questions. He didn't want to lie—because that would give them an excuse to hold him—but so would the truth.

"Has she contacted you? Phone call, text, anything?"

"No."

"Would you help her evade arrest if she asked you to?"

"Don't answer that." Leahy shook his head. "Hypotheticals are pointless. Let's stick to the facts."

Detective Drummond leaned toward Conner. "Where did you change your clothes after you killed Ramsden?"

Oh boy. "I didn't."

"Didn't what?"

"I didn't kill him. Or change my clothes anywhere."

"Who told you Kaylee was at the Marigold Motel?"

"A friend of Kaylee's. I messaged her online."

"What's her name?"

"I don't know." *True.* He wouldn't give them *Aloha's* online persona unless he had to. So far, she was still the only person he knew who'd had recent contact with Kaylee, and he didn't want to send the police her way.

"How do you not know the name of someone you talked to?" Nelson looked pissed.

"Someone gave me her email address. It's an anonymous message board."

"Who gave you the contact info?"

"A guy named Ryan." Conner recited the address, hoping to distract Nelson from asking about *Aloha.* "Another guy named Matt lives there too." The police would eventually find out about the content house, but Conner didn't want to help them.

"Why did you kill Ramsden?"

"I didn't." Conner turned to Leahy. "I have a headache and would like to go home."

"My client has already told you he didn't kill Ramsden," Leahy said. "He has been very cooperative, and you're starting to repeat your questions. So either arrest him or we're leaving."

Conner squirmed. He didn't really want Leahy to push the arrest issue.

"Get out of here," Nelson said.

CHAPTER 26

As Hitch walked out of the courtroom, Nelson was waiting—the last person she wanted to see right now. She had enough to deal with the way her trial was falling apart.

"We need to talk." An urgency in his tone.

"What's the big emergency?" she asked.

Nelson waited until Arroyo was out of earshot. "Ramsden is dead."

"What?"

Several other people left the courtroom and walked past them.

"Not here," Nelson said.

"Want to go to my office?"

"That's not a good idea either. Your office is probably buzzing with talk of the murder. My car's right around the corner on Union. Let's take a short ride."

"Jake, what's going on? I don't have much time."

He grabbed her elbow and led her to the elevator. "How's your trial going?"

"Not that well. I hate when I'm surprised by a witness, especially my own."

They stepped out of the elevator and walked out of the

building, Nelson still making small talk. He opened the passenger door for her, then climbed in the other side. He still didn't say anything as he pulled out of the parking spot.

"Just tell me," Hitch demanded. Her nerves were twitching.

"Ramsden is dead, Conner is a suspect, and you will be questioned."

"Why me?"

"Because you were one of the last people to see Ramsden before he left the bar. And right now, there are no other witnesses from the time he was seen in the bar until Conner found him—or killed him—in a motel room."

Conner found him? That made no sense.

Nelson turned right on Harbor Drive and cruised along the waterfront.

"Conner wouldn't murder anyone." *Unless she'd been completely fooled.* "And why would he kill Ramsden, then hang around and report it?"

"That doesn't work for me either, but stranger things have happened."

"Where's Conner now?"

"I don't know. He lawyered up."

"Jerry Leahy?"

"Yes. But Conner is not my concern. You are."

"Why?"

"I just wanted you forewarned before anyone else on the taskforce talked to you."

Nelson drove onto Harbor Island and parked near the East Basin.

"I wasn't the last one to see Ramsden alive," Hitch said. "DDA Fisher came up just as I was leaving."

"He's already been questioned. And he told us you were with Ramsden."

"I wasn't *with* him," Hitch countered. "I *saw* Ramsden after

I left you. He called me over, and I talked to him for a few minutes. Then I left."

"I can say I came downstairs and walked you out and took you home, if you want."

Hitch jerked her head and glared at Nelson. "Do you think I killed Ramsden?"

"Of course not." He reached over and laid his hand on her shoulder. "I'm just saying it will remove all doubt from the investigation, and the taskforce will leave you alone. You know how messy it can get."

"I know how messy it can get when people start lying. No, thank you." Hitch wondered if he really thought she needed an alibi—or maybe he was setting her up. Both thoughts worried her.

CHAPTER 27

Back in court, Hitch sat at the counsel table, waiting for the jury to be seated. With the testimony so far, she was not certain they would convict Jason Evans. The jurors seemed to be looking at Heather differently, and if they chose not to believe Heather's testimony, they had reasonable doubt. Hitch couldn't trust that Arroyo would call his client to testify. She was sure the rapist would tell on himself—if not with words, with body language. But Arroyo was too smart for that. He wouldn't put Evans on the stand unless he had to. Hitch decided to call her informant. After he testified that Evans told him the sex wasn't consensual, Arroyo's only recourse would be to have the defendant rebut it—or take his chances.

"Please call your next witness, Miss Hitchens," Judge Barenski said. His use of the title annoyed her. Every other judge called her Ms., but not Barenski. He refused to use that term. For years he'd insisted that women lawyers wear skirts in his courtroom. He couldn't get away with that any longer, but he still made his prejudices known. Many female attorneys still wore suits with skirts when he was on the bench. They figured they had a big enough disadvantage with him already. Hitch, on the other hand, didn't care what he thought. Though she understood why female defense attorneys indulged him. Barenski was a conservative judge and usually favored the prosecutor. They didn't need another disadvantage.

"The State calls Aiden Palmer to the stand." In spite of all the prepping Hitch had done with him, Palmer sauntered up to the witness stand as if he didn't have a care in the world. And when he was sworn in, he didn't appear the least bit nervous. His whole attitude came off as cocky, and Hitch wondered how many times he'd done this before. She didn't really know what type of demeanor would be best for a jailhouse informant to persuade a jury. She'd never liked using them to make a case, but this time seemed worse because of her suspicions about what was going on in the prosecutors' office. For a moment, she questioned her decision and almost changed her mind. *No.* She had to get justice for Heather. That meant forcing the rapist to testify and hopefully hang himself.

"Do you know the defendant, Jason Evans?" Hitch asked.

"We shared a cell in county jail."

"How long were you in the cell together?"

"About a week."

"And during that time, did Mr. Evans tell you why he was in custody?"

"Of course. That's the first thing inmates talk about. And everyone says they're innocent and have been railroaded."

Hitch cringed. She'd told him to just answer yes or no and not add anything extra, but he couldn't keep his mouth shut.

"What did Mr. Evans say he was in jail for?"

"He claimed it was for being in Heaven." Palmer smiled, obviously feeling clever.

"Did you ask him what that meant?"

"Objection," Arroyo said. "Hearsay."

"It's a statement against his own interest, Your Honor," Hitch argued. *Arroyo knew her question was legit. He was just trying to interrupt her flow.*

"Overruled." The judge turned to the witness. "Do you remember the question?"

"Of course," Palmer said. "I told him he wasn't making sense. But he gets this smile and says, 'If you knew Heaven the way I know Heaven'. Then he starts blabbering about Heaven. At first, I thought he was wacko, but then I realized he was talking about a person. So I asked who she was, and he said she was a beautiful girl who liked to get raped."

"He used the word *rape*?"

"Yes. He said he raped her."

Shifting noises came from the jury.

Palmer continued. "I said, 'No woman likes to be raped,' and he got that smile again and said, 'She asked for it. She got what she deserved.'"

"Did he know Heather before he raped her?"

"Objection," Arroyo called out. "Assumes facts not in evidence."

"What facts?" Hitch asked. "The defendant told this witness he raped a woman. If Mr. Arroyo is objecting to Heaven and Heather being referred to as the same person, he was the one who established that earlier. So unless his client was talking about another rape he committed …"

"Objection!" Arroyo flew to his feet. "Now the prosecutor is testifying and attempting to prejudice the jury."

Barenski tapped his gavel.

"I withdraw the question." Hitch didn't want the judge to sustain the defense's objection. She turned to her witness. "Did the defendant tell you he knew the woman he claimed to have raped?"

"He said he was Heaven's favorite client. That she had made many videos just for him."

"Did he at any time say he and Heaven planned the experience?"

"No."

"Did he at any time claim she invited him over?"

"No."

"Or that she asked him to rape her?"

"No." Palmer shook his head. "He got off on it."

"No further questions." Hitch turned back to her seat, hoping he'd told the truth.

"Your witness, Mr. Arroyo," the judge said.

"Thank you, Your Honor." Arroyo positioned himself in front of Palmer. "You said you met Jason Evans in jail, correct?"

"Yes."

"So you had been arrested as well, right?"

"Yeah. But it was a misunderstanding."

"It always is."

"Objection." Hitch rolled her eyes. Arroyo knew better.

Before she could give the basis, Barenski said, "Sustained. Please refrain from making remarks, Counselor."

"I apologize, Your Honor. " Arroyo turned back to the witness. "What were the charges that landed you in jail?"

"Shoplifting."

"How long were you in custody?"

"Eight days. But I shouldn't have been there at all."

"And how many of those days were you in the same cell as Jason?"

"Seven. The first day I was in the main holding pen."

"And you're a free man now, right?"

"Right. The charges were dropped for lack of evidence."

"So you were released and the charges dropped after you told someone the story about my client, correct?"

"Objection to the word *story*," Hitch said. "States facts not in evidence."

"I'll rephrase." Arroyo tried again. "You were released and the charges dropped right after you gave the accounting of your conversation with Mr. Evans, correct?"

"Yes. But it's cuz they had no evidence against me."

Hitch wished he would stop saying that. It was only making him sound worse. He would look more credible if he didn't keep trying to convince everyone what a great guy he was.

"The truth is the charges were dropped because you made a deal with the DA, correct?"

"No. I was innocent. I checked out at the counter and paid for—"

Arroyo cut in. "Your Honor, please advise the witness to just answer the question."

"Just answer yes or no," Barenski said.

"No," Palmer said.

Hitch had warned Palmer not to editorialize. Jurors expected these kinds of deals. So Arroyo got exactly what he wanted. He made the jury think he didn't want Palmer to explain, which made the witness look even less reliable. Even with all the theatrics, Arroyo hadn't done much damage and would still have to call his client to rebut the informant's testimony. Hitch felt optimistic for the first time since learning Heather made sex videos.

CHAPTER 28

Tuesday, late afternoon

Conner opened the car door and started to climb out. "Thanks, Mr. Leahy. I really appreciate everything you've done for me." His attorney had given him a ride back to the Marigold Motel and bought him a burger on the way.

"Call me Jerry." He leaned toward Conner. "Keep out of sight, please. The police will likely pick you up again if they don't find Kaylee or come up with another suspect."

"Okay." Conner waved as Leahy drove away, guilt flooding him. He intended to keep searching for Kaylee. She was in even more trouble than he'd realized, and he had to get to her before the police did. Conner at least wanted to be able to coach her for when she was arrested or turned herself in. He didn't want Kaylee to make the same mistakes he had. What she really needed was a defense attorney. Maybe Leahy would help her too.

Conner walked toward his car, wondering if it was safe to retrieve Kaylee's phone from its balcony hiding spot. The patrol units were all gone, but the forensics van was still in the parking lot. He decided to go for it. If anyone noticed him, he would say he was looking for something he'd dropped earlier.

He grabbed a baseball cap out of the Mustang, pulled it low over his forehead, and headed for the corner staircase. As he neared the building, he started the charade, scanning the ground as he walked—just in case security cameras or law enforcement officers were watching. Conner hustled up the steps, his heart pounding more from anxiety than exertion. At the top, he stopped, glanced around as though searching, then reached behind the ceramic pot.

His fingers came up empty. *No!* Had the police found the phone? Conner inched forward, leaned way over, and spotted the phone. He snatched it up, relieved.

As he started downstairs, the feeling was short lived. A tall man in a dark suit came out of the motel office, noticed him, and headed his way. Conner forced himself to relax, or to at least look chill.

"Do you live here?" the man called out. His pinched face and lanky body gave him an Ichabod Crane look.

Conner noticed the bulge of a weapon under his jacket. A detective, as he'd thought. "No. I'm just looking for something I dropped earlier." Conner hit the last step and kept moving.

"Wait."

Argg! Conner made himself stop and turn.

The guy pushed his jacket aside to reveal a badge. "Detective Harrison. What were you doing here earlier?"

Conner's heart pounded so hard, he was sure the cop could hear it. "Just looking for someone. She wasn't here." Conner shrugged and gave a small smile. "Story of my life."

The detective stared at his face for a moment, then waved him on. "Keep clear of this place for a while. It's an active crime scene."

Conner bit back a smart-aleck response and moved toward his car, careful not to look like he was hurrying. He climbed in, resisting the urge to look back and see if the cop was watching him.

A few minutes later, he pulled into a Walmart parking lot, locked the car doors, and took out Kaylee's phone. *Please don't let it be password protected.*

But it was. He tried *birdie*, the name she'd given her first parakeet when she was five. It didn't work. *How many tries before the phone locked him out?*

Conner tried *petunia*, Kaylee's favorite flower. *No go.* Thinking she might be more sophisticated than that, he keyed in her birthday numbers. Another fail. After four more tries, including her middle name, he finally entered *Patricia*, their mother's name.

Bingo.

Conner pressed the text icon and read her most recent message: *I'll be over soon. Dress for it! And we need to get you a better place.* The ID at the top of the screen said *MARS.*

A nickname? For Martin Ramsden? Conner checked the day and time the text had been sent. The night before at 11:25 p.m.

Dress for what? *Oh right.* A rush of emotions overwhelmed him. Rage that Ramsden had somehow coerced Kaylee into a sexual relationship. Curiosity about how Kaylee had met the creep. And guilt about having her phone. The police needed this information to do their job. He would get Kaylee's cell to them somehow—as soon as he found what he needed.

He quickly read through the messages between MARS and Kaylee, which had only started a few weeks ago ... at least on this phone. Their exchanges were entirely about when and how they would hook up.

Conner checked another message thread. *Rona.* The woman he'd met at Beachside Boogie. Her last two texts said *What's cooking?* and *u ok?* He scanned previous messages, but they were just comments about a streaming show they were both watching. Conner started to call the number, then froze. If he used Kaylee's phone, it would be harder to deny that he'd ever had it. And he didn't want the police to think his sister had made calls from it after leaving the motel. If she was in trouble, they needed real information. And he had to remember to wipe off his fingerprints!

Panic gripped him. Once he put the phone back, they could track where it had been. So he couldn't take it home. Or anywhere.

He just needed the data. A clone app could transfer the files to his phone. But then, if he was arrested or the police got ahold of his cell ...

No. He needed to download the files to his computer, then to a flash drive. And his laptop was under the seat. Or it had been that morning. He reached for it, grateful to feel its cool exterior. Conner chuckled. The Mustang had been sitting in a parking lot filled with cop cars. The whole neighborhood had been safe that day.

Conner dug through his console for a phone-charger cord and plugged the cheap Android into his laptop. Once the icon displayed, he clicked through a few options, and the transfer began. It took less than a minute. Kaylee either hadn't had the phone long or hadn't used it much.

But how could he get it back into the motel room without being seen? *Impossible.* The evidence techs were still in there. Could he sneak the phone into the front office somehow? He'd have to think about it. Conner tucked the problem into the back of his brain and let it go. An idea would come to him if he focused on something else.

And right now, he needed to know if Kaylee was alive and well. He desperately wanted to hear her voice.

Using his own phone, he called Rona. "It's Nate Conner. Kaylee's brother. We met recently at the Beachside."

She was silent for a moment. "How did you get my

number? I mean, you're really cute and all, but I have a boyfriend."

"This is about Kaylee. Have you seen her or heard from her?"

"No. I told you that. Yeah, I've texted her, but she didn't respond. Why?" A worried gasp. "Did something bad happen?"

How much to tell her? Nothing, just yet. "Yes. But I think Kaylee's okay." *Unless she'd been kidnapped. Or seriously injured.* "Who would she run to in an emergency?"

"I'm not sure." Distress in Rona's voice now. "She's been drifting away from me for a while."

"What about the other woman you were with that night? The singer?"

"Selene? They broke up months ago."

What? "You mean as friends?"

"Don't be naive. Kaylee's bi. Or at least she experiments. But I didn't get a sense she was ever really in love with Selene." A long pause. "I think Kaylee mostly needed a place to stay."

Conner couldn't think about the weirdness of all that right now. Or maybe ever. "Text me Selene's number. And her address." Just in case Selene wasn't in the data he'd transferred, he'd have it.

"I doubt Kaylee's there. And I don't actually know the address. But it's in La Mesa somewhere."

"But you'll text the phone number? And her last name, please."

"She goes by Selene Gomez. Her legal name is a whole string of stuff I can't remember."

No help. In San Diego, Selene Gomez was as common as Kate Smith. "Have you been to Selene's home? Could you take me there, if needed?"

"I think so. But I was only there once because we usually met at the club. But seriously, Kaylee wouldn't—" A loud clang in the background. "Oh heck. Sorry. I just knocked over my latte cup. So glad it was empty."

"Where *would* Kaylee go? Any new friends? Or out of town—"

Rona cut in excitedly. "I just remembered a guy she mentioned once. Trevor something. He lives near the beach, and Kaylee mentioned he was lit with cash. And that he had a serious crush on her." Rona laughed. "Everyone does."

"Thanks. I'll be in touch." Conner hung up, eager to put Kaylee's phone back. But a strategy hadn't magically popped into his head. He drove to the motel and parked across the street at a convenience store. No matter what he did, they would suspect him. But as long as they couldn't prove it, he'd be all right.

He heard Hitch's voice in his head giving him a hard time. "Sorry!" Conner pulled on his baseball cap and a windbreaker from the back seat and climbed out.

A young teenager came out of the little store. *An errand boy!* Conner hurried after him as he moved toward the sidewalk. "Excuse me."

The kid turned. "What? I didn't take anything."

Conner almost laughed out loud. Better yet. "I think you did. But I'll forget about it if you do me a favor. I'll even throw in ten bucks." Without the shoplifting leverage, he would have offered him twenty.

"What favor? I don't do sex with guys."

"No!" Conner gestured emphatically, then pulled Kaylee's phone from his pocket. "I need you to take this across the street to the Marigold Motel office. Hand it to the person behind the counter and say, 'Room two-oh-six.'"

"That's it?"

"Yep. Just walk out and keep going." Conner pulled out his wallet, hoping he still had some cash. A ten, a five, and two singles. *Oh boy.* "Do we have a deal?"

"Sure." The kid held out his hand. "Easy money."

Conner gave him the phone and the ten. "Don't cheat me. I'll be watching."

"Whatever."

The kid jogged across the street, dodging traffic like only a teenage boy would. Suddenly feeling exposed and vulnerable, Conner climbed back into the Mustang. Security cameras were everywhere. He watched the errand boy go inside the motel. *Sweet Baby J!* The phone was back where it belonged. Conner had no way of knowing if the kid would do as instructed or if the clerk, whoever was on duty, would turn the phone over to the police. But why wouldn't they?

A minute later, the kid came out, glanced over at Conner, then jogged toward the sidewalk, headed in the same direction he'd been going before. Conner started the engine, eager to get out of the neighborhood and never come back. A moment later, the detective who'd stopped him earlier walked out of the motel office. *Oh no.* Had he been there when the kid handed over the phone? The cop glanced in Conner's direction. Panic filled his belly. But he'd parked behind a van near the back of the store, and the kid hadn't seen the Mustang. Or had he? Conner eased out of the lot and onto a side street, forcing himself to drive slowly.

He wanted to go home to Nico's where he felt safe. But he had to try and reach Kaylee's contacts while he was in town. Why drive out there just to turn around and come back?

He drove aimlessly for a while, then realized he was headed toward the courthouse ... and Hitch's nearby office. But he couldn't ever tell her about having Kaylee's phone. She would hate feeling compromised. He wouldn't tell Jerry Leahy either. They would just have to trust that the source of his information was valid.

A few blocks later, Conner parked on the street near an internet cafe. He would make calls from his car, then go inside to get online and conduct more research, if needed. He was eager to contact the people Rona had mentioned.

He found Trevor in the phone data but with no last name and no address. The rich dude and Kaylee had exchanged a series of text messages that were sexually flirtatious and concluded with an invitation for Kaylee to visit his home. Kaylee had responded: *Yaas! Give me 20 min heads up before you get here.* She'd added a kissy-lip emoji.

Where was *here*?

Conner checked the date of the text. Three weeks earlier. Had Kaylee been staying at the Marigold? He wished he'd asked the clerk. Too late now.

Conner called Trevor's number, but no one picked up, as he'd expected. People his age didn't answer their phones. But Conner wanted to talk in person so Trevor could hear the urgency in his voice. He left a message: "This is Conner, Kaylee's brother. I really need to find her. Please call me."

He tried Selene next and left the same message, then opened his laptop. Scanning the download of Kaylee's messages, he came across someone named Chris who'd texted Kaylee about not leaving dishes in the sink. The texts were dated five weeks earlier. Obviously someone she'd stayed with, at least briefly, between the content house and the Marigold Motel. No last name, no address, and no texts before or after those few days. His sister had been so desperate she'd been sofa surfing with strangers. The thought broke his heart.

Was that how she'd ended up in a motel room with Ramsden?

CHAPTER 29

Hitch arrived at Leahy's office a few minutes early, so his secretary, Gabriela, escorted her inside. "Jerry said to bring you in here, so make yourself comfortable."

"Thanks, I appreciate it. I know you're working late." They all were, and Hitch was glad to finally be done with court for the day.

"I just spoke to him, and he's on his way. There's water in there." Gabriela pointed to a small fridge, then left, closing the door behind her.

Hitch glanced around at Leahy's artifacts, then sat in a comfortable leather chair across from his desk. It felt great to be off her feet and out of the lobby, where there was less chance of running into someone she knew. She thought about the threatening call she'd received. Someone was watching her and knew she was investigating the informant situation, which only confirmed her suspicions and made her more determined to find out what was going on. She hadn't told anyone in the DA's office yet, but who could she trust? A few months earlier, she would have shared her concerns with Nelson, but now she wasn't sure what side he was on. So she'd confided in Leahy. She didn't know what Leahy really thought of her conspiracy theory about the snitches, but maybe the phone call would give some cred to her suspicions.

The door opened and Leahy walked in, apologizing. He explained that he would've been back sooner, but his client had suffered a seizure, so he'd waited until the paramedics arrived.

"Is he all right?"

"He was doing better, but they took him to the hospital to be examined." Leahy took a seat.

Hitch needed to get down to business. "You have the video from Beachside Boogie?"

"Yes. There's very little footage with Conner in it, but at least it's not damaging." He popped a flash drive into his computer and motioned for Hitch to come around to his side of the desk. "Here, Conner is attempting to get Burton's attention as he heads for the door." Leahy started the video, and they watched the scene. "And there"—he pointed to the screen —"someone stops Conner. Then he turns around and heads to the front door."

"That's exactly what Conner said he did." Another layer of tension left Hitch's body. Her trust in the young man had been validated.

"I'll go through the whole thing again later and see if I notice anything else," Leahy said. "And I want Conner to watch it with me to see if he recognizes anyone of interest. Maybe it will give us a lead."

"Good idea. What about the video from the jail?"

"They don't have one."

"They have no recording at all?"

"It's blank."

Hitch balled her hands into fists. *The corruption!* "How do they explain that?"

"They don't. The sheriff commander who runs the jail said he would 'look into it.' We both know what that means."

"Yeah. He'll stall until he can come up with a good coverup."

"Have you heard any scuttlebutt in the DA's office?"

"No. But I get the feeling people are avoiding me. Maybe I'm just paranoid, but ..." Hitch paused, wondering again if she should say anything about the threat she'd received.

"But what?"

Hitch told him about the phone call.

"You have no idea who it was?" Leahy asked.

She shook her head. "I didn't recognize the voice. It sounded disguised. Thinking back, it seems like the man spoke slowly and deliberately, almost as if he was reading the lines."

"If those involved are on to you, you'll have to be careful."

"I don't want to lose my job over this, but I can't work for people who blatantly violate our constitution. That's not what I signed up for."

"Do you have any allies in your office?"

"Not anyone I know for sure I can trust. But I'll see what I can find out on my own. With Ramsden dead, there will be lots of turmoil. Maybe someone will feel free to talk about what they know."

Hitch left Leahy's office and walked toward the Central lockup. Her stomach growled as she passed a street vendor, and she promised herself she would get something to eat on the way back.

At the jail, she showed her badge and asked the clerk to check the records for when Conner had been booked. She had read his case file and jotted down the name of the arresting officer, as well as the deputy who'd booked him and signed the property log—Fernando Vargas. There was no mention of a knife.

"Is Fernando Vargas here?"

"Let me check."

A few minutes later, a uniformed deputy approached her. He looked so young, twenty-five at most, a rookie.

"Can I help you?"

Hitch introduced herself. "I'm doing some follow-up on a case in which you signed the inmate's property log. I'd like to ask a few questions."

"Who was the arrestee?"

"Nathan Conner, and it was eight months ago."

Hitch noticed a slight tightening around his eyes before he shook his head. "I don't remember the booking. We've had hundreds since then. What is it you want to know?"

"He claims he had a pocketknife with him when he was brought in, but there's no record of it."

"If he had a knife, I would have written it down. That's not the kind of thing I would've missed." Vargas sounded defensive. "A lot of prisoners claim they had items that they didn't. Mostly they say money. I guess they think they can get some easy cash from the county by claiming we stole it. It never works, but they keep trying."

She tried to placate him. "You're right. I prosecute criminals every day. Truth is not their strong point. I just don't want any loose ends." Hitch paused for effect. "Since the knife he *claimed* he had turned up as a murder weapon."

Vargas flinched. "No wonder he claimed it was stolen."

Hitch gave him her card. "If you happen to remember something, please call my cell. The number is on the back."

CHAPTER 30

"Oh my God!" Nicole burst into tears, then covered her face and sobbed into her hands.

Conner wanted to comfort her, but he'd learned not to disturb his older sister when she was in that mode. He silently waited her out, knowing he had more bad news to share. So far, he'd only told her about the dead man in the motel room and Kaylee being in the wind.

After a minute, Nicole mumbled "Enough," then got up and opened a bottle of white wine. She poured two glasses and brought them back to the table. "They arrested you, didn't they?"

"No. They just took me in for questioning." Conner took a long drink of wine. Not his favorite, but he would take any comfort he could. "Leahy, my lawyer, was with me the whole time. I'm sure it's the only reason they let me go."

"I think I love him."

"Me too."

They laughed and clinked their glasses.

"What else?" Nicole squeezed his arm. "I know there's more."

He hadn't told her about Kaylee's stay in the content

house, and he wouldn't mention that he'd taken her phone from the crime scene. Not yet. "I've reached out to everyone Kaylee's been in contact with in the last three weeks. No one has gotten back to me yet, but I'll find her."

"The police will find her first, and she'll be held without bail. Ramsden is a big deal in the DA's office." Nicole gulped her wine. "Both of you facing murder charges at the same time. What in ever-loving hell?"

Their mother's expression. Conner smiled sadly.

His phone rang, and he snatched it off the table. It was a number he'd called earlier. *Trevor!* He answered quickly. "This is Conner."

"Trevor Gorman, returning your call. But only so you'll stop bothering me."

"Hey, sorry. But I need to find Kaylee. Have you seen her?"

"Uh, not in a month or so."

His tone was off. *Was he lying?* "Has Kaylee contacted you at all?"

"No, man. But you sound upset. What's the deal?"

Trevor was definitely high on something. Conner didn't exactly trust him, but he needed information. "The police are looking for Kaylee, and I really want to find her first."

"Yeah, that girl is trouble." A deep sigh. "She has a friend named Rona, but that's about all I can tell you."

"I've checked with Rona." Conner wanted to see if Trevor would tell him the truth. "Has Kaylee ever been to your house?"

A long pause. "Why?"

"Because she's hiding out somewhere. And I know you invited her over three weeks ago."

"So? She never showed."

But according to their texts, Kaylee had expected Trevor to pick her up. "Did she have a car?"

"How would I know? I need to get back to——"

133

Conner cut in. "How did you meet Kaylee?"

"I'll let her tell you."

"Why can't you? I mean, are you trying to cover for her? I know about the content house."

"Then ask them."

Conner had tried that. "Do you know how Kaylee connected with Martin Ramsden from the DA's office?"

A long silence.

"I really can't help you. Don't contact me again." Trevor ended the call.

CHAPTER 31

Tuesday evening

Hitch sat at her desk, eating the tacos she'd picked up and waiting for everyone else to leave. One by one, they headed out. She frequently worked late, and it wasn't unusual for her be the last one in the office, with the exception of Ramsden, who had often stayed late too.

He'd been so ambitious, especially when it came to ensuring a winning record. After he'd been promoted to chief deputy DA and put in charge of their division, the stats had showed an increase in convictions. He'd had to approve every case that was filed, and the DDAs had reported to him daily. He'd encouraged plea deals, but he'd also wanted plenty of trial wins. Those made headlines. Whenever anyone lost a case, he'd called them into his office and conducted a strategy session. Then he'd tightened his oversight of the next three or four trials the attorney handled. Hitch had left one of those sessions knowing she'd better not lose another one for a while. She'd also developed a little animosity toward her supervisor.

An attorney walked past and said "Goodnight."

"Goodnight, Ian." Hitch looked around. She'd been tracking her peers' exits and was pretty certain Victoria Wu was the only attorney left in the building. *Vic might make a good ally.* She was idealistic, seemed to look up to Hitch, and didn't get involved in the day-to-day office drama.

Hitch walked over to her cubicle. "I see you're working late again."

"Yeah, a frustrating trial. How about you? You're in the middle of a trial too, right?"

"And things are not going that well. It's a rape case, and there's no DNA." Hitch sat in Vic's visitor chair and lamented. "Juries have come to expect everything to be like *NCIS*. Too much television with forensics that don't really exist. And get this. The victim just revealed, on the stand today, that she posts sex videos on OnlyFans." Hitch shuddered a little. "I was blindsided. It shouldn't have any bearing on what the perp did, but juries have a hard time getting past that sort of thing."

"That could be devastating to your case."

"I know. But enough about that. How are you doing with all this sudden chaos?"

"I can't believe Ramsden was murdered."

"It's pretty awful." Hitch stood back up, wanting to make sure she could see if anyone approached … before she brought up the real reason for her visit.

Victoria sighed and fiddled with her necklace.

"Are you all right?"

"I am." Victoria paused. "I'm concerned about my trial. Ramsden said he'd turned up a witness and I was supposed to interview him this afternoon so he could testify tomorrow."

"What's the problem?"

"Ramsden never gave me the information about the witness, so I don't know who it is or how to reach him."

"Did you talk to the investigator?"

She nodded. "He doesn't know anything about it either."

Hitch took a deep breath. "Do you know if he's a jail informant?"

Victoria's eyes shifted. "I don't know. Why do you ask?"

"Just curious."

Victoria was quiet for a moment, then said, "We seem to have many of those in our cases. I never realized how often that happened."

Hitch wasn't sure yet how much to say, but she'd heard concern in Victoria's voice. Maybe she suspected something too. "We get a lot more informants than we used to."

"How long has that been going on?" Victoria asked.

"About a year and a half."

"Isn't that when Ramsden became supervisor?"

She was suspicious! "Yes. What are you saying?" Hitch wanted Victoria to say it first.

"It just seems that whenever a case isn't going well, a witness, usually an informant from jail, seems to appear." Victoria scowled. "I've had it happen twice in the last six months, and I know others have too. Although, no one else seems concerned about it. I thought about talking to you because I trust you, but then I thought I was being ridiculous."

"I wish you had. I have the same concerns." Hitch nodded, feeling vindicated.

"And another thing. The case I'm working on now had Ramsden pretty upset. The defendant burglarized the home of an eighty-year-old woman. She saw the burglar, but he didn't know it. So we had a great witness. It looked like a slam dunk until the victim had a stroke. She can't even talk now."

"How did Ramsden handle that?"

"Not well. He said, 'We can't afford to lose this one.'" Victoria mimicked his nasal voice. "When I told him there wasn't anything I could do, he got pretty upset. Then he suddenly said, 'Never mind. I'll take care of it.' The next day, he called and said we had a new witness."

"Do you think his witnesses are lying?"

"I don't know, but it doesn't feel right. What do you think?"

Time to share her concerns. "Even if they are telling the truth, if they've been planted in jail to elicit information from someone who already has counsel, that's not legal." Hitch nodded at Victoria. "I'm sure you're familiar with *Massiah v. United States,* in which the Supreme Court found the government couldn't use informants to deliberately elicit information without the defendant's lawyer present. It's a clear violation of the constitution."

"I know. I wondered about that too. It just seems too convenient." Victoria swallowed hard. "Do you think Ramsden was planting informants in the jails?"

"I think it's possible, maybe even likely."

"What do we do now? We can't just let it go."

"We have to get some proof first." Hitch glanced around, then cautioned, "Before we talk more about this, let's make sure we're alone."

Victoria nodded. They stepped out of the cubicle, turned in different directions, and walked up the two aisles until they reached the front of the office. No one else was there.

"What now?" Victoria asked.

"I'm not sure."

"We could check the files and make a list of all the cases where informants were used at trial or were possible witnesses. See if we can find a trail back to Ramsden."

"That would take too long," Hitch countered. "We just need to find a couple of witnesses who will point the finger at Ramsden, or whoever is setting it up. Maybe it's his investigator. Or maybe Ramsden had a deputy in the jail working for him. He couldn't have done it all on his own. So we need to find out who was helping him."

"But how?"

"I have an informant on my trial now. I'll start with him and see if I can get any information."

"I can check back for the last one I used. And I know Ian had one a couple of weeks ago. Maybe I can find out who it was."

"Just be careful. I'm already into this up to my eyebrows, but I don't want you to get into trouble."

"I have an idea." Victoria hurried toward the back of the room.

Hitch followed her. "Where are we going?"

"Ian probably has that file in his desk. I'll check it."

"He's not supposed to keep the files in his desk." Hitch scowled. "They should be returned to the shelf after the trial is completed."

"I know, but Ian keeps them until after sentencing. He's too lazy to put them back, and he says no one ever checks for them anyway."

Victoria stepped into Ian's cubicle and opened his file drawer. She shuffled through folders, then pulled one out. "Here it is." Victoria sat down and perused the paperwork. Hitch tried to read over her shoulder.

"The informant's name is Darius Williams."

She'd heard that name recently, but not in connection to her rape case. Hitch spotted movement near the outer door. "Quick, put the file away. The night custodian just came in."

Victoria tucked it into the drawer, and they strode casually back to her cubicle. They watched the custodian work his way toward them, emptying trashcans as he went along. When he left the room, they gathered up their stuff and exited the building.

Hitch climbed into her car, but before starting it, she called and left a message for Aiden Palmer: "Meet me at my office before court tomorrow morning at eight sharp."

CHAPTER 32

A few hours earlier

Conner headed for his room, opened his laptop, and searched Facebook for Trevor Gorman. He sensed the guy had lied and knew a lot more about Kaylee than he'd admitted to. Particularly her connection to Ramsden. That relationship was deeply disturbing. A terrible thought hit Conner, landing in his gut like a punch. What if Kaylee had been trying to protect him? The prosecutor might have coerced her into sex by threatening that her brother would spend his life in prison for murder unless she hooked up with him. Was that why he hadn't been charged with Troy Burton's death? And why Kaylee had killed Ramsden? To free them both from his grip?

Conner jumped to his feet and paced the small room, taking deep breaths. The cannabis oil in the vape called to him. He desperately needed to calm his anxious nerves. A benzo would be even better, but no doctor would write him a script for one. He sat back down and forced himself to focus. His Facebook search had produced three men named Trevor Gorman who lived in California, with one in La Jolla. That matched Rona's description of him as "lit with cash." But Gorman hadn't shared much personal information and rarely posted. Conner checked Instagram, but Trevor wasn't listed on that media site. Was he older?

Conner's phone rang, and he checked the ID. *The Roadhouse.* They probably wanted him to work, and he needed the money. And a decent burger. *What the heck.* He answered the call, and as expected, a busboy hadn't shown up for work. He told Wally he could be there in thirty minutes.

"Where on earth do you live? I need you now."

"Sorry. I hate being this far out of town, but it's the only place I've got. I'll leave now." Conner hung up before Wally told him not to bother. A busboy shift meant he would make tips, and he desperately needed some cash. And a place to stay in town. Driving back and forth was costing him time and gas money.

He didn't get home until midnight, but he was too wired to sleep so he moved on to Plan B in his search for Trevor Gorman. Conner hadn't done any hacking in a few years, but finding someone's address was easy and might not involve anything sketchy. But first he went back to Facebook to see if Gorman's page linked to any websites, blogs, or outdoor exercise apps that posted routes. Unless the domain owner paid for privacy, most online hosts were listed in the ICANN directory, which contained mandatory address information. But Gorman didn't host a website or blog, so Conner shifted to workout apps. After checking Strava, he found Gorman on GORUCK and scanned the maps he'd posted. The guy walked the exact same route every day. Conner laughed out loud. What was the point of the tracking app?

But it paid off for him. Gorman always started and ended

his route from the same place, and a quick search of Google Maps produced the address. Conner plugged *Trevor Gorman* and the address into a DMV license-renewal application. The file didn't process, but it wasn't rejected for a mismatch either. Now he knew exactly where to find Gorman's house, which was on the beach in La Jolla.

Maybe he would find Kaylee there too.

CHAPTER 33

Wednesday morning

By seven, Hitch was at her desk in the DA's office, as were five
other prosecutors. The office would be full before eight, so she
decided it was a good time to check the computer records to
see if Conner's sister had any charges filed against her. Hitch
typed in *Kaylee Conner* and found an entry from two months
earlier. The charges, three counts of solicitation, had been filed
by Fisher, Ramsden's minion. The solicitation by itself was
unusual. More often, prosecutors would file drug possession or
prostitution charges as well. It must have been a pretty weak
case. She needed to pull the file if she wanted more
information.

Hitch retrieved the paperwork from the file room and
checked her watch: *7:23*. Plenty of time before Palmer arrived.
She sat down at her desk and opened the thin folder. Fisher
only had the case for two days before Ramsden took it over.
Why would a chief deputy work on such a low-profile case? Supervisors
usually only took on the big stuff that made headlines. Maybe
the john was someone important. Hitch googled the men's

names listed and found no one significant. *Maybe one was a friend of Ramsden's.* She wanted to search for a connection and wished she had more internet skills. Hitch jotted down the names, hoping Leahy might be able to help her. She was tempted to copy the file and take it with her, but that could get her into real trouble. It took only a few more minutes to peruse the rest of the paperwork and discover that Ramsden had dropped the charges five days after they were filed.

A strange case, indeed.

Hitch returned the folder, then glanced through yesterday's notes from the Evans trial. It was almost eight, and Aiden Palmer hadn't shown up yet. He finally arrived at seventeen after. "You're late," Hitch said.

"I had to take a bus. You should've picked me up if you wanted me here on time."

Like an Uber driver? Fat chance. "Have a seat."

"Why am I here? I thought we were done with my testimony."

"There are a couple of issues," Hitch said. "Please sit. We don't have much time."

Aiden took a seat and started fiddling with the antique hourglass on the corner of her desk. It was the only thing on there besides a battery-operated pencil sharpener, several pencils, and the file she was working on.

Hitch stared at him until he stopped. "You testified that you didn't make a deal in exchange for your testimony against Evans. But that's not true, is it?"

"I didn't make a deal." Palmer scowled. "I said I would testify, and the charges were dropped. That's how it works, right?"

"Were you telling the truth about what Jason Evans told you?"

"Of course."

Everything with this guy was "of course." Like saying it made it true.

"Who did you give the information to about your conversation with Evans?"

"An investigator from the DA's office. I don't remember his name."

"What did he look like?"

"I'm not sure. I wasn't feeling that great when he came to see me."

Liar. "Do you remember anything about him? Tall? Short? Fat? Skinny?"

"Medium height, in decent shape, short brown hair. Maybe thirty or forty years old."

That described most of the male investigators in the office. "But he came to you in jail?"

"Yeah."

Hitch sharpened a pencil. "Did you talk to him before you were placed in the cell with Evans?"

"No."

"Be honest. This is important."

"I am. He said Fisher wanted me to plead out my shoplifting charge, and I said no."

"How did Evans' name come up?"

"I told him I'd heard something that was probably useful, and I was willing to testify."

"You'd already talked to Evans?"

"Yeah."

An unspoken deal. She was afraid to ask, but she had to know. "Did he tell you what to say when you testified?"

"No. That was all Evans." Palmer looked disgusted. "The guy was proud of what he did. He wasn't just confessing. He was bragging."

Hitch wished Palmer would have said that during the trial instead of giving all that other unsolicited detail. But at least she was more comfortable that his testimony hadn't been solicited and her case was solid.

CHAPTER 34

Wednesday morning

In the middle of cleaning parrot cages, Conner's phone rang. He glanced at the ID, happy to see it was his attorney. He shed his gloves, hurried out of the aviary, and answered the call.

"Can you come into my office?" Leahy asked. "I've got the security footage from the Beachside Boogie the night Burton was killed. I'd like you to review it."

"Uh, sure." Anything to be done with the birds. "Can I ask why? I mean, it backs up what I said about that night, doesn't it?"

"Yes. But I want to see if you recognize anybody connected to Burton or see anything that looks suspicious. His killer was likely in the club that night. Or waiting for him outside."

"I'm on my way."

⸻

After spending his busboy tip money on gas, Conner vowed to find a place to stay in town, at least while he was searching for

Kaylee and trying to solve Burton's murder. He was spending too much time on the road. Maybe Darius would let him crash on his couch for a while. That would save him a lot of driving.

By the time he arrived at Leahy's office, his stomach was growling for lunch. The defense attorney greeted him warmly, something he still wasn't used to.

"Hey." Conner took a seat. "Thanks for getting the video from the club. For everything you've done for me."

"You're welcome." Leahy chuckled. "Now that you've sat down, I need you to come around and watch it on my monitor."

"Sure." Conner didn't know what to expect, but he was braced for boredom. "How much are we looking at? I mean, time-wise."

"I've marked a twenty-five-minute section in which you and Burton are both on the main camera."

Not a worst-case scenario, Conner thought. He might get through that. He hustled around the desk, realizing he'd forgotten to take his meds again. *Oh heck.* Focusing would be challenging, and he owed Leahy his full attention. He would put a note on his bathroom mirror when he got home. *If he remembered.* Conner suppressed a laugh.

The first ten minutes were tough, watching a bunch of strangers pass through the center section of the club. Then he caught sight of himself heading through to the karaoke area, a big grin on his face. *Oh yeah.* His first time hearing real music since he'd left jail. On the monitor, he passed a woman in red, who turned and watched him as he walked away. *Did he know her?* "Pause it and back up, please."

"Yeah, she's checking you out," Leahy said with a laugh.

"Can you zoom in?"

"A little." Leahy enhanced the image.

Conner stared at the pretty woman. "No. Sorry. I've never seen her before."

Leahy restarted the video, and Conner went back to watching strangers, his impatience and frustration mounting. To keep calm, he settled into a pattern of rotating his focus to different sections of the crowd.

Another five minutes and he spotted Troy Burton coming out of a bathroom. Conner felt a flash of anger, then remembered the man was dead. Burton paused by the wall for a second, checked his phone, then looked around as if waiting for someone.

A tall, young guy strode up, wearing a familiar jacket. Both men turned and started toward the back room. *Darius!* What the heck was he doing with Burton? "Pause again."

"You know him?"

"Since high school." Conner felt deflated. "Darius Williams. He's the one who told me Burton was planted in my cell to get a confession."

"So he knew him. I'm not sure what that means."

"Me neither. But I feel betrayed that he's hanging with the snitch who ruined my life. I thought he was a good friend."

Leahy was quiet for a moment. "Maybe it's an opportunity to get information."

"I guess I could try." Conner shook off the weird vibe. "Let's get through the rest of this video."

The only other person he recognized was Selene as she headed for the restroom. He remembered that she'd been sitting with him and Rona at the time, so nothing suspicious there. But she did look upset. Maybe she just had *resting bitch face.* Too bad, because she was gorgeous.

Conner's stomach growled, and Leahy offered to buy him lunch. Conner forced himself to say, "No thanks. I'm good. Besides, you bought me a burger yesterday."

"How about this? I'll make you earn it." Leahy pulled out his wallet and handed Conner a twenty. "You can run across the street and get us both a sandwich at Porky's. It'll give me more time to prep for a trial this afternoon."

After they ate, Conner headed toward La Jolla. He felt compelled to see the house, to see Trevor Gorman in person. As he parked near the address, his mouth dropped open. The house was a tri-level, modern version of a California Spanish classic. The huge windows were covered with curtains, not allowing the occupant to enjoy the view, like a fishbowl with a lining. Conner assumed the side facing the ocean had even more glass. Was it covered too? That would be a shame. It also wouldn't allow him to peek inside.

Conner got out of the Mustang and sauntered up to the front door, enjoying the vibe of the rich neighborhood, a whole other world than the Marigold Motel. How had Kaylee met this guy? She sure had a wide variety of friends and hangouts.

No one answered his knock, so he rang the doorbell, pressing long and hard. A strange electronic version of Michael Jackson's "Beat It" started playing. Conner chuckled, thinking he might like Gorman if he got to know him. Or he would hate him. Conner didn't hear any movement inside or dogs barking, so he headed for the back of the house, which was really the front, because it faced the ocean. To get there, he scooted, then climbed over an assortment of basalt boulders. The neighborhood association probably didn't allow fences, so homeowners used unfriendly landscaping to keep people from accessing the beach from their properties.

A flagstone patio lined a back wall of tall sliding glass doors, and a set of concrete steps led down to the sand. For a moment, Conner stared at the ocean, loving its peaceful power. He would never live anywhere he couldn't see and feel this regularly. Resisting the urge to wander onto the beach, he turned toward the house. No window treatments back here. He stepped up close and peered inside, careful not to touch the glass. The space was immaculate, like a showroom no one lived in. So different from the clutter and chaos he'd grown up in.

But in the middle of all the beige and off-white, a spot of orange. Conner scooted to the left a few feet, hoping for a better view, and leaned in again. A pair of panties tucked into the edge of the couch. The end table nearby held reading glasses and a computer tablet. That's where Gorman sat, his comfort zone. Was he a panty sniffer? Were those Kaylee's? Orange was her favorite color.

A seagull cried out, startling him, and his nose bumped the glass. An alarm went off, wailing loudly enough to be heard for miles. *No, no, no!* Conner bolted, scrambling back over the boulders. When he reached the front walk, he forced himself to saunter, not a care in the world—in case anyone was watching. He climbed into the Mustang, wishing he hadn't parked out front. For the moment, he had to get away and not encounter any police. But he would call and/or confront Gorman again. The man knew something about Kaylee, and Conner intended to get that information.

CHAPTER 35

Wednesday morning

"The State rests," Hitch said, feeling a weight lift off her shoulders. The trial wasn't over, but her responsibility mostly was.

The judge looked at the defense attorney. "Please call your first witness, Mr. Arroyo."

"I would like to call Dr. Lavinda Thomas to the stand, Your Honor."

A dark-haired woman in her late forties was sworn in, and Arroyo offered her curriculum vitae into evidence. For an hour, the defense attorney attempted to establish Dr. Thomas as an expert, and Hitch tried to discredit her on *voir dire*. The jury looked bored, and so did the judge, but Hitch wouldn't stipulate to her credentials. Dr. Thomas wasn't a well-known expert to the court.

The judge asked for any objections to the witness' qualifications, to wit, Hitch made a few regarding her experience. But Judge Barenski ruled Thomas an expert in sexual behavioral disorders.

"In your clinical practice, have you worked with any men who have been convicted of rape?" Arroyo asked.

"Yes. I spent six years studying inmates who were labeled sexual deviants and another four years with ex-cons with rape convictions."

"How many men with rape convictions would you say you dealt with over the last ten years?"

"Five or six hundred."

"In the conclusions of your last study, you separated these men into two different groups. Would you tell us what they were?"

"I know the experts used to believe rape was an act of violence only and had nothing to do with sexual gratification. There have been some recent studies and theories that proclaim all rape is about sexual gratification. However, I have done extensive research and have worked with many rapists, and I've discovered there are two types of rapists. One group, the majority, commit an act based in violence. That is the main purpose of the act, not sexual gratification. For the others, the act is committed for the sole purpose of being gratified, not just for themselves, but for their partner as well."

Bull puckey on both fronts. Hitch couldn't wait to discredit this crackpot.

"Wouldn't that require consent on the part of the woman?" Arroyo continued.

"It would, or at least the belief, on behalf of the man, that he had consent."

"Were any of the men involved in role-playing of a rapist-victim scenario?"

"Yes, quite a few actually. Most of whom fell into the *gratification* group."

Where was Arroyo going with this? A rape was a rape. It didn't matter what kind of pleasure the perp got out of it. And leading scholars on the subject claimed rape was *always* about sexual gratification, with violence and domination as a bonus. Hitch jotted down a question for cross.

Arroyo continued. "What other findings did you discover regarding those involved in role-playing rape scenes?"

"In some situations, the perpetrator forced their victims to role-play a rape scene, and in those cases, the act was about domination. However, there are many couples who role-play the same sorts of scenes, and it's a turn-on for both, as well as a consensual act." Dr. Thomas' tone shifted into lecture mode. "The problem is that engaging in these kinds of acts can be risky. If the woman changes her mind, how is the man to know? Part of the whole role-play is for the woman to say no or to act afraid. How would the man know she'd changed her mind?"

Irrelevant! Heather and Evans were not a couple. Hitch jotted down more notes.

"Let me give you a hypothetical," Arroyo said. "Assume a man watched rape videos over the course of a few months, videos that a woman specifically produced for him. Then he communicated with her, requesting more videos—until one of them suggested they make it more real. Would it be reasonable for the man to think it was a consensual act?"

"Yes, if both parties agreed to it."

"And if he was acting out a behavior they had shared many times previously through videos, would it be reasonable for the man to think that when she cried out for help, that she was just acting?"

"Yes, that would be reasonable. Especially if she was a good actress."

"No further questions."

"Cross?" the judge asked.

Hitch eagerly stood and turned to the witness. "Dr. Thomas, there's a difference between what may be *legally* consensual and what is in a person's mind, correct?"

"Yes. But people can only act based on what their perception is."

"So if someone perceives things a certain way, even if that perception is inaccurate, that person will behave according to what he perceives?"

"Absolutely."

"And you're saying those actions are justified as long as the person believes his own inaccurate perceptions?" Hitch was leading her into a minefield.

"I'm saying they will act accordingly. It's all a person can do because it's all the information they have." The witness clearly empathized with her subjects.

"But he would possess other information, based on thirty-plus years of living on this earth, correct?"

"Yes. But if whatever experiences he's had previously still lead him to the same conclusion, he will act on his perception at the time."

"Let me give you a hypothetical: You own a new Mercedes and you let Joe Blow drive it on several occasions. You never tell Joe Blow he can have the car or even that he can borrow it whenever he wants. However, Joe Blow likes the car a lot and decides he wants it for himself. So he goes to your house, takes the Mercedes, and leaves town. Would that be an illegal act?"

"The law is your expertise, but if he believed I consented to him having the car, then it would not be wrong in his mind."

"But it would still be illegal, correct?"

"If you say so."

"Let me see if I've got this right. You're testifying that it's all right for a man to *rape* a woman as long as his perceptions justify it in his own mind?"

"Objection," Arroyo spewed. "Misstates the facts."

"Withdrawn," Hitch said. "No further questions."

Arroyo's next witness was Heather. Hitch knew he would use her to authenticate a video of herself role-playing a rape scene. It would be damaging, but she didn't think it would be enough to get a not guilty verdict. At least she hoped not.

Heather took the stand again, and Arroyo stood in front of her. "Mr. Evans was a regular customer of yours, correct?"

Hitch wanted to object on the basis that Heather was now his witness and he couldn't ask leading questions. But then Arroyo would label Heather a *hostile* witness. That only meant the witness was contrary to the legal position of the defendant, but the word *hostile* never sounded good to a jury. So she let it go.

"Yes," Heather said.

"How many of your videos did Mr. Evans subscribe to?"

"I don't know offhand."

"He had been a customer for about six months, correct?"

"Yes."

"And over that time, he subscribed to at least one new video every week, correct?"

"That sounds right."

"You made many videos for him that included rape scenes, correct?"

A slight pause. "Some."

"How many?"

Heather took a deep breath. "The last three months, they were all rape scenes."

"So once a week for three months. That's approximately twelve rape-scene videos, correct?"

"That's about right."

"And in those videos you would beg the attacker to stop, correct?"

"Yes."

"Heather, have you done any acting?"

"I was in the drama club in high school, and I did a couple of plays."

"Have you taken any drama classes at the university?"

"My first year, I took one class, but I didn't continue after that."

"But you used the skills you obtained in those classes when you made your videos, right?"

"I suppose." She looked annoyed and tried to hide it.

"Are you a good actress?"

"Not especially."

"Let's let the jury decide." Arroyo removed a flash drive from his pocket and handed it to the court clerk. "This is marked as *Defense Exhibit #3*. I'd like to offer it into evidence once this witness authenticates it."

"Proceed." The judge nodded.

Arroyo showed the video on a screen he'd already set up. The jury squirmed in their seats, obviously uncomfortable with the content.

"Is that you in the video?" Arroyo asked.

"Yes."

"Who filmed it?"

"I did."

"How?"

"I have a camera set up in the room, and I act in front of it."

Arroyo paused the video and used a laptop pointer to direct attention to a spot on the screen. "This shadow of a man, who is that?"

"A roommate. He helped me with the video."

Arroyo played a little more of the scene, then stopped it again. "And this man dressed in a hoodie who came at you while you screamed? Is it the same man?"

"Yes."

"You're screaming and saying 'no,' but you're not actually afraid, are you?"

"No. It wasn't real."

Arroyo continued to play the recording, pausing and asking questions. "In each of these scenes, you act afraid, correct?"

"Yes."

"And in each one, you beg for the attacker to stop, right?"

"Yes, but—"

"Thank you. No further questions."

Judge Barenski glanced at Hitch, then said, "I have to leave a little early for lunch today, but I need a quick break now. We'll take a ten-minute recess."

CHAPTER 36

As she left the courtroom, Hitch checked her three voice messages. Jake Nelson, Victoria Wu, and Conner all asking her to call. Conner had an urgency in his voice, so she contacted him first.

"I need you to do something for me," Conner said.

Hitch was hesitant. "What?"

"I found a connection between my sister and a rich guy who lives in La Jolla. I went to his house, and he wasn't home, so I—"

Hitch interrupted. "You didn't do anything illegal, did you?"

"No. Well, I did set off the alarm, but I didn't really do anything wrong."

"Dang it, Conner. You need to stay out of trouble."

"It's all good."

"You were obviously snooping around and probably trespassing. If he has alarms, he probably has cameras."

A pause. "I just wanted to talk to him. I have to find Kaylee, and he knows something."

Hitch took a deep breath. She wanted to find his sister too. She hated the thought of any girl caught up in that terrifying world. "What can I do?"

"I need to know if this guy has a criminal record. Can you run a background check?"

"I'll see what I can do. What's his name?"

"Trevor Gorman."

"That name sounds familiar."

"You know him?"

"I've just seen his name recently." She thought for a few seconds but came up blank. "Sorry, I don't know where, but it will come to me."

Conner told her what he'd learned about Gorman and gave her his address in La Jolla.

"I'm in the middle of a trial right now," Hitch said. "But I'll do some research at lunch."

Hitch hung up, checked the time, and headed back to the courtroom. She would respond to the other calls later.

Heather took a seat in the witness stand for redirect. Hitch wanted the jury to hear Heather testify that she never encouraged Jason Evans.

"Did you at any time agree to have in-person contact with the defendant?" Hitch asked.

"No." Heather shook her head. "Never."

"Did you at any time or in any manner tell him where you lived?"

"Never."

"Did you want the defendant to attack you?"

"No!" She shuddered.

Hitch continued asking questions along the same lines, making sure it was clear to the jury that Heather was not a willing participant. After she was done, the judge excused the jury, and they broke for lunch. Hitch was glad. It would give her time to check on Trevor Gorman. *Where had she seen that name?* The question gnawed at her.

As she walked back to her office, she returned Nelson's call, relieved when he didn't answer. She left a quick message, hurried into the DA's office, and went straight to Victoria Wu's desk.

"Hi, Victoria. I got your message but didn't get a chance to call. What's up?"

Victoria stood and glanced around, then spoke softly. "I did a little research on that information witness of Ian's, Darius Williams—"

"Did you say Darius?" Now she remembered. He was a friend of Conner's.

"Yes. Do you know him?"

"I know a little *about* him," Hitch corrected. "But I didn't know he was an informant."

"He's testified in two recent cases. The first time his charges were dropped, and the second time they were severely reduced."

Hitch wondered if Conner knew that about Darius. *Not likely.* She wasn't sure what it meant, but she would have to warn Conner.

"Thanks, Victoria."

Hitch went to her desk and started a search for Trevor Gorman. It was always a chore trying to find information on her computer, but she had finally mastered a few things. As long as she didn't have to be creative, she could find her way around the DA files, and she knew how to search by name. She typed in *Trevor Gorman* and discovered two separate cases, both charging him with soliciting a prostitute. Both cases went away without ever going to court. The first was dropped because the prostitute couldn't identify him, which seemed bogus. The second case was dismissed because the charges were dropped against the prostitute, and therefore, no case. *Oh, jeeze.* That's where she'd seen Gorman's name. He was the john in Kaylee Conner's case.

Hitch picked up her phone and hit the redial on Conner's call. As soon as he answered, she said, "We need to talk. I have information you'll be interested in."

"What is it?"

"Can you meet me after work?" Hitch asked.

"Where?"

Hitch hesitated, then said, "My house."

"Okay. Text me the address."

Yeah, right. "Just jot it down. I'm in a hurry."

"I was trying to make it easier for you."

"Well, you didn't." She gave him the address, set a time, and hung up.

CHAPTER 37

Wednesday late afternoon

Feeling rattled and unsure of what to do next, Conner headed for Lucky's, a favorite hangout. Or it had been. He hadn't been to the tavern since his release, and he hoped the regulars remembered him.

He stepped inside and instantly relaxed. Old Man Dave was still on the barstool at the end of the counter, and Katrice still towered over customers from behind the bar. The only TV was set to CNN, but the volume was down, as always. He loved the quiet—compared to sports bars and redneck hangouts where talking heads blathered about the fall of America. Here, the only sounds were soft voices and the clink of billiard balls tapping into each other. *Home!*

As he approached the counter, Katrice spotted him and threw her arms into the air. "Conner!"

He grinned, a warm feeling rolling over him. "Hey, Katrice."

"Where the heck have you been?"

He slid onto a barstool, trying to decide what to say. He

almost lied and said he'd been in Seattle with his sister, then changed his mind. The meetings he attended preached "honesty in all things," so he'd give it a try. "I took a state-mandated timeout."

Katrice nodded. "What for?"

"I was in the wrong place at the wrong time." True, but not necessarily honest. So much for his new policy.

"With the wrong person?" She raised an eyebrow as she poured a tap beer.

"Yeah."

"Then that's your takeaway. Steer clear of the wrong people." Katrice set the beer down for him. "First one's on the house. Welcome back."

"Thanks."

Katrice lumbered to the end of the bar to check on Old Man Dave. The slightly younger Dave, a crazy cyclist, wasn't around.

Conner took a sip, savoring the cool bitter taste. But he would only drink half. He still had to drive home. And figure out how to buy some gas. He needed another bussing shift at the restaurant to earn some cash. But for now, his boss had him working on-call only, no regular shifts until he was clear of suspicion. He hadn't heard from his friends in dark suits lately, but he would. Kaylee's phone suddenly showing up at the motel would motivate them to look at the security footage. And that one detective had seen him and talked to him. It was only a matter of time before they questioned him again. Conner decided he had to tell Leahy about the incident. Honesty in all things.

He took another long drink of beer, then left it on the counter as he headed for the pool tables in back. Another middle-aged regular—Craig? Greg?—looked up from his game. "Conner. It's about time. You're the only one who actually challenges me."

Conner put two quarters on the table and waited for his turn. Greg beat him the first game because Conner was rusty and put the eight ball in the wrong pocket on a bank shot. But he wouldn't let that happen again. "Five dollars on the next game?"

"I shouldn't." Greg shook his head. "But what the hell? You're on."

Conner didn't have the cash, but he wasn't too worried. He barely won the next round, then suggested another bet and ended up with ten dollars.

A sense of discomfort came over him. *Was it guilt?* For playing pool instead of searching for Kaylee? Instead of working to find Burton's killer and clear himself? Or had he just forgotten how to chill? Jail kept everyone on edge. Relaxing could be dangerous on the inside.

"I'm outta here." He shook Greg's hand. "Good games."

"Don't be a stranger."

"I won't."

Conner hustled out, thinking he would call Leahy, get some gas, and drive out to Gorman's house again. The man had to be home sometime, and Conner had a couple of hours before his meeting with Hitch.

On the sidewalk, Seth Atkins and his enforcer waited for him, blocking his exit.

Conner's pulse pounded in his throat. "Hey, Seth." He tried to sound casual. And failed.

"You got my money?" Seth stepped closer.

Again, Conner's instinct was to lie. But why delay the inevitable? "No. But here's the thing. I've got a job and a connection—"

Seth's fist landed in his gut before Conner could finish. He fought the urge to moan and bend over in pain. "I can get it tomorrow." Conner tried to scoot sideways, but the enforcer blocked him.

Another blow smashed into his face. The pain blinded him, and the sound scared him. *Was his nose broken?* Before he could run, Seth slammed him again, a shot to his left eye.

"Be a man of your word and have it tomorrow," Seth growled. "I expect to hear from you. Don't make me chase you down again. And don't make me harass your crazy bird sister for it."

Seth winked and walked away.

CHAPTER 38

Conner knocked fifteen minutes ahead of schedule. Hitch opened the door and said, "You're early."

"That's better'n being late, isn't it?"

As he spoke, she noticed his black eye and fat lip. "What the heck happened to you?"

"A fist came at me, and I didn't duck fast enough."

Hitch felt bad for Conner. He was brash and sometimes reckless, but he had a good heart and was trying to go straight. "Come on in."

Conner hesitated, then stepped inside. For a long moment, he looked around, seeming to take in the whole atmosphere.

"You seem uncomfortable. Are you all right?"

"Yeah. I've just never been in a lawyer's house before. Never thought I'd be in a prosecutor's place, for sure."

"We're just people. We live like everyone else." She looked him over again. His nose was swollen too. "Who did the number on your face?"

Conner explained about Seth Atkins and the money he demanded. "I'm not worried about myself, but now he's threatening my sister, Nicole, and I can't have that."

Hitch decided to take the conversation outside. She led him

toward the slider, but stopped when they passed the kitchen. "Would you like something to drink?"

"You got a beer?"

"How about a soda?"

"That'll do. Pepsi, if you got it."

Her favorite. Hitch grabbed two cans of Pepsi from the refrigerator, then set them down and dumped some ice into a kitchen towel. She handed the ice to Conner. "For your pretty face." *Oh heck.* She hadn't meant to say that out loud. She spun away from him, grabbed the sodas, and headed outside. Conner followed, and she offered him a seat under the bamboo structure.

Again, he seemed to soak up his surroundings. "Nice yard."

"Thanks. I like it here." Hitch got right to the business at hand, telling him what she'd learned about Trevor Gorman, not sure how Conner would take it.

He didn't seem fazed. "So that's how Kaylee and Gorman are connected. We need more information. Is there anything else you can do from your office? Check out his file? Or do you have a database on criminals, something like that?"

Hitch tilted her head. "Look, I'm lucky to have gotten you what I did. I'm completely lost when it comes to technology. I don't even text. I've learned how to operate the programs I need to use at work, but anything beyond that is out of my wheelhouse."

He looked stunned, then amused. "I'll be glad to help. Maybe we can learn something else about Gorman." He pulled a laptop from his backpack and made a face. "I tried earlier, but when I have to use my phone for a hotspot, it's so slow. And this Mac is almost as old as I am. Do you have a laptop?"

"Yes." Hitch wasn't sure this was a good idea. She got frustrated pretty easily when she tried to learn new tech stuff. But she knew she had to sooner or later. "I'll go get it."

When she returned, she noticed Conner had scooted their chairs closer together. *Hmph.* She sat down and handed the device to him.

"Wow, this is fast," Conner said, as it started up.

"It's new and supposed to be easy to work. But I lost my tutor, so I haven't used it much." Nelson had encouraged her to buy the contraption, and they'd fought each time he tried to help her. She knew it had been more her fault than his, but she'd hated the whole ordeal and had been embarrassed by her mental block. But this might help get her past it. She didn't care if she looked computer ignorant with Conner. Maybe she could just get him to do the work and possibly learn a little during the process.

Hitch wanted to help Conner find Kaylee, but even more important, she wanted to stop the corruption in the DA's office. Maybe solving one thing would get them closer to the other. She hoped she was doing the right thing by working with Conner, but even if she wasn't, she was in too deep now and had to keep going. "How do you suppose Ramsden and Kaylee met?" Hitch asked.

"You said he was the DA on her case when she was arrested for prostitution. Isn't that it?"

"It seems he had to have known her before. Why else would he take her case? It was a nothing crime." Hitch pondered a moment. "Maybe he was protecting Trevor Gorman, the john, a rich guy he wanted something from. We need to find a connection between those two men. If there is none, then it's more likely Ramsden already knew Kaylee."

"How do we find that out?"

"We just keep digging, I guess. Ramsden was planning a run for DA. Maybe it was about a campaign donation."

Without comment, Conner started a new search on Hitch's laptop.

"Maybe I need to ask Detective Nelson to weigh in on this," Hitch suggested, musing out loud again.

"Are you crazy?" Conner stared, open-mouthed. "He wants to put me away."

"He's not a bad guy."

"He was a real jerk when he questioned me."

"Oh, he can be that all right. But he sincerely wants to get at the truth. You're better off with him than lots of others in the department."

Conner decided to start with the county's property-tax database and check out Gorman's address. He couldn't believe Hitch wasn't tech savvy. She was an attorney! But just because someone was smart, or even brilliant, with memory and strategy processes, didn't mean their brains could handle logistics. He was *kind of* good at everything but didn't excel anywhere.

"Tell me what you're doing as you go along," Hitch said. "I want to learn."

That surprised and pleased him. "Glad to. I think you'll like all this stuff once you get better at it."

"We'll see."

"What I did was to key *San Diego property tax* into the search field." He pointed to the bar on the browser, then hoped he hadn't insulted her. "The county's website loaded, so I keyed in Gorman's address." The file loaded as he talked, so Conner scrolled through it. "You just have to keep finding the input area and entering the thing you're looking for." He gave her a soft smile. Hitch's vulnerability in this setting was sweet, and he wanted to put his arm around her. *Not a good idea*, he self-corrected.

"What are we looking for now?" she asked.

"Something unusual or revealing about how he makes money."

"Do you suspect he isn't legitimate?"

"The only thing I know about him is that he lives in a nice house and is likely rich. So that's the only jumpstart I have." Conner focused on the monitor, noting the property-owner details. "He doesn't actually own that nice beach house. Robert Zimmers does."

"I don't know the name."

"Me either." Or what it meant. Zimmers could be his father or his business partner. But the information didn't seem important to finding Kaylee. It had been more than twenty-four hours since she'd left the crime scene, and time seemed critical. "I'm not sure what's next."

"I just remembered what I wanted to tell you." Hitch touched his arm.

A tingle pulsed toward his heart. He took a gulp of soda.

"Your friend Darius Williams is an informant."

"No! Don't say that." He didn't want to believe it, but her deadpan tone was convincing. Conner felt betrayed again. "He's the one who told me about Burton working with the DA to convict me."

"Maybe that's how they knew each other." Hitch leaned toward him. "We have to figure out which investigator Ramsden was sending out to make contact with these defendants."

Conner stifled a yawn.

Hitch scooted her chair away and stood. "If you're tired, you should go home. We can work on this tomorrow."

"I can't afford the gas to drive out to Nico's, just to come back in the morning." He'd prepared for a rough night. "I planned to sleep in my car. Probably in a Walmart parking lot. I have to keep searching in person. Kaylee's life could be in danger."

Her expression was hard to read, but her eyes were busy thinking, he could tell. Finally, she said, "Why don't you stay here in my guest bedroom."

She'd surprised him again. "Thanks, Ms. Hitchens. I needed something to break my way."

"Just keep it between us, okay? My association with you could get me fired." She hesitated, then said, "And call me Hitch. All my friends do."

CHAPTER 39

Thursday morning

Conner woke in a strange bed and had a flash of panic. What had he done? Who had he hooked up with? But he was alone. And the room was minimalist, in shades of beige and sage. *Oh yeah.* He'd stayed over at Hitch's. She'd felt sorry for him— being broke and beat up—and let him stay over. Going to sleep had proved challenging, and he'd been awake late, searching online for information about Trevor Gorman and Martin Ramsden.

Conner swung his feet to the floor and glanced at the laptop on the small table. Hitch had let him use her faster machine, but he still hadn't learned much. Except that Ramsden had done at least four interviews in his election bid for district attorney, and now the media and internet were buzzing with speculation about his death. The name of the motel had leaked, but the cause of death was still under wraps. Maybe he should do an interview about it—and earn a sweet guest fee.

Conner sauntered into the adjacent bathroom to pee, and

the sight of his black eye and swollen nose startled him. His face looked worse than it had last night. But it hurt a little less. Still, he had a headache and hoped Hitch would offer him some coffee.

A knock on the bedroom door, followed by, "Conner! Get moving. I have to leave soon."

He stepped over and opened the door. "Can I hang out for a bit and make some—"

"No. You leave when I leave. We're not roommates."

"Okay. I'll be ready in three." He caught her staring at his naked chest and smiled. "Thanks again for letting me stay."

As they were heading out a few minutes later, his phone rang. *The Roadhouse again.* He wanted the shift and the money, but he didn't really feel up for it. Conner forced himself to take the call. "Hey, Wally."

"I need you for a lunch shift. Can you be here by eleven? You'll be done by two, and you'll make tips. Assuming we get a crowd."

"Sure. See you then." Conner hung up, realizing he didn't have his work pants with him. *Shoot.* But he didn't want to drive out to Nicole's just for pants. He would stop at St. Vincent's and pick up a pair for a few dollars. Or maybe find some in the free bin. He couldn't wait to get his own apartment near the beach.

"I have to work a lunch shift," he said, as he and Hitch walked out to their cars.

"Good. It'll keep you out of trouble."

As soon as she drove away, he called Leahy. He had to get this over with, and he knew from past experience he should be upfront with his lawyer, assuming he could trust him. He decided Leahy was trustworthy. At least Hitch thought so, and that was enough for him.

"There's something I think you ought to know," Conner said.

"I'm finishing up a motion I need to file this morning." Leahy sounded rushed. "Can you stop at my office? I'll be done in about ten minutes."

"Uh, sure. I can be there in fifteen." Conner thought it might be better in person anyway. That way he could watch his attorney's expression and see just how bad he'd screwed up. He would know in an instant if the guy still wanted to represent him.

When he neared Leahy's office, Conner searched for street parking without a meter and had to walk six blocks. He was fine with that since he had more time than money right now.

Conner walked into Leahy's outer office just as the attorney handed some paperwork to his assistant. "Please make four copies and bring them into my office when they're ready." He turned to Conner. "Come in. I have about ten minutes before I have to leave for court."

Leahy directed Conner to his inner office, letting him go first, then closed the door behind them. "Have a seat." He pointed to a chair and then sat down behind his desk.

Conner didn't speak right away, not sure this was the best idea after all.

Finally, Leahy asked, "How bad can it be? Just spit it out."

Conner told him about taking Kaylee's phone and putting it back, watching the lawyer's face as he explained. But he saw little change in the guy's expression. When Conner was done, Leahy only asked for a couple of logistical clarifications.

"You don't seem that upset," Conner said.

"I'm not happy with what you did." Leahy sounded calm. "But it's your life you're screwing up, not mine. You made my job a little harder, but more important, you made it harder for the investigators to figure out what really happened. And you risked being arrested again. They're going to assume you changed something on the phone to cover up what you, or your sister, did to Ramsden."

"I didn't do anything. I just want to find Kaylee."

"I know that, but the cops will assume otherwise. You didn't do yourself any favors by taking that phone." Leahy paused. "I'm glad you told me though. It'll be easier to deal with the fallout when it happens. They probably have security cameras that recorded your presence, but don't admit to anything. If you're questioned, just tell them you're invoking your right to remain silent and you want me present during questioning. Do you understand?"

"I got it."

Gabriela opened the door and handed the documents to Leahy.

He thanked her, then stood. "Conner, try not to commit any more crimes until we get this batch taken care of."

"I have to find her, so I'm—"

His attorney put both hands up, palms out. "Please don't tell me about any crimes you plan to commit. There are different rules governing advance notice of future crimes and my knowledge of the ones you've already committed." He put his hands down and walked to Conner's side of the desk.

Conner stood, and Leahy gripped his shoulder. "I mean it, kid. Stay out of trouble."

Conner left, not sure what to think, except that he had to be more careful. Locating Kaylee felt like an emergency, and if that meant getting into trouble, he would deal with it. He hurried back to his car, drove to St. Vincent's, and found a cheap pair of black pants. So far, his luck was holding out.

The three hours of bussing tables passed quickly, and the food servers, all men, tipped him a total of twenty-two dollars. Not bad, considering he'd also made wages that would show up on a paycheck soon. Conner walked out the back door, hoping to get called in to work again soon, and jogged down the alley. In the parking lot, Detective Drummond stood by the Mustang.

"Nate Conner. Just the ex-con I wanted to see."

The sound of his voice sent a chill down Conner's spine. This guy had been a jerk the last time he'd been questioned. "What's up?" He wanted to sound unconcerned, but he held back his instinctive grin.

The cop pointed to his dark sedan. "Get in the car. We have to talk."

"I'd rather talk right here."

"Get in. Detective Harrison is meeting us at the department."

Oh hell. That was the guy who'd spotted him at the Marigold. They were leaving Detective Nelson out. Not a good sign. Hitch had said Nelson could be trusted to find the truth. Conner felt like these guys just wanted to make a case against him because he was an easy target.

For the third time in a week, Conner sat handcuffed at the small table in the windowless room. This time felt worse, and dread filled his chest. "I'd like to wait for my lawyer." They'd let him make a call, but Leahy hadn't answered, and his message box had been full.

Drummond laughed. "We can hold you for three days, so settle in."

A smart-ass comment about boredom popped into his head, but he shut it down—then tried to channel what Hitch or Leahy would advise him to say. "I have a job, and I'd like to keep it. Please be reasonable."

The other detective nodded. "Then tell us where you found your sister's phone."

"I'm not at liberty to say."

"Why not?"

"Advice of counsel."

"Your lawyer doesn't understand how this works," Harrison drawled. "If you cooperate with us—and have nothing to hide—we go easy on you."

Conner smiled. "I appreciate that."

"How did you tamper with the phone?" Drummond cut in, anger flaring. "What did you delete?"

Conner was silent.

"I saw you at the motel," Harrison said, sounding calm in comparison. "Why did you go back?"

"Unfinished business."

"Be specific."

"It's too personal." Conner's plan was to be either vague or silent.

After an hour of hammering him, they left him alone in the dark with no water. His throat was dry and scratchy from swallowing so hard, and his wrists hurt from the cuffs. Conner took long slow breaths and told himself he would survive. He just had to stay quiet and not panic.

They were gone for what seemed like hours. Conner had no idea what time it was. His stomach growled with hunger, his head pounded, and his bladder was about to burst. When Drummond walked in, Conner snapped, "I have to pee. Please."

"Not until you tell us something relevant." Drummond sat and downed a gulp of Pepsi.

Conner would have killed him for it. Good thing he was cuffed. He took a long breath and stayed silent.

Harrison leaned toward him. "Give us an easy one. Like, who assaulted you and why."

They'd been over this a few times already. Still in pain from the last beating, Conner had no intention of ratting on Seth.

Even if Seth went to jail, he would simply send his enforcer. And that guy would snap him like a twig.

"Let's talk about Ramsden," Conner said. Being on the offense would at least distract the detectives for a while. "Have you figured out what he was doing in that sleazy motel?"

Drummond leapt to his feet, reached across the table, and grabbed Conner by the throat. "You're not worthy to mention his name, you little piece of—"

Conner coughed from deep in his lungs and struggled to catch his breath. Little white stars floated around his eyeballs, and he couldn't speak.

Drummond didn't let go. "You stabbed him, didn't you? You caught him banging your sister and you killed him. Just admit it, and we can all go home."

Conner closed his eyes and slumped in his chair. He wasn't unconscious—yet—but they might as well think so.

Twenty minutes later, a front desk clerk stepped into the interrogation room and announced, "Attorney Jerry Leahy is here to see his client. He's prepared to file a grievance if you don't release Nate Conner."

Yes! God he loved that man. Leahy had seen his missed call and figured out that Conner was down here in the hellhole again. Probably because he hadn't answered his phone in hours.

"Don't look so happy," Drummond warned in a soft, threatening voice. "I've asked DDA Fisher to file murder charges. So we'll be seeing you again real soon."

CHAPTER 40

Thursday mid-afternoon

When the trial concluded for the day, Hitch asked Heather to come to the DA's office.

"I thought I was done testifying." Heather looked worried.

"You may have to be recalled. I hope not, but just in case, there are a few things I want to go over with you."

As they walked back, they chatted about Heather's college courses. Hitch avoided having conversations with witnesses in public settings. You never knew who was lurking. She'd learned that lesson the hard way when she'd spoken to a colleague in the women's restroom at the courthouse. Someone in a stall had overheard, and she'd almost lost her job over it.

When they reached the office, Hitch found an empty conference room and led Heather inside. As she sat down, Heather checked her phone.

"This won't take long," Hitch said.

"Good. I have class in an hour and a half, and I'd like to get something to eat before then."

Hitch sat across from her. "I need to understand your living situation. Are you still in the same house where you were attacked?"

"No way. I had to move. Once Evans found me I no longer felt safe." Heather closed her eyes for a moment as stress flashed on her face. "I figured the owner wouldn't want me there either."

"Did the landlord ask you to leave?"

"Quite the opposite. My rape put his house on the map. But I couldn't stay there after what happened."

"What do you mean 'put his house on the map'?" Hitch felt totally befuddled.

"Even though the house lost its anonymity, people in the business lined up to get a room. I heard he even raised the rent for everyone who was already there."

Hitch scowled. "Why would someone want to live there after what happened to you?"

"They wanted to use the notoriety to pitch their videos."

Hitch realized she'd stumbled onto something she knew nothing about. She chastised herself for not keeping up. First OnlyFans, and now this. "Did everyone in the house make videos?"

"Yeah. It's called a *content house*. There are all kinds, ranging from mansions with rich people trying to get famous, to the kind of place I was in. We each lived our own lives and did our own thing, but we could help each other if we needed another person in a video, or if we needed special filming."

"And that's what you did in the attacker video Arroyo played in court?"

Heather nodded.

"How did you find that house? That living situation?"

"My friend from school, who was making money on Only-Fans, told me about it. She was living there at the time. When I first moved in, the tenants were all students working their way through college, but then it started to change. With seniority, I got to move into the guesthouse out back. I loved the privacy, but it made me vulnerable." A memory darkened her expression, but Heather continued. "Zayne, the man in the video, and I were the only ones left from when I first moved in. Others had come and gone, but they kept getting younger."

"You mean minors?"

"There was one girl for a while who was only seventeen. But she didn't stay long. She was drop-dead gorgeous, and the owner gave her a lot of attention. I'm pretty sure he was smashing her." Heather shook her head. "She won't stay pretty much longer if she doesn't quit using to numb herself for the sex work. I tried to help the girl the first time she was there, but she didn't stay long enough."

"You mean she left and came back?"

"It happens."

Hitch hated the thought of another young girl ruining her life with drugs. "If she's underage, maybe we can get her help. Do you know her name?"

"It won't help you find her. I just know her OnlyFans profile. And she turned eighteen, so she's an adult now."

"Just the same, I'd like to follow up." She'd never heard the slang *smashing* before, but she knew what it meant. And she wanted to go after the pig landlord who had taken advantage of a minor. It wasn't too late for that. "What's the owner's name?"

"I don't know. Zayne is the house manager, and he would know, maybe even his address. Zayne collected the rent for him."

"Did the landlord come to the house to pick it up?"

"Sometimes, I think. I only saw him once."

"Can you describe him?"

"No. My encounter with him was very brief, and I barely remember it. I didn't even know he was the owner until a few days later, so I didn't pay much attention at the time."

"How do you know he was involved with the young girl?"

"She told me she didn't have to pay rent with money. Zayne also mentioned that the owner was jealous of him making a video with her. She helped him in a couple scenes of his big hit—*Fifty Shades of Zayne Gray*."

"What's the girl's profile name?"

"Special K."

She'd heard that name, and she knew where. As soon as she left the conference room, she called Conner. He didn't answer, so she left a message: "We need to talk. It's important. Call me."

CHAPTER 41

Thursday evening

Leahy gave Conner a ride back to his Mustang for the second time in two days. "I won't forget what you've done for me," Conner vowed. "If I ever win the lottery or come into some real money, I'll find a way to repay you."

"Just live a good life and do nice things for people less fortunate." Leahy reached over and squeezed Conner's shoulder. "That's all I need from you."

"I will. I promise." Conner swallowed hard, feeling emotional. It had been a long stressful day. And it wasn't over yet.

He climbed into his car, started the engine, and plugged his phone into the mini-charger he kept handy. The cell had gone dead while he was in the interrogation room. And he strongly suspected a tech person at the police department had copied its contents while they held it. He would have.

Stomach growling, he drove straight to the Beachside Boogie. But not to party. He hoped to find Darius, who had a lot of explaining to do. Conner didn't have time to waste.

Detective Harrison had said they planned to file charges and pick him up again before the weekend. Finding Troy Burton's killer had to be his priority.

Darius was in the karaoke room as usual. He sat near the back with a pretty blonde woman Conner didn't know.

"Hey!" Darius looked happy to see him.

"We need to talk." Conner gestured for him to stand. "Can we step into the hall?"

"Why so serious?" Darius reluctantly pushed out of his chair.

"Because my life is on the line." Conner turned to the woman. "Please excuse us." He grabbed Darius' arm and steered him toward the door. On the way out, he pulled his phone and charger out of his front pocket. It was at fifty percent now, and he had a voice message. And a few missed calls. He would deal with all of it as soon as he confronted Darius.

In the hall, Conner launched right in. "You met with Troy Burton, right here in this hall, the night he died."

"So?"

"He's the rat who turned on me. Why were you friendly with him?"

"We knew each other. That's all."

"How did you know each other?"

"Jail." Darius acted annoyed, but he was clearly uncomfortable.

"What did you talk about?"

"What's the deal? You're acting like a jealous boyfriend."

Ha! "I'm about to be charged with Troy's murder. If I don't figure out who actually killed him, I'm toast."

"Settle down. He just wanted to ask me about—" Darius

stopped and pressed his lips together.

"What? I need to know!" Conner raised his voice, not caring what Darius thought of him. The guy didn't seem like much of a friend anymore.

"You wouldn't understand."

"Try me."

A look of guilt flashed across Darius' face.

And suddenly Conner understood. "You're an informant too. That's why your charges were dropped." He stepped toward Darius. "Why?"

"They labeled me a *career criminal* because of a few theft charges. I was looking at five years."

Conner understood, yet snitching wasn't a choice he would ever make.

"They also offered to make all my fines go away. That debt was killing me." Darius put his hand over his heart. "But I'm done with that life now. All of it. I swear."

"Who made the offer?"

"I can't tell you."

"You have to." Conner grabbed his shoulders and locked eyes with him. "I'm looking at a murder rap. Or two. So life in prison."

Darius looked pained and conflicted. Finally, he said, "He calls himself 'Buddy,' but that's not his real name."

"But you can describe him?"

"Of course. I'm good with details, and I saw him right after I talked with Troy."

Yes! Conner had suspected that Ramsden's grunt guy had been paid to silence Burton. Now he was sure. "I need your help, Darius. Maybe tonight. But I have to make a call first." Conner pulled out his phone again and saw that the voice message was from Hitch. "I have to listen to this. But don't go anywhere without me."

Darius gave him a look. "Did you see my date?"

CHAPTER 42

Hitch changed into pajamas, sat on the sofa, and turned on a standup comedy special. Ten minutes later, her doorbell rang. *What the heck?* She checked the time: *10:05.* She grabbed her keys with the pepper-spray canister and unlatched the trigger before peeking through the peephole.

Conner stood there, his eyes wide with anxiety. Hitch yanked open the door. "What are you doing here at this hour?"

"I have someone you need to hear from." Conner shifted to the side, revealing another young man standing behind him. "Can we come in? Please. This is important. And you said you wanted to talk."

"I didn't mean ..." She gave up the thought and stepped aside, so they could enter. She was curious to know what this was about. And furious at the same time. "Where have you been? You didn't answer any of my calls."

Conner stopped in the entry. "I was detained and questioned. Again. And my phone went dead." He smiled in an attempt to be charming. "But I brought Darius Williams with me."

As if that was supposed to make her feel better. This was an intrusion into her privacy. She never should've invited

Conner to her house. He had no boundaries. Why would he bring a known criminal into her home? And at this hour! She changed her mind about listening to them right now. "Conner, it's late. Why don't we do this tomorrow?"

"Because Detective Drummond plans to charge me with murder tomorrow. And it took a lot of talking to get Darius to come here tonight." Conner's shoulders sagged, as if he'd realized his mistake, then he rallied and tried again. "He's an informant too. And—"

"Was," Darius corrected. "I'm a new man."

Hitch fought the urge to roll her eyes.

Conner plowed on. "Darius worked with someone from the DA's office, and he wants to watch the video from the club to see if he can spot him. Leahy gave you a copy, right?"

Hitch nodded.

"Good. Because Darius saw *the investigator* there that night." He used air quotes when he used the label. "If Ramsden's grunt guy is on the recording, Darius will recognize him."

Hitch was intrigued. "My laptop's on the table with the flash drive in it. You go set it up. I have to get dressed."

When she returned, wearing jeans and a t-shirt, the two men were already studying the video. Conner was seated, and Darius stood behind him. Hitch stood nearby and watched with them.

About halfway through, Darius said, "Back it up."

Conner pressed the keyboard and scrolled back.

Darius pointed at a thirty-something man in a fedora. "That's him. The dude who contacted me about snitching for Ramsden."

"Did he say *Ramsden* specifically?" Hitch pressed.

"Not at first, but later he talked about him more freely. Buddy acted like some big shot because he was working for *the man*. He liked to name-drop. I'm sure Ramsden never knew that." Darius turned to Hitch. "I can't believe he's dead."

But Hitch was deep in her own thoughts. Darius' testimony could be a big help in exposing the corruption in the office, which Hitch suspected went deeper than Ramsden. They needed more evidence. She tapped Conner's shoulder. "I need to show his picture to a few people. Is there a way you can isolate it and save it as its own file? Maybe move it to my phone?" *Was she wishful thinking?*

"I'm already on it." Conner clicked a few keys and suddenly a large image of Fedora Man took up the screen. "Do you know him?"

"No," Hitch admitted. "He's not an in-house investigator, but we also use private contractors when we need them."

"Now what?" Darius asked, shuffling nervously. "I'm on shaky ground here. I don't want to be pulled into this any more than I have to." He moved to the end of the table to face Conner. "You know I want to help you, Bro, but if this guy killed Troy for talking too much, he could come after me."

"We'll do everything we can to keep you out of this," Hitch said. "But right now, I need more information." She asked Darius to sit down, but he stayed on his feet, restless. She questioned him about cases, dates, and times, including what he knew about other informants. She learned that four regular snitches were either getting information after the arrestee had a lawyer or were making up stuff to exchange for a good deal for themselves. The investigator didn't seem to care whether the information was true or not.

"Do you know the names of the other snitches?"

"I knew Troy Burton, and he once referred to another guy as Sammy."

"Did the investigator ever give you his name?"

"He said to call him Buddy because he was my *new best friend*." Darius rolled his eyes. "I know that isn't his real name." Darius started to pace.

"You seem anxious, and I'm sure there are other places

you'd rather be," Hitch said. "Why don't you watch the rest of the video, then be on your way."

Darius stepped back so he could see the monitor, and Conner played the video to the end. But nothing else of interest showed up. When Darius started to leave, Conner stood as well.

"Conner, can you stay a few minutes? There's something else you need to know."

"Oh right. Your message." He walked Darius out, then came back to the table and looked at her expectantly. "What is it?"

"Didn't you say Kaylee went by the name Special K?"

"Yeah. Why?"

"I know of a house where a girl called *Special K* lived for a while. She's about the same age as Kaylee. She lived there twice, in fact, but not for long each time. And she's not there now."

"Where?" Conner asked, his eagerness a little heartbreaking.

"I can't give you the address because of confidentiality. Also, it's a content house. Do you know what that is?"

"Yeah." He nodded solemnly. "How do you know all this?"

"A woman who lived with her is the victim in the trial I'm on right now." Hitch suddenly wanted a drink. She'd never get to sleep after all this. "I'll ask Heather if she's willing to talk to you. She liked Kaylee and wanted to help her. Maybe she'll even introduce you to the house manager. You may get more information that way."

"So call her."

"Not now. It's too late."

"Then text her. If she's awake, she'll probably answer. And if she's not, she won't hear the text come in."

Hitch tilted her head and scowled at Conner.

"Oh, that's right. You don't text." He held out his hand.

"Here, give me your phone. I'll do it. Every minute we waste might put Kaylee in more jeopardy."

"I doubt if Heather is willing to take you there tonight."

Conner was undeterred, his arm still outstretched, waiting for her phone. "If I chat with her tonight, we can set up something for tomorrow. Or she'll see my text first thing in the morning. It'll get things moving." His voice shook a little as he spoke. "I have to find Kaylee. I'm so freaking worried."

Hitch handed him her phone.

"What name is she under?"

"Heather."

Conner keyed in a message with stunning speed. He hit send and looked up, seeming impatient already.

"What did you say?"

"I just told her to contact you as soon as possible, that it was about Special K, a matter of life and death."

"You didn't have to be quite so dramatic."

Before he could respond, Hitch's phone rang in his hand. He glanced at it. "Apparently, she's still up." He handed Hitch the cell.

"Heather, I'm sorry to bother you so late. But I'm here with Kaylee's brother, and he's desperate to find her. Would you be willing to help him?"

"Kaylee?"

"The girl you know as Special K. Or at least we think it's her. I'm putting you on speaker now." She'd finally learned how to do that.

"Do you have a picture of Kaylee?" Heather asked.

"Yep." Conner reached for his phone.

"Text it to me, and I'll see if it's a match."

"Coming at you from my number." Conner glanced at Hitch's cell, then quickly sent the photo.

A few seconds later, Heather said, "That's her."

"Will you take him to the content house?" Hitch asked.

"And introduce him to anyone who knew her? I'm sure they'll sympathize with his concern."

"Tomorrow, after my classes. I'll text a time and place to meet." She hung up.

"Thank you," Conner whispered, his eyes tearing up.

"No problem. Just get me the landlord's name while you're there." He looked so sad and beat-up. And she knew he was still too broke to buy food or gas. "You can stay here again. But don't ever bring anyone over here. Or mention my address."

"I promise." He grinned. "You're a goddess."

CHAPTER 43

Friday morning

Hitch made coffee, then pounded on the guest room door. "Conner! Get up. I have to go to work." She waited a moment, then pounded again. "I made coffee. And I'll fix some toast or something you can take with you. Move it!"

She went back to her bedroom and dressed for the day, then called Nelson. "Hey. How are you?" She needed something, and it couldn't hurt to play nice.

"I thought you were ignoring my calls," Nelson said.

"I've been busy. Lots of crazy stuff going on." She hesitated. "I need your help." Hitch hated to ask him for fear he would think she wanted to start dating again, but he was the only person she knew who could do this favor and get back to her quickly.

"Want to meet and talk about it?"

"Maybe. But first, I'll send you a photo. Can you find out who the guy is? Check him out in your system?"

"Just the image? No name?"

"Yes."

"I can run facial recognition software, but unless he has a record, I won't get a match. We're not the feds." Nelson went quiet for a moment. "Is this official business?"

"Not exactly. It may end up that way, but right now, it's an educated hunch."

"I'll see what I can do."

"And, Jake, please keep it to yourself. I don't know who the players are yet."

"You're being pretty secretive."

"Because I know something is wrong, but I don't want to point fingers yet. If I'm right, I'm sure you'll be glad you helped me."

He was silent for a moment. "I'll let you run with it for now, but don't get in over your head. Remember, I'm here if you need me."

Hitch hung up, attached the image of Buddy to a text—just as Conner had shown her—and sent it to Nelson. Now to deal with her sleepy houseguest. The thought made her smile.

Half an hour later, Hitch dropped her satchel on her desk and walked back to see Victoria, who was focused on her monitor.

"Good morning." Hitch stepped into her workspace. "Are you busy?"

"I just finished typing a motion to suppress." Victoria clicked her keyboard. "And now it's printing. What's up?"

"I want you to look at something." Hitch tapped the photo of Buddy on her phone and held it out. "Have you ever seen this guy?"

Victoria studied the image. "Yeah. Fedora Man. He met with Ramsden one evening last week. I was the only one still in the office. Ramsden came in by himself about seven-thirty, glanced around and probably didn't see me back here, then went into his office. That guy came in about ten minutes later and headed straight to Ramsden's office."

"Are you sure it's the same guy?" Hitch glanced at the entrance. "From here, he might've been too far away to get a good look at his face." She trusted Victoria, but Hitch thought like an attorney. Everything had to hold up in court.

"It was him." Victoria made a face. "I went to the file room, and when I came out, he was walking toward the restroom. As he passed by, the creep looked me over, practically drooling, and said, 'Nice!' I wanted to stick my foot out and trip him, but I didn't."

"I have to figure out who this guy is. I already knew that he was connected to Ramsden, but that's it."

"How did you make the connection?"

"He seems to be the go-between for Ramsden and the informants. He presents himself as an *investigator*. I know he's not one of ours, but he could be a contractor."

"That's easy to check." Victoria tapped a few keys, then turned her monitor to display a short list of private investigators they'd used recently. "I only searched back to the time Ramsden became supervisor. Is that okay?"

"Makes sense." Hitch was fascinated by what Victoria could do on the computer—and so quickly. As she stepped around the desk to watch, she decided it was time she became more proficient.

"One of the four is a woman and another is African-American, so that only leaves two." Victoria googled the first one and opened a website with his photo. The guy was too young to be Buddy. The second didn't have a website, but Victoria found his Facebook page. The guy looked like a throwback from the sixties: long hair, beard, and too old to be Fedora Man.

"If he's not working for the DA's office, he could be Ramsden's personal friend," Hitch speculated. "Without his name, we can't check to see if he's actually an investigator. My guess is that he probably isn't. He's more likely a criminal who couldn't get a license if he wanted to."

When Hitch arrived at the coffee house in Pacific Beach, Nelson was already seated on the patio. He stood and greeted her.

"Nice place," Hitch said. "How'd you find this?" As soon as she asked, she regretted it. He'd probably spent time here with another woman. She hated that she still cared and wished he wasn't so charming.

Nelson seemed to sense what she was thinking. He tipped his head and smiled. "I know a cop who lives nearby. I have coffee with him occasionally. Nice view, don't you think?"

Hitch looked at the ocean. "Can't beat it." They sat down. He'd texted her earlier, and she'd managed to open the message—thanks to Conner's patient coaching. "What did you find on Buddy?"

Before he could answer, the waitress walked up with a black coffee for him and a latte for her. Hitch shook her head.

"I had to get something for myself. And I know what you like." Nelson smiled and shrugged. "Their sandwiches are really good too. We may as well have lunch while we're here."

After a quick glance at the menu, Hitch ordered a jalapeno burger, then tried again. "Tell me about Buddy."

"He has a criminal record from about five years ago. Receiving stolen property, plus a drug possession. Nothing since. He spent a few months in jail, did a treatment program, and completed his probation. That's not to say he's clean, he just hasn't been caught again."

"You must have gotten a name."

"Oscar Kolinder. He tries to pass himself off as a private investigator."

Hitch scowled. "But if he has possession and theft on his record, he wouldn't be able to get licensed."

"He works under someone else's license. Oscar Kolinder, his father."

"Well, that's legal, right?"

"It would be if his father were still alive, but he died two years ago. Junior must be paying his license fees to keep it current, which is *not* legal."

"Please don't bust him yet," Hitch said. "There's far more to this than investigating without a license." She hesitated, then decided to lay it out. "He might be the one who murdered Troy Burton and Martin Ramsden."

"Whoa!" Nelson stared, open-mouthed. "What are you keeping from me?"

He sounded both perplexed and irritated, and Hitch hesitated again. Yet she knew he was as committed to his job as she was to hers. Also, she and Conner might be impeding his investigation. *Still* ... "Why should I ever trust you again?"

"Please." He reached over and squeezed her hand.

His touch electrified her, and she pulled back.

"This isn't about our relationship," he pressed. "It's about two homicides. Let's help each other close these cases and convict the right people."

It was time. "I think Ramsden was corrupt and planted informants in jail. And he made deals with other ex-cons who were willing to say whatever he needed them to in court."

Nelson pushed his hands through his hair. "Oh man. I hate to believe it, but that explains a few things. Including why the ADA is leaning on the taskforce to bring him a case against Nate Conner."

"He's not a killer." Hitch believed it and needed him to as well.

"I'm still neutral on that subject." Nelson gave her a look. "But the whole thing with Conner's knife is hinky. A deputy at the jail told me you'd been asking about Conner's possessions at his booking. And he mentioned that the ADA wanted that inquiry shut down."

The second guy in command. "Ramsden was trying to frame Conner. And it sounds like his boss is either part of the corruption or part of the coverup." Hitch sipped her latte, trying to choose her words carefully. But they came out blunt anyway. "I think Ramsden sent Oscar Kolinder to kill Troy Burton."

Nelson stared and shook his head. "Seriously? What's the motive?"

"He'd used Burton as a snitch several times, with Kolinder as the go-between. Maybe Burton talked too much about their arrangement or even tried to blackmail Ramsden. He was that greedy and stupid." She couldn't help grunting in disgust. "I don't know the exact motive. But you can bring Kolinder in and lean on him."

"With what?"

"That image I sent you? It's from the security footage at the Beachside Boogie the night Burton was killed. It puts Kolinder at the scene."

"A lot of people were there. What else have you got?"

"Another informant who worked with Ramsden to provide false testimony." *And not much else.* Hitch realized how thin her case sounded. "But maybe now that you have Kolinder as a suspect, you can connect him to Ramsden's murder too. Maybe he's in the motel's security footage. Or a witness saw him."

Nelson seemed to mull it over. "Drummond is leading the taskforce, and he really wants to nail Conner for it. And Harrison saw him return to the motel. We all know Conner took his sister's phone from the room, then brought it back. If he has nothing to hide, why would he do that?"

"Maybe he just wants to find his sister." Hitch leaned forward. "Your turn to share. Tell me about Ramsden's crime scene. Cause of death, for example."

"Stabbed with a knife."

"And you still have Conner's knife in evidence lockup?"

"Correct. But still, it's the same method."

"What about the time of death? Conner probably has an alibi."

"I can't help you with that." He squeezed her hand. "I know the guy is pretty, but don't fall for him."

Hitch rolled her eyes. "Don't insult me."

A long moment of silence.

Finally, Nelson said, "I will tell you this. I've been leaning away from Conner as the suspect for Ramsden's murder. My colleagues aren't happy about it, but there's no trace of Conner at the scene. And there was no trace of blood on his clothes when he was detained immediately after calling in the dead body."

Hitch knew all that, but she was relieved to know Nelson was still objective about doing his job.

The food server brought their sandwiches, and Hitch waited until he'd walked away to ask, "Will you round up Kolinder?"

Nelson shook his head. "Not yet. I'll tail him for a while first. Maybe set up a sting."

"Great idea. I'm sure Ramsden wasn't in the informant-scheme alone, and I'd like to take down his accomplice. Or accomplices."

"I'm more interested in Kolinder as a murder suspect, but we'll see who we round up in the sting. And whether they want to inform on each other."

Hitch laughed at the irony, then dug into her burger.

CHAPTER 44

Friday afternoon

Conner pulled into a little strip mall and parked on the east side of the movie theater. He was early, but he hadn't wanted to take chances with traffic on Friday at quitting time. He leaned back and checked Instagram on his phone, then switched to reading the news and looking up every few minutes.

Heather showed up fifteen minutes late in an old Subaru and hurried over to his car. He recognized her from the photo she'd sent him. Conner leaned over and opened the passenger door. She climbed in, looking fabulous, and said, "Sweet ride."

"Thanks. I'm Conner."

"I figured." She buckled in and turned to him. "I've been having second thoughts about this all day. I haven't been back there since I was sexually assaulted. So let's move this along. And if I get flaky and have to go sit in the car, you'll know why."

"Okay." Conner started the engine. "I'm sorry that

happened to you." *Wait. That wasn't politically correct.* "I mean, I'm sorry some guy did that to you."

"Thanks for clarifying. The crime did have a perpetrator." A pause. "But I don't think he'll be convicted." She sounded matter of fact and a little sad.

He didn't know what to say. "Where to?"

"Take a left out of the parking lot. It's only a few blocks from here."

The ranch-style home sat on an oversized lot with palm trees lining both sides and a guesthouse partially visible in back. The driveway held three cars, so Conner parked on the street. He glanced at Heather. "Ready?"

"Yeah. Zayne is expecting us."

As they neared the door, a guy in his early thirties opened it and motioned them to come in quickly. Conner glanced up at a security camera as they crossed the threshold.

"I hope they added one to the guesthouse too," Heather commented.

Conner hadn't known what to expect, but the setup in the living room surprised him. It was an open floor with no furniture and studio-style cameras set up around the room.

"For group dance scenes," Heather explained. "Or group sex. They pull out floor pillows for that."

"Hey, no trade secrets, please." Zayne smiled, but he was serious. "Let's sit in the kitchen."

Conner tried not to think about Kaylee in this house, making sex videos. But a naked Heather popped into his brain. So did Aloha. Would he get to meet her? He shut down the thought. *Focus!*

They sat at the table, which held a small cardboard box.

"I'm glad you're here," Zayne said. "K left a few things when she split so suddenly, and I wanted to get them back to her." He pushed the box toward Conner.

"Why did she leave on short notice?" Conner asked. Then he remembered Aloha had said they kicked her out for using.

"She had a few problems, but I was willing to work with her on the drug issue. We all use. It's just a matter of moderation." He smoothed his already perfect hair. "But K's girlfriend wanted her to get out of the video business. And she kept showing up here. She wanted K to get clean and go live a sweet little prudish life. I got tired of it."

"What girlfriend? Do you know her name?"

"K just called her Sweet-Cheeks. I don't think she wanted us to know."

Argg! Conner's frustration flared. "Where did Kaylee go from here? To live with her girlfriend?" That didn't mesh with the Marigold Motel.

"I don't know. Sorry." Zayne shook his head. "She was secretive about that. In other ways, she seemed quite open."

Conner reached for the box. "What's in here?"

"Some hair products, a stuffed tiger, a collection of buttons, and a journal."

Conner tipped the box toward him and grabbed the lavender book. He flipped through to see if Kaylee had used it —and found it half filled. It was all he could do to put it back in the box and make himself wait to read the pages.

"What else can you tell me about Kaylee?" Conner leaned forward, but he had no expectations anymore.

"She's gorgeous, sweet, and funny—but rather troubled. I hope you find her and get her some counseling."

Heather finally spoke up. "Is anyone else here who might know Kaylee?"

"No. They're all new."

"What about Aloha?" Conner asked. "I messaged her, and she told me Kaylee had been kicked out. So she knows her."

"Aloha isn't here." Zayne stood. "And you shouldn't be either. I try to keep strict privacy and security measures in place for the content providers." He turned to Heather, his expression hard to read. "Your assault was a turning point. Yes, we're all making more money, but our security is shot, and we're moving soon."

Heather got up and walked out without a word. Conner thanked Zayne for his time and started to follow her, box in hand. Then he remembered Hitch's request and turned back. "Do you own this house?"

"No." Zayne stood too. "I just manage it."

"Who's the owner?"

Zayne looked wary. "GRZ Properties. Why?"

"Just curious."

As he headed for the car, a female voice called out, "Are you Conner?"

He turned. Walking up the path from the guesthouse was a gorgeous girl with long dark hair and bronze skin. *Aloha!* "Yes. Hi. Aloha, am I right?"

She nodded and gestured for him to meet her halfway. "I don't want Zayne to see us talking." She shrugged it off. "No big deal though."

"I'm still looking for Kaylee."

"I know. And I remembered a guy named Chris that she mentioned. He wasn't a boyfriend, just someone she hung out with. She might be there."

"Do you know his last name or how to contact him?"

She shook her head. "Sorry. But I think he works at Urban Outfitters." She backtracked. "Or maybe it was Urban Beach House."

Another dead end. But her mention of a boyfriend prompted Conner to ask, "What about Jay, her ex? Do you know where to find him?"

"I never knew him." Aloha grimaced. "But K wouldn't go back to him. She said he sexually abused her."

Conner felt sick. His heart couldn't take any more. "Can I give you my phone number? In case you think of something?"

She shook her head again. "But good luck."

Conner dropped Heather off at her car, feeling guilty. "I'm sorry about taking you there. I didn't mean to cause you pain."

"I'll be fine. I hope the journal helps you find her." She got out and hurried to her own car.

Conner opened the lavender notebook and read the first page.

S, the sweetie, gave me this journal and begged me to write about "the trauma," as she calls it. I've never really talked about it, but she thinks this will help me find peace. And live happily ever after with her. LOL! But I'm not much of a writer, and I think I have to be medicated to do this. More later.

Okay, that's better. A cannabis gummy, chased down with some peach schnapps. But now that I have a nice warm glow, I hate to waste it on reliving the worst day of my life.

Conner had to stop. Kaylee was probably talking about their parents' deaths. It had been the worst day of his life too. He couldn't read this right now. It might devastate him. He had to stay focused. And strong. And figure out where the hell Kaylee was. This wouldn't help him. He flipped through a few pages, skimming for a reference to a woman named *S* or any clue to a place she considered safe. But he couldn't help noticing phrases and chunks of text. Kaylee had witnessed the tragedy! And somehow she believed it was her fault. *Oh no!*

Hands shaking, Conner kept turning pages, forcing himself to skim. Six pages in, the narrative changed, and Kaylee recounted a dinner *with S and her family*. He skipped that too, flipping through to where the entries stopped. He wanted to go back and read every word, but this was Kaylee's private journal. He had to respect that. At least for now.

CHAPTER 45

The same afternoon

Hitch watched Arroyo stride into the courtroom, his shoulders back and chin high. When he reached the table, he looked her directly in the eye and grinned, as if he had some secret knowledge.

It was all an act. Hitch knew he was worried. The case was going her way now. Heather had been rehabilitated as a witness, and the informant's testimony had made Evans look like a sleaze. Arroyo's only recourse would be to call his client to testify—a defense attorney's nightmare. Evans was especially risky. Arroyo would have schooled him in how to behave on the stand, but Hitch was good at getting witnesses to show their true personalities. She'd been studying Evans throughout the trial and was sure she could push his buttons. She had to, because if Evans came off as credible, they could lose. She had no intention of letting Heather down.

Once the jury was called in and the preliminaries taken care of, Hitch waited to see if the defense would rest, or if Arroyo would call his client.

Arroyo called Evans to the stand.

Hitch suppressed a smile and picked up a pencil. She was ready.

Arroyo started with the basics. "Do you know Heather Davis?"

"Yes."

"How did you come to know her?"

"I stumbled across her OnlyFans site, and I thought she was beautiful, so I subscribed to her content. Over time, she started making special videos for me. She said she liked to make attack—"

"Objection, hearsay," Hitch said.

"Sustained."

Arroyo picked back up. "What kind of content was in the videos?"

"A man would surprise her and sexually assault her."

"How many of those did she make?"

"Twelve, I think."

"Did you ever meet Heather Davis in person?"

"Yes."

"Did you have consensual sex with her?"

"Yes."

Hitch let them run. She would damage Evans on cross.

"How did you meet her?"

"We arranged for me to surprise her at her house and act out a scene from the videos in real life."

"How did you make that arrangement?"

"Messaging through the app."

"Do you have those messages?"

"Some."

After establishing the communication between Evans and Heather/Heaven, Arroyo handed the defendant a phone. "Please read this message."

"I'd really like to meet you and fulfill my fantasy."

"Who wrote that?"

"I did," Evans said.

"Please read Heaven's response."

"That would be very expensive."

"At any time, did Heather, aka Heaven, tell you she didn't want to act out the video?"

"No."

"When you came into her house, did she tell you to stop or indicate that she didn't want you there?"

"She didn't do anything different at the house than she did in the videos. I expected her to say those things because that was part of the act." He glanced over at Heather, and she glared back.

"Did you believe she wanted to have sex with you?"

"Sure. She was always so agreeable and interested when we communicated and when she made the videos for me."

"Why do you think she suddenly cried rape?"

"Objection," Hitch said. "Speculation."

"Sustained," Barenski said. Evans continued to speak, so the judge turned to him. "Don't answer the question."

Arroyo resumed. "Did Heather fight you during your sexual encounter?"

Sexual encounter, BS. It was rape.

"She struggled a little, not really enough ... er ... as much."

"No further questions." Arroyo sat down.

"Cross, Miss Hitchens?"

"Thank you, Your Honor." She got up, taking her time, and stood in front of the defendant. "The message you read earlier that you claim came from Heather, it said 'expensive,' correct?"

"Yes."

"That could've been a remark just to be flippant, right?"

"Maybe. But it wasn't. She was serious."

"But you never established a price, correct?"

"No. But I—"

"In fact, you never had any further conversations or messages about meeting in person, correct?"

Evans hesitated, and Hitch wondered if he would lie. The defendant glanced at his attorney, then said "No."

"Based on that brief exchange, you decided Heather wanted you to rape her?"

"Objection."

"I'll rephrase," Hitch said. "Based on that brief exchange, you determined that Heather wanted you to break into her house, threaten her with a knife, tear her clothes off, and have sex with her?"

Evans face flushed, and his eyes sparked. For a split second, he couldn't conceal a slight smile.

Hitch assumed the jury saw the excitement in his face, and she hoped at least a few noticed how he moved his hands over his crotch to hide his physical reaction.

"Yes," Evans finally said.

"Heather never gave you an address or told you where she lived, did she?"

"No."

"How did you find her?"

"On the internet."

"You couldn't just google it, so how did you find it?"

"I ran a search."

"What kind of search?"

He shrugged. "Nothing special."

"How would you explain that? Considering my technical support people couldn't find Heather connected to that address."

"I'd say I'm smarter than they are."

"Objection." Arroyo spoke loudly, but it was too late. Evans had already shown how smug he was.

"Withdraw the question," Hitch said. She started to walk to her seat, then turned back. "One other thing. You said Heather didn't struggle *enough*. What did you mean by that?"

"Not like she did in the videos. The whole point is to make it seem like she was surprised and resisting."

"You had a knife to her throat, correct?"

"Yes."

"A real knife, not a fake one, like in her videos?"

"It looks real in the videos."

"Could it be that Heather was too afraid to respond?"

He shrugged, but his hands went to his crotch again. "She liked it."

Bingo. No juror wanted to hear that. "No further questions."

Hitch called Heather back to the stand for the limited purpose of clearing up the messages. "Did the defendant ever ask you to meet?"

"Yes. I get that from almost every client."

"Did he suggest that you act out the video?"

"Yes."

"How did you respond to that?"

"I told him it would be 'too expensive.'" She put air quotes around the words. "That's the basic answer we all give when a subscriber wants to meet in person."

"So you never intended to meet him?"

Heather shook her head. "No. I have never met with any of my fans, nor would I."

"Did the defendant ask you for your address?"

"Yes. But I ignored it."

"So you never told him where you lived?"

"No."

"Is your name associated with the address of the house you were living in where the crime took place?"

"No. I don't receive mail there, no utilities are in my name, and it's not on my driver's license."

"No further questions."

CHAPTER 46

Friday afternoon

Both sides rested. It was time for Hitch to give her closing, but as she often did, she waived her right to argue until rebuttal. Hitch expected Arroyo would try to hammer home the issue of consent. She was prepared.

Arroyo rose to make his closing argument, then walked over and stood in front of the jury box, as was his style. He was known for how well he could handle jurors. He always looked them in the eyes when he gave his arguments, smiling at the appropriate times, and evoking sympathy when needed. He was good.

"Beyond a reasonable doubt. That's the prosecutor's burden. She must prove to you that Jason Evans raped Heather Davis. In a few minutes, the judge will give you some jury instructions. Listen carefully as he explains the elements of the crime of rape. Most important, he will tell you that the prosecutor must prove the act was not consensual. If it was consensual, Mr. Evans did not commit a crime. He does not dispute that they had sexual intercourse. We do not contend that his sexual interests are not unusual, but that in and of itself does not make him a rapist. Nor do we pretend Ms. Davis' job is normal. Let's look at the facts."

Arroyo shifted his feet and used his fingers to lay out his points. "Jason found Heather online in a setting that allowed him to harmlessly engage in his sexual fantasies." A pause. "She provided lots of material for him, encouraging his proclivities." Another pause. "When he asked for an in-person encounter, she didn't say no. In fact, she set a baseline. It would be *expensive.* He was willing to pay and in fact did pay her. Heather testified that he paid her three-hundred dollars. Perhaps she expected more, but—"

"Objection. Arguing facts not in evidence."

"Sustained," Judge Barenski said. "Tread lightly, Counselor."

Arroyo continued with his argument. "Heather testified that her name was not connected to the house where she was living. There is no testimony that indicated he could have followed her to the content house. There is no evidence suggesting Jason could have possibly obtained her address from anyone—because there were no records of where she lived and no mutual acquaintances. And yet somehow, magically, Jason knew where to go. Who had her address? Heather did. Reasonable doubt." He glanced briefly at the victim.

"The prosecutor will argue the sex was not consensual. That Heather said no and struggled to get away. But Jason testified that Heather agreed to have sex with him in the same way she had been doing on the videos she made. She had performed this scenario every week for over three months. That's a minimum of twelve times. In every video, she said 'No' and pretended to fight off her intruder."

Arroyo's voice pitched higher, indicating empathy with the defendant. "How could he know she suddenly meant for him to stop? How would any reasonable person know? They wouldn't. In fact, there is testimony that Heather didn't struggle as much as she did in the videos, suggesting again that she was consenting. Once again, it gave Jason reason to believe she continued to agree to the sex."

Now his tone dropped into lecture mode. "Couples engage in unusual sexual practices all the time. As long as they both consent, it is perfectly acceptable. This is the kind of sex play that can be confusing, since the whole intent of the act is to pretend to be scared. You've seen the video. We all know what a good actor Heather is. That certainly would raise reasonable doubt in my mind."

Hitch noticed that Arroyo seemed to be addressing the men on the jury, looking more directly at them than the women. He only had to convince one man—who had been in a situation where he wasn't sure what a woman wanted. Dread filled Hitch's stomach.

"Heather, herself, admitted she lies. She testified that she lies to her clients when they ask her questions she doesn't want to answer. She performed sex acts for Jason for months. We don't know what happened when Jason arrived at her home. Perhaps she changed her mind. But how would he know that? How would any reasonable person know that? They wouldn't. Reasonable doubt." Arroyo nodded slightly, then walked back to his chair.

It wasn't a great legal argument. But it didn't have to be if Arroyo could convince one juror that the sex had been consensual. That was all he needed, and Hitch was worried.

She stood but remained at the counsel table. She had to separate herself from Arroyo's performance. Approaching them would seem like she was emulating him. Hitch hoped remaining at the counsel table would tell the jury she was so confident in her argument she didn't need theatrics.

"Let's examine the *real* facts. The defendant came to Heather's residence, surprised her, held a knife to her throat, and forced sex on her while she pleaded for him to stop. No matter what kind of spin the defense wants to put on it—that's rape." She gave it a moment to sink in.

"Jason Evans raped a young woman and wants to blame the victim. It feels like a throwback to the fifties. She was asking for it? Really? There is no evidence that Heather consented to being raped. In a message, Heather used the term *expensive*, but she explained that was an off-hand remark to end the messaging. And it did in fact end the conversation. There were no more exchanges regarding any agreement to meet in person. If the defendant had any of those messages, doesn't it seem logical he would have produced them? Just as he did the other ones?" The jury was listening intently, and Hitch felt a surge of confidence.

"The defense implied that because her address was hard to find, Heather must have given it to him. But there is no evidence whatsoever that she did. The defendant didn't testify Heather gave him her address. Why do you suppose that is? Because she did not. He said he found her address online, but he wouldn't tell us how. And we know by his own statement that he is very adept on the computer."

Hitch softened her tone to empathize with the victim. "Heather has a job some of you may not agree with, but she is not a prostitute. What she does to earn money to pay her way through college is legal. It wasn't easy for her to come forward and report what happened. She knew once information about her work came out, she would be judged for it. Please don't make her sorry she reported this crime."

Hitch paused again, looking at each of the jurors. "The defendant broke into Heather's house, put a knife to her throat, and raped her while she begged him to stop. He wants you to believe that this young med student invited him over to do that." She shook her head. "He's asking you to believe that her begging, screaming, and struggling were not clear signs that she wanted him to stop. The defense kept talking about reasonable doubt. The judge in his instructions will explain that does not mean all doubt is removed. I'm confident that when you review the evidence and weigh his testimony against hers, you will come up with a verdict of guilty." Hitch returned to her seat.

Judge Barenski cleared his throat and gave his charge to the jury. He kept his voice at an even keel as he doled out the instructions, starting with the Judicial Counsel of California Criminal Jury Instruction on reasonable doubt. Hitch had heard these instructions so many times she could quote them by heart. The judge explained that the jury should not be biased against the defendant just because he was charged with a crime, and that he was innocent until proven guilty. Everyone knew what those words meant. The tough ones came moments later when the judge said, "Proof beyond a reasonable doubt is proof that leaves you with an abiding conviction that the charge is true. The evidence need not eliminate all possible doubt because everything in life is open to some possible or imaginary doubt."

Had she left the jury with an "abiding conviction" that Heather did not consent?

Judge Barenski continued with the instructions for the rape. "The defendant is charged in Count 1 with rape by force in violation of Penal Code Section 261. To prove that the defendant is guilty of this crime, the people must prove the following …"

Hitch tuned out again. She knew the elements as well as her own address. She had to prove Heather and Jason weren't married and that sexual intercourse took place, neither of which was in dispute. The other two elements were the ones in contention. Was it by force, and did Heather consent? Hitch listened for the buzzwords, "a woman must act freely and voluntarily." Then the judge explained that even if she did consent initially, she could change her mind and it was no longer by consent if she "communicated through words or acts to the defendant that she no longer consented to the act of intercourse, and a reasonable person would have understood that her words or acts expressed her lack of consent." There was no doubt in Hitch's mind that Heather had not given consent, but had she herself done enough to convince the twelve people sitting in the jury box?

The judge went on with the rest of the jury instructions. This was the most boring part for the attorneys, but the jury seemed to listen intently, all eyes focused on the judge except for one woman who kept glancing around the courtroom. That usually meant the juror had already made up her mind and didn't care to hear anything more. The question was: Which way she was leaning? Hitch had given up long ago trying to figure out how jurors' minds worked. She had polled many a juror after a hung verdict and was always surprised by their reasoning, or lack thereof.

The judge finished speaking and excused the jury for deliberations. Hitch gathered up her things and left the courtroom, hoping she'd done enough to get justice for Heather. She checked her messages as she walked back to her office. She had one from Conner, one from Nelson, and one from a number she didn't recognize. Conner and Nelson had both asked her to call them. She listened to the other message.

Hello. This is Fernando Vargas. We met at the jail a few days ago. We need to talk.

Hitch immediately returned his call, but there was no answer.

CHAPTER 47

Friday evening

Heart aching and anxiety mounting, Conner drove toward the ocean, the only sight and sound that could soothe him. Poor Kaylee. No wonder she was so troubled. Blaming herself for their parents' deaths all these years. Why hadn't she told anyone? They could have helped her. Guilt, of course. She had probably thought her siblings would blame her too. What a terrible secret to carry. Conner felt more determined than ever to get her into rehab where she could get counseling—for everything.

He parked at La Jolla Shores, his favorite place in the world, and felt a little better. He watched the burnt-orange sun slowly descend into the ocean and tried to empty his mind. But it wouldn't cooperate. Ramsden's death mystified him. Kaylee looked like the obvious suspect, but she wasn't a violent person. And her anger about the past had been directed at herself.

Maybe the act had been self-defense. Ramsden might have tried to force her into having sex. Or maybe he'd been violent with her, and she'd fought back. With a good defense attorney

—and a jury sympathetic to her trauma—she could stay out of prison. And Conner knew a good lawyer.

But first he had to find her. That meant finding her girlfriend. S, Sweet-Cheeks, whoever she was. Or so he hoped. Kaylee might have left town completely. Had she gone to stay with Gina in Seattle? Conner texted his middle sister, but hesitated before sending it. If Kaylee wasn't there, Gina would be alarmed. She might even call him and want to talk. He wasn't ready for that conversation. Besides, Gina would have let him or Nicole know if Kaylee had shown up.

What if someone else had stabbed Ramsden and Kaylee had witnessed it, then ran? The killer might be trying to find her and silence her. Troy Burton had been stabbed too. Maybe an ex-con seeking revenge had killed both men for putting him away. That's what the police thought. Only they believed Conner was that ex-con.

The ocean disappeared into the darkness, and his anxiety boiled to the surface again. Time to get back to work. Conner left the seaside park and headed north. No harm in driving by Trevor Gorman's house. He was more likely to be home in the evening.

A dim light glowed at the edge of the front window coverings. That didn't mean anyone was home, but Conner parked and hustled up to the door anyway. He rang the doorbell and waited. Shuffling noises started in the back of the house and grew louder as someone approached the door.

Gorman's voice sounded above him. "What do you want now?"

Conner glanced up at the intercom speaker. Was Gorman stoned? His words had been slow and measured, but not sloppy like a drunk's. That might work in Conner's favor. "Kaylee is in danger," he called out. That should get the guy's attention. "I need to find her before the police do. Or before Ramsden's killer does."

A long moment of silence. Then a soft click and Gorman opened the door. The thin man in his forties stared at him. "You both have the same eyes."

"I know." Conner smiled. "Can I come in?"

"Sure. I could use some company. Living alone gets to me sometimes." Gorman stepped aside. "That's why I pay for girls like Kaylee."

Conner bit back a response and hurried into the foyer. He would let this privileged pervert say whatever he wanted … as long as he provided information.

"Let's go sit in the lower level. The moon over the ocean can be lovely."

They passed a massive kitchen with a built-in bar. "Something to drink?" Gorman asked.

He'd better not. "No thanks." But he was starving. "Can I have a snack? Crackers, an apple, anything easy." Conner was never too proud to ask for food. His mother had believed most people enjoyed providing sustenance to others. Not eating what they offered robbed them of the joy.

"Sure. Just help yourself. If I go in there, I'll end up eating everything in sight."

The munchies. Gorman was trippin' on weed. Conner opened the stainless-steel refrigerator and saw mostly leftover takeout containers. *Ugh.* He moved a few and found a jar of salsa. Now if the guy just had some corn chips. *No.* Too messy and noisy. Conner grabbed a banana from the bowl on the granite counter, wolfed it down, then headed for the wide steps leading down to the living space.

Gorman was seated on the end of his leather couch, the exact spot Conner had predicted from his earlier visit. The place where he'd spotted the orange panties. In the dimly lit room, Gorman stared at the ocean, mindlessly sipping from a tumbler. The dark liquid could have been anything.

Conner sat in the middle of the couch and wondered if he

should ease in or just be blunt. He'd been direct the last time they'd talked, and it had scared Gorman off. He decided to go slow. "How did you meet Kaylee?"

"Answer this question first. Did you come here yesterday? And set off the alarm?"

Honesty in all things. "Yes. I'm sorry. But I just wanted to talk."

"You are persistent. I admire that." Gorman finally turned to look at him. "I need a little more sativa to get through this. Would you like to join me? I only have edibles."

Yes, indeed. That sounded awesome. "I'd love to, but I have a long drive home." God, he hated being sober and responsible.

"Kaylee never turned down anything." Gorman popped something into his mouth, then talked around it. "Ecstasy was her favorite. It made the sex so much more intense."

Conner didn't want to hear about his sister's sex life, but apparently it was the core of her relationships. "How did you meet Kaylee?"

"I became aware of her videos on OnlyFans. She's so beautiful. And so compelling. I can't put it into the right words, but I wanted to consume her." Gorman sipped his drink. "So I sent her a message and offered her five-hundred dollars to meet me in person. She checked out my references, doubled the price, and we set it up."

"How did you guys get busted for prostitution?"

Gorman snapped his head toward Conner. "How do you know about that?"

"I can't reveal my sources." If he mentioned working with a lawyer, Gorman would probably kick him out.

"Then I'm not telling you about that sorry incident." Gorman sighed. "It's not important. A friend made it go away."

"Deputy DA Martin Ramsden?"

Another head snap. "You're quite informed. Are you

working with the police?" Gorman's eyes went wide. "Are you wearing a wire?"

"No! I'm trying to keep the police from picking up Kaylee and charging her with Ramsden's murder." Conner had a wild thought that scared him. What if Gorman was the killer? His body tensed. "How well did you know Ramsden?"

"We go way back." Another sip. "We invested in real estate together, as a sideline. But I continued on my own and made better investments." Gorman smiled. "But donating to Ramsden's campaign was one of my best. It's nice having a free pass with the DA's office." His expression went dark. "But he's dead now, and that's shameful."

So cold. Had he killed Ramsden? A jealousy thing involving Kaylee? Was his sister in this house somewhere?

"You said Kaylee was in danger," Gorman reminded him. "What do you mean? Or was that just hype to get my attention?"

Conner treaded lightly. "I'm genuinely worried. Somebody killed Ramsden. Stabbed him, I think. And Kaylee likely witnessed it. I think she's in hiding because she's scared he'll come after her too."

"It was probably an ex-con. They sometimes take it personally when a prosecutor gets them locked up."

Conner felt restless and uncertain. None of this was helping him find his sister. "Do you have any idea where she would go?"

"Kaylee knew a lot of people. Many of them would do anything for her."

Now they were getting closer. "What about her girlfriend? Kaylee called her Sweet-Cheeks."

"Oh yeah. Selene."

Rona's friend? "You mean Selene Gomez? I thought they broke up."

"They did. And they got back together."

"Where do I find her?"

"I don't know. But try searching using her whole name." Gorman paused. "Selene Maria Gomez Ramsden."

"What?" Conner jerked forward, and spit flew out of his mouth. "She's related to Martin Ramsden?"

"His daughter."

CHAPTER 48

A year earlier

Kaylee glanced across the table at Selene's father. He was handsome, but loud and full of himself. Her mom on the other hand seemed detached, like someone who'd taken a hefty benzo. And Aria never looked at her husband directly. Not a happily married woman. But she was dark-eyed and sexy like Selene.

"What are you studying?" Mr. Ramsden asked, staring intently at Kaylee.

Oh right. Selene had told them she was a student at Grossmont College. Kaylee had been—just long enough to get her GED, which Selene had pushed her to do. She loved her girlfriend's ambitions for her. They filled Kaylee with temporary confidence and a sense that her life could mean something. But not yet. She wasn't ready to be an adult.

"Kaylee?"

"Oh sorry, Mr. Ramsden. I was thinking about my sociology class. I like it enough to consider changing my major." She'd said the first thing that popped into her head.

"Please call me Martin. And keep in mind, there's no money in social work," he lectured. "You should think about becoming a lawyer. You can always take some *pro bono* cases to help the underprivileged."

Selene, seated next to her, patted Kaylee's leg under the table. "Ignore him. Dad thinks everyone should be a lawyer. Or a banker."

"There's nothing wrong with money," Ramsden countered.

Aria suddenly leaned over and locked eyes with Kaylee. "You're pretty enough to be a model. But it's not a long-term plan. I advise you to study technology. It's the future."

"Sound advice, Mom." Selene gave a cursory smile.

Kaylee hoped they were done with that subject. She just wanted to get through this mandatory meet-the-family nonsense and go out clubbing. Dancing was her joy. Well, other than sex and drugs. She tried to suppress a grin.

"What's funny?" Aria sounded upset.

"Me," Kaylee said quickly. "I'm so bad at math. I can't imagine myself learning how to code software."

"Too bad." Aria shook her head. "But nursing is a great job too. And you can always find work."

"Leave her alone," Selene said with a laugh. "Just because I've always wanted to be a surgeon doesn't mean other young people have their lives figured out."

"Of course." Aria got up and began picking up dishes.

Kaylee looked at her uneaten food. She'd been a bad guest, but she'd been too nervous about the whole scene to be hungry. Then the molly had started to kick in. The effect would be in full glory by the time they hit the club.

"Does anyone want dessert?" Aria asked.

Kaylee shook her head, and Selene got up to help clear the table. When the look-alike women left the dining area, Mr. Ramsden stood and gestured to her. "Come join me on the patio where I can smoke a cigar. We'll get to know each other better."

Why not? He was a powerful man, and he was looking at her the way all men did.

———

Ramsden watched Kaylee sit on the patio love seat and resisted the urge to slide in next to her. He really wanted to, just to feel her leg against his. She radiated warmth, vulnerability and sexuality—all in a stunningly gorgeous package. And those green eyes!

He eased into a chair nearby and took out a cigar giving him something to focus on so he didn't stare at her. No wonder Selene was in love. *Let it go,* he told himself. This girl was too young. Too naive. He had to steer clear. But he would run a background check just to make sure Selene wasn't hooking up with a criminal. "Would you like a cigar?"

The girl laughed, a musical sound that made his heart leap in his chest.

"Hard pass." She inhaled deeply. "But I like the smell."

Unlike Aria, who hated the cigars. His wife had been so distant lately, Ramsden thought she might be having an affair. So humiliating. And such bad timing. "Where are you from, Miss Kaylee?"

"You mean, like, where was I born?"

So young. "Exactly."

"Right here in San Diego County."

Not a good sign. "Tell me something about your family."

Kaylee laughed again. "We operate Nico's Parrot Rescue, so we're not in your league."

Ramsden didn't care. He planned to run for DA, and after that, governor. He had campaign contributors lined up, but he needed to improve his division's conviction rate. And to keep his family together. A divorce or a Selene scandal could ruin him. So he would keep an eye on this girl.

CHAPTER 49

Saturday morning

Hitch woke early, padded into the kitchen, and pulled out the full-sized coffee maker she rarely used. One cup of Krups was all she usually had. Conner would drink the rest when he got up. Hot, cold, he didn't seem to care. As long as he could put some kind of sugar in it. He was such a kid. But she had to admit she enjoyed his company. Quite a change of pace from all the take-themselves-too-seriously gen-xers in her office. She chuckled. Including herself.

She took her coffee out to the back patio and tried calling Vargas again. Still nothing. She sat back and enjoyed the morning sun while she read the newspaper. But her serenity didn't last long. She started thinking about Kaylee and where she could be. And what kind of danger she could be in. Nelson had said he would tail Kolinder, but he had to find him first. Conner still thought Kaylee's girlfriend would be with her or know where she was, so they had to find Selene. Ramsden's daughter. What a shocker that had been. Conner had called her late the night before with the news, and she'd invited him to stay over again so they could get an early start on their mission.

Hitch decided to try a computer search like he'd shown her. She keyed Selene's full name into the search bar and pressed enter.

Links came up for Selene's Facebook page, an Instagram account, and something called TikTok. But after Hitch clicked on a link, she didn't know what to do next. Frustrated, she was about to give up when she remembered a program they used at the office to find information about people. She knew the user-name and password and just had to remember the name of the program. It was *verify*-something. That was it—*verifyinfo.com*. She brought up the site and keyed *Selene Gomez Ramsden* into the space where it asked for a name.

She knew the next part took a few minutes, so she went inside and poured another half cup of coffee. By the time she got back to her laptop, she'd received a report in her office email account. Hitch decided to try the searches for Kaylee, Ramsden, and Gorman as well. After she'd processed all the names, it suddenly hit her. There would be a record of her searches! How would she explain that? *Oh well.* She hit *print* and went inside to retrieve the reports.

She picked up the one for Kaylee, which wasn't as long as the others. The only address it showed was Nicole's.

"That's a really loud printer." Conner wandered into her home office, sleepy-eyed. His hair was disheveled and he was shirtless.

Hitch took a deep breath. *Stay focused.* "Yeah, I know. It's old." She paused. "Question."

"Yes?"

"We have a program at the office that lets us research indi-viduals. We're not supposed to use it for personal stuff, and I sort of did."

"You *sort of* did?"

Hitch felt herself flush. "Will someone be able to check and see if I used it inappropriately?"

"Probably. It likely shows a record of all searches. Even if it doesn't, a techie certainly could find it if he wanted to."

The printer kept clanging and spitting out documents.

Conner scowled at it. "Who all did you run?"

"Besides Selene, I did Kaylee, Gorman, and Ramsden."

Conner stepped toward the printer to get the documents, but Hitch stopped him. "I'd better do this. I've already violated enough rules." She carried the papers to her desk and collated them, making four stacks, then stapled each bunch together.

Conner had started pacing, obviously impatient. "Did you get an address for Selene?"

"I don't know if it's current, but the report lists an apartment in La Mesa not far from Grossmont College."

"I'll get dressed and suck down some coffee."

Hitch decided they would take her car, and Conner cheerfully climbed into the passenger seat. A first for any man she'd known. On the drive, Hitch updated him on what she'd learned from Nelson. "But if you get questioned again," she warned, "you can't reveal that you know any of this."

"I won't." He reached over and touched her arm. "Thanks for telling me. I'm relieved to know Detective Nelson is putting the brakes on framing me for both murders."

After a long moment, he added, "Nelson is more than a friend, isn't he?"

Hitch was surprised the question didn't bother her. "We used to date. But at this point, we're just friendly colleagues."

"It's good to have an inside source."

At the two-story apartment complex, they checked the mail-boxes and found Selene's name on unit nine. They walked around to the side of the building and passed doors for six, seven, and eight.

"There it is." Conner scooted over and knocked.

They had already decided they would be direct with Selene if she came to the door and assertive if Kaylee was the one who responded. When no one answered, they waited a few seconds and rapped again.

"Do you want to wait or come back later?" Hitch stepped away.

But Conner was still at the door, with a small set of tools in his hand.

"What are you doing?"

"I'm going in."

"We can't do that."

"Maybe you can't, but that's what I'm doing."

He was reckless. Hitch started to walk away, then stopped when she heard the door open. She pivoted and followed him inside, all the while telling herself it was crazy and stupid. In the small, cluttered living room, clothes were strewn about, and a pair of orange panties hung from the ear of a five-foot-tall, paper mâché giraffe. *What the—?*

Conner trotted off and checked out the bedroom. "No one's here," he called out.

"I can't do this." Hitch spun around and bolted for the exit. "I'll wait in the car. Don't get caught."

She hurried to her Mazda, then moved it around to the side, so she could see the entry to Selene's apartment. As she waited and watched the door, she glanced at the report on Ramsden. But she couldn't focus. If anyone did show up, she likely wouldn't have time to warn Conner, but at least she would see them coming. Two young men walked along the corridor toward apartment nine. Hitch held her breath. But they strolled past the door and around the corner to the stairs. *Whew. Come on, Conner. Hurry up.*

It seemed like she'd been waiting twenty minutes for Conner to come out when her phone rang.

"Hello. This is Fernando Vargas."

Finally! "Thanks for calling back."

He was quiet for a moment.

Hitch prompted him. "You said we needed to talk. Do you know something about the knife they took from Nate Conner?"

"Not the knife, exactly." He took a deep breath. "But that video from when Conner was booked should not have been blank."

Hitch glanced at door nine again. No movement. "Do you think it was erased?"

"I think it was switched."

"Any idea who did it?"

"The only one I know who had access to that video prior to the defense subpoena was DDA Martin Ramsden."

Clunk. Another piece of evidence fell into place. She'd known he was dirty, and now she might have proof. "Did he sign in to see the evidence?"

"Yes, but not under that case."

"Then how do you know he had access to Conner's booking video?"

"Because I saw it in his hand as he slipped it into his jacket. He didn't realize I was there and could see him. I caught a glimpse of the file date on it, so I went and checked. There was another recording in its place. So I played it. Nothin'. It was blank."

"Why didn't you report it?"

"Who would believe me? I had messed up. Even if they believed me, I shouldn't have allowed the recording to be heisted. But more likely, they would think I was covering my own butt, that I didn't check to make sure it was intact before I filed it. Either way, I was screwed."

His assessment was likely accurate. "When did this happen?"

"A few weeks ago."

"When did the knife disappear from the property locker?"

"It never made it to the locker."

"How is that possible?"

"I had only been on the job for a week, and to tell you the truth, I was overwhelmed. It was a crazy busy night at the jail, so I didn't get to the paperwork until much later." A long pause. "I'm not sure what happened to the knife. I remembered a knife from that arrest, but I started to question myself because, as I said, so many arrests were going down. I didn't know how, but I thought maybe I had mislaid it somewhere. So when I filled out the paperwork, I left it off."

"But you're sure there was a knife?"

"Yes. I noticed it because of the initials carved into the handle."

"Why are you telling me this now?"

"I can't, with good conscience, let someone go down for a murder they didn't commit." He made a noise in his throat. "And then Ramsden died. So he can't get me fired as revenge."

"Are you willing to tell the police and the court what happened?"

He hesitated. "I'll lose my job if I do."

"Maybe there's a way to spin it," Hitch said. But right now, she couldn't think of one. "Thank you. I'll be in touch." She hung up and called Jerry Leahy with the news. Hitch decided not to tell Conner until they knew they would be able to use it.

After a few more minutes, Conner finally came out of

Selene's apartment. *Thank goodness.* He glanced around, then started to walk in the direction the car had been parked earlier.

"Over here," Hitch called out, as she started the engine.

Conner jumped in, and they drove off.

"This is too crazy," she said. "I hope it was worth it because we could both end up in jail over this. I can't believe I let you talk me into doing it."

"This was your idea!" He gave her a teasing smile. "You want to know what happened in that motel as much as I do."

Hitch headed west on I-8. She knew Conner was right, but she needed to stay within the law or it wouldn't do either of them any good. "Did you find anything? And if you took something, please don't tell me."

"I didn't. But Kaylee was definitely living there at some point. I found a closet that had several orange shirts—her favorite color—and I found notes in her handwriting. Also, there were empty bottles of peach schnapps in the trash. She at least spent time there."

"But nothing that might tell us where she is now?"

"No. Sorry. But I noticed there were no overnight bags in the closets, so I'm wondering if they packed a few things and went somewhere else. After I get my car, I'll go stake out the place. Maybe I'll catch Selene or Kaylee coming back."

"I have another idea." Hitch took the 805 off-ramp.

"Where are we going?"

"I found an address for a house in Del Mar that Ramsden owns. It's a long shot, but it might be a hideaway for them."

"I'm game."

"Good. But we're not breaking into this one."

"Right."

"I mean it, Conner. You'll end up right back in jail with no ability to help Kaylee. Not to mention, you'll look even more guilty for the murders."

Conner didn't respond.

Hitch eased off the gas and moved into the exit lane. "Then I'm not taking you there."

"All right. I won't break into it while you're with me."

"Meaning, you'll do it later?"

"Only if I have to."

Hitch kept driving.

CHAPTER 50

Months earlier

Kaylee grabbed clothes from the closet and shoved them into a travel bag. She would sort out her wardrobe later. Right now she had to get out of Selene's apartment. The woman was making her crazy.

"Where are you running to this time?" Selene taunted from the doorway. "Back to the content house?"

"At least they don't try to control every aspect of my life!" Kaylee fought back tears. She hated arguing with people she loved. She'd seen too much of it from her parents, who had loved—and hated—each other to the bitter end.

"I don't want to control you," Selene argued. "I just want to help you."

"I don't need your help. You're my girlfriend, not my damn social worker." Kaylee grabbed a handful of clothes from the small dresser, shoved those in too, and headed for the bathroom. She always forgot her shampoo.

Selene followed her. "The content house will be your death.

They don't care about your drug use or whether you get Hepatitis C or if some subscriber rapes you." Her girlfriend was shouting now. "Zayne just cares about making money. And the landlord just wants to screw you like everyone else."

"Including you," Kaylee snapped back.

"This isn't just about sex for me, and you know it!" Selene grabbed her shoulder and spun her around. "I love you! I want what's best for you. I want a life with you." Her dark eyes blazed with passion.

Kaylee loved her for it. But Selene was too much of a good thing. And too moody lately. Kaylee needed out. "But I want a *whole* life. And that includes using ecstasy sometimes. And being spontaneous. And having sex with strangers just for the newness of it."

"Sometimes? You're high every day. And it's not just molly. Rona told me you tried heroin."

"So?"

"It's dangerously addictive. Everyone knows that."

"It's also really beautiful." Kaylee laughed, remembering how peaceful she'd felt. The first-time joy of feeling nothing but love. No anxiety. No guilt. No anger. No disappointment. For hours! Yeah, it would be easy to become a junkie. *Had she just said all that out loud?*

"But the euphoria doesn't last." Selene broke into tears. "And heroin will kill you. I'm a biology student. Trust me on this. "

"I'm starting to think aging is over-rated." Kaylee pushed past her out of the bathroom, threw her shampoo into the suitcase, and zipped it closed.

"Please don't go," Selene pleaded. "You need counseling to get over your trauma."

"Not this again!" *And you didn't just get over trauma. You learned to live with it.* "Please don't cry. I'm not saying we can't see each other. I just can't live with you 24/7."

Selene pressed a notebook into her hands. "Use this journal. Write about your experiences. You won't find peace until you do."

CHAPTER 51

Saturday noon

Ramsden's beach house in Del Mar sat in a cluster of palm trees. A six-foot hedge surrounded the property, creating privacy. Conner thought the neighborhood seemed like the kind of place where people didn't know each other and didn't want to. "Park here," he said. "We don't want them to see us."

"I know what I'm doing," Hitch mumbled, as she pulled over. "Sorry."

She shut off the engine. "Actually, I've never done anything like this before. We have investigators who track down witnesses and information leads." She held out her keys to show him a tiny canister. "But I carry mace everywhere."

"Smart." Conner smiled. "But I don't think you'll need that. Kaylee witnessed a murder, and Selene is grieving her father's death, so they're probably both in shock. I don't blame them for hiding out from the police and the media."

"If they're even here." Hitch reached for her door handle. "I don't see any cars or movement in the house."

"Their vehicle could be in the garage." Conner climbed out, and they started toward the house. "Ramsden must have made a lot of money if this is his second home."

"I heard his wife came with a bundle, but that might be just a rumor." Hitch paused, as if remembering something. "And that night he was drunk, he told me she'd just left him. I hope Mrs. Ramsden's not here."

"Maybe she'll be helpful."

Hitch hesitated again. "What exactly is our objective?"

Conner turned to her. "To help Kaylee however we can. If she witnessed the murder, she needs to go to the police. And hopefully with Jerry Leahy at her side."

"What if she won't go?" Hitch grabbed Conner's arm. "Now that I've enlisted Nelson's help, I have an obligation to tell him what I know."

"I understand. But she's my little sister. She'll listen to me." As soon as he said it, Conner had doubts. Kaylee wasn't the same person she'd been a year ago when he saw her last. But still, he wanted to bring her home to Nicole's, where they could support her while she got treatment.

He and Hitch stopped at the walkway and looked at each other. "Let me do the talking to start with," Conner said. "I'm family, so I'll seem less threatening."

"Okay."

He knocked, then leaned against the door to listen. "I hear footsteps," he whispered. "Someone is moving around."

But no one came to the door. Conner knocked again. Still nothing. "Selene," he called out. "It's Nate Conner. I need to talk to you."

He put his ear to the door again, but the movement had stopped. "Selene!" Conner shouted this time. Maybe she had earbuds in and was listening to music.

He grabbed the doorknob and turned. It wasn't locked. He

looked at Hitch. "I'm going in." Conner stepped inside and called out again. "Anybody home? Selene? Kaylee?"

Beyond the foyer, the house opened up into a great room with a kitchen off to the side. A tall, dark-haired woman suddenly rushed into view. "What the hell are you doing?"

"Sorry to barge in." Conner flashed her a charming smile. "I thought maybe you had earbuds in and didn't hear me knock." He moved toward her. "Nate Conner, Kaylee's brother. We met last week at the Beachside Boogie."

Her dark eyes flashed. "Kaylee's not here. And you can stop right there." She stepped sideways, blocking a hall leading toward the bedrooms.

A shiver ran up Conner's spine. She was hiding something. But he had to play it cool as long as he could. "I need to find her before the police do. Can you help me?"

"I haven't seen Kaylee in weeks." Selene crossed her arms. "Why are the cops looking for her?"

Her tone was too casual.

"They want to question Kaylee about a murder she likely witnessed, but that's—"

"I don't want to be involved. Please just leave." Selene stared past him. "And take that woman, whoever she is, with you."

Conner glanced over his shoulder to see Hitch standing timidly in the foyer.

"Can you at least tell me where I might find her?"

"No. Sorry. Kaylee has burned through most of her friends."

Conner tried a long shot. "I know she called you from the motel after your father was murdered."

Selene's body stiffened and her eyes hardened. "You don't know anything about it."

Did that mean she did?

Hitch eased up by his side. Conner kept his eyes locked on

Selene. "You're someone Kaylee counted on. Just tell me where she is. I want to get her into rehab, then bring her home so her family can be supportive."

"She won't go." Her voice trembled. "Believe me, I've tried."

Moaning sounds came from the interior, the rooms Selene was blocking the entrance to.

Was that Kaylee? Was she in pain? "What's going on?" Conner demanded.

"Nothing. That's my sick dog. Now get out." Selene started toward him, pointing at the front door. Conner braced himself, with no intention of retreating.

The moaning got louder, and a weak female voiced called out. But the words were unintelligible.

"I think that's Kaylee," Conner said.

Hitch stepped forward and locked eyes on Selene. "I'm an attorney, and I think it's important that you understand the long list of crimes you're committing." She grabbed Selene's arm and tried to turn her away from the hall. The big woman didn't budge.

Hitch kept talking, her tone intimidating. "If you're holding Kaylee against her will, you can be charged with kidnapping. That's a very serious crime. You may be doing this because you love her or you think you can help her, but your intentions are immaterial. The act in itself is enough to get you a felony conviction with a prison sentence and a strike. Do you really want to spend eight years in a state prison?"

That should shake her up, Conner thought.

When Selene didn't respond, Hitch went on. "Eight years! That's a long time to be stuck in a cell and not see your family or Kaylee."

"I don't have any family left, and Kaylee doesn't love me. What difference does it make?" She spoke softly now, sounding eerie. "Eight years. That's a joke." Her eyes stared off into space.

Hitch glanced over at Conner. He assumed she was thinking the same thing he was. Selene was off her rocker and possibly dangerous. He bolted past her and down the short hall. The moaning sounds came from the room at the end. He grabbed the door handle, but it was locked. *Damn!* He glanced back and saw Selene charging him.

"Why is it locked? I want to see Kaylee!"

Selene grabbed his arm and tried to drag him back down the hall. "We'll call the police!" Conner threatened. *Would they?* They were the intruders.

Selene froze for a moment.

Hitch went on the offensive, diverting the woman's attention again. "You must have something to hide or you would've called them yourself by now. Being a DDA's daughter won't protect you from whatever is going on here. You can't hide behind Martin Ramsden this time."

"I don't need my father!" Selene barked back.

Whoa! Hitch had hit a nerve.

She must have realized it too and doubled down. "He was totally corrupt and would be headed to jail if someone hadn't killed him."

"Corrupt? How quaint." Selene let out a bitter laugh. "He was a predator. An adulterer. A girlfriend-stealing pig. He deserved to die."

For a moment, they all went silent.

CHAPTER 52

Five days earlier

Kaylee couldn't get into sex with Martin, but she didn't mind it either. She was floating in that lovely bubble of euphoria that only H could give her. She mindlessly did what he wanted, because he paid for the room—as long as she kept her body exclusive to him. But what he didn't know couldn't hurt him.

By the time he flopped on his back, panting and sweaty, her bubble had developed a leak, and the joy was slowly oozing out. Kaylee headed for the bathroom. Martin would want to go again soon, with a little help from Viagra. But in the shower, she could be alone, letting the warm water soothe her battered body. Her thoughts drifted to Selene. She was a better lover than her father, equally intense, but more giving. The thought made Kaylee giggle. Both father and daughter would explode if they knew she was hooking up with the other. But they would never find out. Kaylee always took a bus or an Uber to Selene's apartment and refused to tell her where she was staying. Selene had barged into the content house one too many times and ruined a good thing for her.

Kaylee stepped out and towel-dried her hair. She heard water running in the room next door and wondered what time it was. Martin had shown up in the middle of the night, but maybe it was morning by now. Not that she cared. But the proximity of her motel neighbors was getting to her. She wanted a nicer place with more privacy. Maybe it was time to press for one. Her visits to Trevor's house had triggered a longing for a better life. But that meant getting clean, and that was too unbearable. She'd tried detoxing once, and it had almost killed her with intense pain, nausea, and disassociating. So she would just enjoy the ride for now.

Kaylee stepped out of the bathroom, wearing only a towel. Where was her favorite robe? She'd left and lost so many of her things with all the moving around.

"Hey, sexy girl. Get over here." Martin was sitting up now, stroking himself.

"You're a machine," she said, in her seductive voice. "And soon to be the DA, a very powerful man." She sashayed over to the bed. "I think your mistress needs to live in a nicer place."

"You'll have to earn it." He grabbed her hair and pulled her onto him.

Ten minutes later, the door burst open, and a cold breeze blew across her body. Martin froze in place, and Kaylee snapped her head toward the intruder. "Selene!"

Oh no! She'd forgotten to lock the door again. Kaylee scrambled out of the bed, reaching for a t-shirt.

"You little liar!" Selene lurched toward her, then stopped and stared at the bed, open-mouthed. "You're cheating with my father!"

For a moment, her girlfriend seemed too stunned to move.

"It's not like that," Kaylee whined. *So lame.*

"Shut up!"

Martin was sitting up now and grabbed a sheet to cover his junk. "Sorry, Selene. I thought you two broke up."

"She's the love of my life! How could you?"

Martin shook his head. "She's a junkie whore, and you deserve better."

The words stung so much, Kaylee cried out.

Selene rushed toward the bed, her words an outraged hiss. "You cheated on Mom and ran her off, and now you're screwing and slut shaming my girlfriend. No one will even miss you." She pulled a knife from her shoulder bag and lunged at her father.

Kaylee stared in horror as the blade plunged into his chest. *Oh my God!* She wanted to run from the sight. But she was naked and high and had nowhere to go. Her mind reeled.

The next five minutes were a blur as Selene vacillated between snapping orders and trying to soothe her.

"Get dressed and grab your things."

"You can't stay here. The police will blame you and lock you up."

"I'll take you someplace safe."

"Why aren't you packing? Oh hell. Just put your hood up and let's go."

They rushed out into the early morning light. In shock, Kaylee didn't care where they went, as long as they got away from all the blood.

CHAPTER 53

Hitch watched in disbelief as Selene broke down, mumbling about killing her father. The woman was obviously having a psychotic break, probably brought on by stress, guilt, and grief. Hitch wanted to pull out her phone and call the police, but she hesitated. Selene was big and dangerous and moved quickly. And they still needed access to Kaylee—if that was even her in the bedroom.

"Unlock the door," Conner pleaded. "Kaylee needs help."

"She's just detoxing. She'll be fine." Selene's eyes darted back and forth between them.

"You're not a pro—" Conner stopped mid-sentence.

Selene was walking away, moving casually into the living area.

Hitch started to follow, wondering if she could sneak a phone call. But she couldn't let Selene out of sight. The woman was a killer.

The sound of a foot slamming into hollow wood made her turn back. Conner raised his leg and smashed the door a second time. The lock hinge broke free from the frame, and the door swung open. Conner rushed in. Torn between responsibilities, Hitch spun back and went after the crazy woman.

Kaylee lay on a bed, covered in sweat, her thin nightgown clinging to her emaciated body. *Oh dear God.* Conner rushed to her. "Kaylee, it's Nate."

"Hey. You're here," she mumbled. "I need water. And aspirin."

A good sign. "I'll take you to a hospital."

"No. They'll give me drugs." Her words were hard to understand, but the meaning was clear. She wanted to stay clean and not take the anti-anxiety meds detox centers gave addicts to get them through the first week.

He noticed a pitcher of water on the nightstand and a plastic cup. He poured some water in the cup, helped her sit up, and held the cup to her mouth. After she'd swallowed half the water, he set the cup down and took both of her hands in his and squeezed. "I'm so happy to see you." His heart was bursting with joy.

She squeezed back. "Me too." Tears rolled down her face. "Selene won't let me out."

"The door's open now, and I'm taking you home."

When Hitch reached the living room, she heard the garage door opening. *No! Selene was fleeing.* Hitch spun toward the entry and bolted out of the house. Selene was backing out of the driveway in a white Tahoe. Hitch ran down the sidewalk to her car, wishing she'd parked closer.

She started the engine with one hand and grabbed her phone with the other. After calling 911, she pressed the accelerator. The Tahoe was disappearing down the street.

A call taker answered. "What is your emergency?"

"A woman who killed her father and abducted her friend is

driving away. The vehicle is a white Tahoe, and the suspect is tall, with dark hair."

"Is the victim in the car with her?"

"No. But this woman is dangerous. I'm following, but the police need to stop her."

"Do you have a license plate number?"

"No. But her name is Selene Gomez Ramsden."

"Got it. Do not get too close, do not interfere, and do not hang up."

But it was too late. Hitch was already ending the call. She wanted to reach out to Nelson. He couldn't do anything at this point to help her, but he needed to know what was happening.

She pressed her speed-dial icon for him, and he answered on the third ring. "Hey, what's up?"

"You're not going to believe this, but here goes." Hitch took a long breath to slow her pounding heart. Ahead of her, the Tahoe made a left turn on Carmel Valley Road. Hitch sped up, not wanting to lose her. "I'm in Del Mar, chasing Selene Ramsden in my car." A strange laugh escaped her body.

"What?"

"She killed her father. Yes, I mean Martin Ramsden, the DDA stabbed in the Marigold Motel. Kaylee Conner was hooking up with both of them. A very strange lover's triangle."

"No kidding?" He seemed too stunned to say more.

Hitch made the left turn as well, taking the corner too fast. "Whoa."

"What's going on?"

She didn't know. Ahead of her, the Tahoe had stopped and was turning around. "I have to focus. I just wanted you to know, in case you want to get out here and intercept Selene from the local police. Bye." She disconnected the call.

The Tahoe was coming back in her direction and speeding up. Hitch eased off the gas and looked for a place to pull off and turn around.

When she glanced back at the road, Selene had crossed the centerline and was heading straight at her. *Oh no!* Hitch jerked her wheel to the right and drove off into the marshes. The Tahoe slammed into the rear side of her car, spinning her in a circle. Hitch pressed the brake and held on for dear life. Thank God the airbag hadn't deployed. Her car came to a stop, and she glanced over at the Tahoe, fifty feet away. It had stopped too, and Selene was getting out.

What the hell? Was the crazy woman coming after her?

Hitch heard sirens in the distance. *Finally!* She locked her doors, then wondered if she should get out and run instead. She hated feeling trapped.

Selene charged at her car, brandishing a knife. Hitch wished she had a gun instead of a canister of mace. But the woman surprised her and shoved the knife into her front tire, then bolted back toward the Tahoe.

The wail of sirens was suddenly deafening. A patrol unit careened into the field and slammed to a stop near the Tahoe. Selene glanced wildly around. Officers jumped from the vehicle, weapons drawn.

Another patrol unit bounced into the field.

Hitch rolled down her window and yelled, "She has a knife!"

But nothing she said mattered anymore. After a moment of hesitation, Selene charged at the tall cop from the first car, her arm in the air.

No! That was suicide!

Shots rang out, and Selene dropped to the ground.

CHAPTER 54

Monday, late afternoon

Hitch heard footsteps and looked up from her desk. Victoria was approaching with a grim expression. Victoria stepped into Hitch's office and whispered, "Can you hang around until everyone is gone? There's something you have to see."

"Sure."

Victoria walked away, and Hitch went back to preparing for her next case, but she couldn't concentrate. Waiting for the verdict in her current trial was excruciating, and the office had been buzzing all day with the news about Ramsden being killed by his own daughter.

For a distraction, Hitch called Conner to see how Kaylee was doing, and he invited her over to see for herself.

"Uh, I don't know. When?" She was stalling.

"Tomorrow night."

It wasn't something she would normally do, but otherwise she would be sitting home by herself, worrying about the verdict. "All right. What time?"

"I have to check on something and get back to you." He hung up.

Another attorney left the office. The blinds were open, and from her desk Hitch could see all the cubicles except two. She stood and walked over to the window to check those two. Empty. She glanced around, then jotted down the names of the people who were still at their desks. She watched as the ADAs filed out, crossing each one off her list, then sharpening her pencil. Finally, the only two left were Victoria and Fisher. Hitch was anxious to leave, but she'd told Victoria she would wait, so she did.

Hitch stood to stretch and saw Fisher come out of his cubicle near Victoria's. Instead of heading toward the main door, he turned and approached Victoria. It was quiet enough in the office for Hitch to hear the conversation through her open door, and she was curious enough to pay attention.

"You're working late," Fisher commented.

Victoria glanced up. "I've got a frustrating case."

"What is it? Maybe I can help."

"Thanks, but I can handle it. I just need to work through some things and make a timeline. It's all good."

"I'm great at timelines."

"If I do it myself, it'll stick in my brain. But thanks." Victoria sounded a little impatient.

"Would you like me to keep you company?" Fisher pressed. "It's been a stressful day, with the news about Ramsden's daughter and all."

"I really appreciate it, but I work better alone. I'll see you tomorrow."

"I'm headed to the Prohibition Lounge. If you get done before eight, stop by. We can have a few drinks."

"Sorry, I won't be able to make it. Thanks again." Victoria pivoted back to her monitor.

Fisher finally got the hint and started toward the front door, glancing back at Victoria several times.

Shortly after the door closed behind him, Victoria hurried over to Hitch's office. "I thought he would never leave."

"He sure was flirting with you," Hitch said.

"I went out with him last night," Victoria blurted, sounding confessional.

"Are you serious?" Hitch realized how critical she'd sounded and backtracked. "I'm sorry. I didn't mean to be so harsh. Uh, I guess the heart wants what the heart wants."

"Eww." Victoria made a face. "I just wanted to pump him for information. I knew he would spill if I asked him. I just had to get him in the right setting."

"So you asked *him* out?"

"I just reminded Fisher I was around, and he did the rest. He's been flirting with me for months. He's a nice enough guy, just rather awkward." Victoria paused and lowered her voice. "I think Ramsden intimidated Fisher into working with him, then held it over his head once he got involved."

"In the corruption?"

She nodded.

"What makes you think that?"

"I looked at the cases with informants, and Fisher has had more than anyone else," Victoria explained. "And there's more. Come to my desk."

As they walked over, Victoria said, "I looked at the investigations for those cases, and outside funding was used for ninety-five percent."

"But that doesn't tell us who the investigator was."

Victoria sat down. "Watch." She clicked a few buttons on her keyboard. "If I follow the entries for the informants, it leads me to their data." She opened a new tab. "Here's Darius Williams, the guy we talked about earlier."

"What am I looking for?" Hitch struggled with the overload.

Victoria scrolled down. "See who the contact was for the DA's office?"

"Oscar Kolinder."

"Same with almost every single case." She brought up more documents for different informants, all with the same results.

"Wasn't that risky for Ramsden?" Hitch commented. "I mean, if all this information is in the records, anyone could find it, right?"

"Not unless they were looking for something specific. And even so, Ramsden could have claimed he used legitimate outside help. He had to employ someone they could relate to and trust." Victoria stopped and blinked rapidly. "It's so weird to be talking about our supervisor in the past tense. And to be building a case against a dead man."

"For me too," Hitch said. "But Ramsden wasn't the only one involved. And none of this proves he did anything illegal, unless we can establish that the informants were paid to lie or that they were planted to get information."

Victoria raised her eyebrows. "Fisher knows more than he's telling."

"What makes you think that?"

"He said some cryptic stuff about knowing more than he should and about Ramsden 'taking care of a snitch who got out of hand.'" Victoria used air quotes. "Fisher also claimed a 'two-time loser' would go down for it. The more Fisher drank, the more he talked." Victoria chuckled. "I kept dumping my vodka tonic in his glass when he wasn't looking. But then he got so wasted, he stopped making sense and couldn't communicate at all. I had to call him an Uber to get him home."

"Did he say anything else about the *snitch who got out of hand?*"

"No. But once when he went to the bar to get us another round, he left his phone on the table, and I checked his history. There were calls to Ramsden and—get this—Oscar Kolinder."

Not enough without the content, Hitch thought. "We all have calls to Ramsden, as well as to the investigators."

"Not like this. Fisher had dozens. I read a few text messages as well, but they were vague."

"Maybe you need to go out with him again."

"I don't think I could take it. In his head, we're already a couple. I can't encourage that." Victoria hesitated. "But if you want, I'll go with you to meet with him. If he realizes how much he already told me, he may be quicker to share other things."

"Call him and set it up."

"He's at the Prohibition if you want to do this now. I'll text him and let him know I'm coming. He'll wait for me."

Hitch had never been to this particular bar and was surprised by the almost-hidden entrance and the front door sign that read: *Law Office, Eddie O'Hare, Esq.* Inside, they headed down a long set of stairs to an underground lounge that looked like it was right out of the 1920s, including a long, tufted sofa bench along the brick wall. Old fashioned, lantern-like lamps glowed throughout the dark space, giving it a vintage, speakeasy vibe.

Hitch stopped for a moment to take it all in. Even the cocktail specials on the board had names like *Sidney Ellis Booty, Fat Guy in a Little Coat,* and *Banana Hammock.* Across from the long bench was a stage, which apparently featured big-band orchestras, but it was too early for anyone to be playing. Hitch made a mental note to come back one night for the music.

The lounge hadn't filled up yet, so she quickly spotted Fisher sitting at the far end of the counter. "There he is."

They hurried over. Fisher's face lit up when he saw Victoria, then lost its glow when he realized Hitch was with her.

"We need to talk," Victoria said. "Over there." She pointed toward the end of the bench, which had a small table and chairs. Fisher picked up his drink and silently followed as they headed over. "This will work," Victoria said. "It's nice and quiet here." She sat in one of the chairs, and Hitch took a seat on the bench, but Fisher remained standing.

"Why are you here?" he asked, glaring at Hitch.

"Sit down and I'll tell you."

Fisher looked back and forth between her and Victoria, then finally sat in a chair next to Victoria.

Across the table, Hitch locked eyes with Fisher. "There's a problem in the DA's office, and you're right in the middle of it."

"Whoa!" He held up his hands. "What are you talking about?"

"Ramsden and his snitches." Hitch waited a few seconds, but Fisher said nothing. So she pressed on. "We know he was trying to jack up his wins so he would look good in his run for district attorney."

"I don't know anything about that." Fisher fidgeted.

"Yes, you do." Hitch used her trial voice. "You had most of those informants on your cases. We have the data, and as far as we're concerned, you are just as culpable as Ramsden. In fact, now that Ramsden is dead, you look even more guilty and will likely get *all* the blame."

A moment of panic hit Fisher's eyes.

Hitch dialed up the pressure. "Oscar Kolinder has been arrested, and I'm sure he'll want to take a deal and tell us everything."

Fisher swallowed hard. "You know about Oscar."

"And the knife that killed Troy Burton." Hitch was fishing now, but she was on a roll and going for it.

"Look, I don't know who killed Burton." Fisher hesitated. "But as for the knife—" He stopped and shook his head.

"Tell us what you know."

He took a breath and pushed back. "Why should I?"

"Charles." Victoria put her hand on his shoulder. "This corruption scheme will hit the fan in the next day or two. You need to decide which side you're on. The sooner you come forward, the better chance you have of getting out of this without prison time."

"That's right," Hitch added. "You're a little fish." *Pun intended*, she thought, but didn't say. "Nobody will be interested in convicting you if you give us the information we need to shut this operation down. You know how it works. And we know there are others involved who are in higher positions. That's who everyone wants to convict."

Fisher looked at Victoria. She nodded. "Please tell us what you know, Charles."

He took a deep breath. "Kolinder did all of Ramsden's dirty work, and I suspected him when Burton was killed."

"Why?" Hitch demanded.

"I heard Kolinder and Ramsden talking about Burton wanting more money and threatening to expose them if they didn't pay. I think Burton found out more than he was supposed to know and tried to blackmail Ramsden." Fisher's voice cracked. "I heard Ramsden tell Kolinder to get rid of him. I wanted to believe that only meant to cut ties with him, then Burton turned up dead." Fisher sighed. "I still wasn't totally sure, but then I heard about the murder weapon."

Hitch's pulse jumped. "The knife that was used to kill Burton?"

"Yes."

"What about it?"

"It's how I got into this mess in the first place."

"Explain," Hitch said. "And we need details."

A long silence.

Finally, Fisher plunged in. "About ten months ago, I was in the booking area of the jail. I had questioned a witness, then stopped downstairs to say hello to a deputy friend I had dated." He looked sheepish for a moment. "While I was there, a patrol officer brought in a guy for possession of stolen goods. He'd been caught in some kind of scam involving a refund for tools."

He was talking about Conner. "Do you know the guy's name?" Hitch asked.

Fisher shook his head. "They took his property to bag it, like they always do. But then I saw the other booking deputy stick the guy's knife in his own pocket. I assumed he was just stealing it for himself. Cops take things from evidence lockers all the time." He shrugged and continued. "But I went to Ramsden the next morning to report it anyway. And while I was in his office—to my complete surprise—the deputy came in and laid the knife on Ramsden's desk. I knew it was the same knife because it had the same fancy initials engraved on it." Fisher rocked in his seat, a man with a lot of burden to get off his chest. He kept talking and staring at the wall behind her.

"Ramsden tried to cover it up, saying the knife was evidence that he needed to see, but I knew it was a lie, and he knew that I knew. We never talked about it after that, but he took me under his wing and saved several of my cases with last-minute informants. Eventually, I was in the thick of it." Fisher finally looked Hitch in the eyes. "When I told Ramsden I didn't want to use any more informants, he threatened that if I didn't cooperate, Kolinder would make sure it looked like the whole thing was on me. He said the operation was bigger than any of us."

"Geez, Fisher." Hitch shook her head. "Do you know who else is involved?"

"There's the deputy who got Ramsden whatever he wanted from the jail—inmates' cell phones, IDs, and of course, informant testimony."

"His name?" She hoped it wasn't Vargas.

"Darrell Yates."

"Who else do you know about?"

"The district attorney."

It felt like a body blow. "DA DeFazio is a part of the corruption?"

"Not exactly. He didn't find out about it until recently, but he wanted to shut it down and keep it under wraps, instead of exposing anyone."

Hitch understood the DA's concerns. "That would mean all the cases in which we used informants would have to be retried." But there was more to it. "Exposure would also mean acknowledging the corruption happened on his watch, and DeFazio would be done politically."

"Exactly." Fisher looked a little lost and pathetic.

"Are you willing to come forward?"

"I think I should."

"Good. I have just the guy you need to talk to." Hitch turned to Victoria. "Stay with him, please. I need to make a phone call." Hitch walked away, but kept them in her sight. She called Nelson, who answered on the first ring.

"Hi, beautiful."

Really? "Hey, I have information that will help resolve the Burton murder."

"Did your boy-toy confess?"

"Why are you back on Conner? I thought you were tailing Kolinder. Never mind. Can you meet me?"

"Now?"

"Yes."

"Where?"

"My office. No one will be there, and we need privacy."

"Now you're talkin'.."

"Just be there in ten minutes."

Hitch asked Victoria to ride with Fisher to make sure he didn't get cold feet, then headed out, arriving a few minutes before they did. Nelson drove up just as she exited her car.

"Thanks for coming," Hitch said.

"You call, I come."

"I have a witness who's about to show up. He said he'd talk, but it might be better if you wait here with me just in case he changes his mind."

Nelson squinted. "Who is this witness?"

Hitch gave a brief overview of Fisher's role.

"What does that have to do with the Burton murder?"

"He saw Deputy Yates take Conner's knife during the booking, then give it to Ramsden."

Nelson finally looked intrigued.

In her office, Fisher told his story again, giving even more detail, including information about how and where to find Kolinder. He seemed relieved when he finished, even though he knew Nelson had recorded it.

"Are you going to arrest me?" Fisher asked.

"No. But I expect you to stick around town."

"I'm not going anywhere, except home." Fisher got up to leave.

Nelson walked Victoria to her car, then returned. He stood next to Hitch's chair and smiled down at her.

"If all this checks out, your boy-toy will be off the hook."

"Please stop calling him that."

Nelson reached down and touched her cheek. "You look so stressed. Let's go back to my house, share a bottle of wine, and relax in the hot tub."

The offer was tempting. As she considered it, an image of her sharing the tub with Conner flashed across her mind. Hitch shook her head, trying to toss out the visual. *What was that about?*

Not important. But it had clarified that she really didn't want to start up with Nelson again. She couldn't trust him with other women. "I think it's best if we just stay friends."

CHAPTER 55

Tuesday morning

Conner took a seat in Leahy's office, curious about why he'd been summoned. At one point, he'd told the attorney he would do anything to repay him, so maybe Leahy was calling in a favor.

"Relax, Conner. This is good news." Leahy smiled. "With your permission, I'd like to file a motion to have your conviction overturned."

"Heck yes!" Conner grinned so widely his cheeks hurt. "That could change my life and open a lot of doors that have been closed to me."

"No guarantee," Leahy cautioned. "But with the evidence Hitch is collecting about Ramsden's corrupt informant scheme, I feel upbeat about our chances. If the court determines there was corruption, every case with an informant will be challenged. I want to be the first one filed."

"Awesome sauce!" Conner could not believe his good fortune. "I know I've said this a few times, but I want to repay you somehow. I can mow your lawn anytime. Or every time. Or run errands. Whatever you need."

"The court appointed me, so I'll get paid. Besides, as I've said before, all the payment I need from you is for you to live a good life, stay out of trouble, and pay it forward."

As he sauntered out of the office building, Conner realized he was whistling. He stopped long enough to laugh, then picked back up. A woman passing by glared at him, but he didn't care. He wanted to celebrate, but he had to work a lunch-hour dish-washing shift next. Even that thought didn't faze him. But he did need to find a better a job. He had a lot of debt to pay.

In the Mustang, he started the engine, wondering how he would kill an hour of time. His phone rang, and he glanced at it. *Nicole.* "Hey, sis. I'm headed for work soon. What's up?"

"Some strange news."

What now? But he wasn't worried. Nicole sounded happy.

"The parrot rescue just received an anonymous donation for two grand."

"Wow." Conner shut the engine back off. "That's great news. Maybe you can finally buy the solar panels you've wanted."

"I could. But I won't." She paused for effect. "The donor specifically indicated the money should be used to *pay my employee's debt.*"

"What? You don't have any—" Conner stopped. "Except me."

"And you owe Seth two grand. Or so he thinks."

"Holy pancakes!"

"I hate giving that thug the money," Nicole grumbled. "But I know you won't press charges against Seth, and he'll probably beat you up even worse next time. So how do we do this?"

Conner was too stunned to speak. Had Jerry Leahy made the donation? *No.* He didn't know about Seth. But Hitch did. "Uh, I'll call Seth and set it up. Thanks, Nicole. I love you."

"Nice to know, but I still expect you to clean cages."

"Always." Conner hung up so she wouldn't hear him choking back tears.

CHAPTER 56

Tuesday evening

As Conner stepped into the house, he heard Kaylee's laughter, a musical sound that lifted his heart. He turned to Nicole, who'd been out in the aviary and walked in with him. They both grinned. "She's back."

They headed for the kitchen where Gina and Kaylee were hugging and looking happy. Kaylee turned to them. "Gina showed up. A family reunion." She grinned. "I should've tried a sympathy play earlier."

"I know," Gina said, sounding guilty. "I should come down more often." She moved toward Conner and gave him a big hug, then hugged Nicole too. "But I'm staying nearly a week."

"We should have a picnic at La Jolla Shores like we used to," Conner suggested.

"I'd love that." Gina beamed.

They all turned to Kaylee.

"Oh yeah. I'm in." She let out a worried laugh. "But it'll have to be tomorrow. I'm headed to rehab soon. Serenity Acres is holding a spot for me."

Conner squeezed her hand. "Good decision. I'll support you in any way I can."

"Then be prepared to smuggle peanut M&Ms into the place on visitation days."

They all laughed, then went quiet. A detective had come to the house that morning and taken Kaylee's statement about the previous day's events. The brief episode had left her shaken, but the worst of the detox was over.

"Please come back and stay with me when you're out," Nicole said. "As your stand-in parent, I'd like another chance to properly launch you into the world."

"I messed up my first one pretty badly."

Conner wanted to talk about her journal entries, but he heard a car drive up. "That's probably Hitch. I'll get the door." She'd wanted to meet Kaylee, and his sister had agreed.

After Conner brought Hitch into the kitchen and made introductions, they all sat down and Nicole handed everyone a Pepsi. Conner raised his in a toast. "To new beginnings."

"I'll second that," Hitch said. "But I feel like I'm intruding on a family gathering, so I won't stay long. I just wanted to officially meet you, Kaylee."

"It's a pleasure." Kaylee smiled. "I appreciate what you did for me. And I'm sorry about Selene's craziness. I seem to be a magnet for intense people."

Conner gave Kaylee a shoulder hug. "You're young. You'll get better at figuring out who to hang out with and who to avoid." He laughed. "I'm still getting there myself. But my newest friends are both lawyers, so I think I'm moving in the right direction."

His sisters all laughed. Dang, it was good to have everyone together.

"And thanks for getting Jerry Leahy to help both of us," Kaylee said. "He's wonderful." He'd sat with Kaylee during her interview at the police station that morning.

"I wish I could be more involved, but as a prosecutor, I have to …" Hitch trailed off, then laughed. "I'm starting to think I'm on the wrong team."

"So how did your rape trial turn out?" Conner asked. "Did Evans get convicted?"

"I don't have a verdict yet." Hitch's expression was grim. "And it's been too long. I'm worried."

Kaylee cut in. "Evans? Do you by any chance mean Jason Evans?"

Hitch leaned forward intently. "Yes. Why? Do you know him?"

"He's my ex-boyfriend."

Conner snapped his head toward Kaylee. "He's Jay?"

"Yeah. And he raped me too."

They all turned to stare at her.

"I know, he was my boyfriend." Kaylee's expression tightened. "So no, I didn't report it. Our legal system seems to think that if you've ever willingly had sex with a man, he's entitled to more of it whenever he wants."

Hitch nodded. "I wish I could argue otherwise, but I'm afraid you're mostly right." She reached across the table and patted Kaylee's hand. "I'm sorry you went through that. Would you be willing to discuss it with me on the record? Not now, but when you're up for it?"

"I'll tell you right now." Kaylee pulled her shoulders back, sounding determined. "Selene was right about one thing. I have to start talking about all the crazy stuff I've been through."

"Are you sure?" Nicole looked worried. "Recovery is a process, and you have all the time you need."

"But I have to start somewhere. And if Jason is on trial for rape, Hitch needs to hear this."

"It's actually too late for—"

But Kaylee was already talking. "Jay had always been sexually aggressive, but then he started talking about acting out a rape fantasy. He wanted me to play the part, acting scared and saying no." Her voice caught, and she took a drink of Pepsi. "I said I wasn't into it, but I *might* go along *one time* so he could have the experience and move on."

Nicole stood. "I'll be back. But go ahead." She moved toward the hall.

Conner realized she was too upset to listen further. He didn't blame Nicole.

"There's not much more," Kaylee said. "Two nights later, Jay snuck up on me when I was in bed, held his hand over my mouth, and forced himself on me. I was totally not in the mood and feeling kinda sick, so I struggled and tried to tell him to stop. But that really psyched him up, and it got worse." A tear rolled down her face, but she kept it together. "When he did it a second time, I broke off with him."

"How old were you?" Hitch asked.

"I had just turned seventeen, and he knew it."

"If you're willing to testify, I'll look into pressing charges for rape," Hitch said. "The longer we keep him in jail, the better."

"I don't know." Kaylee shook her head. "Talking here is one thing. Being questioned in court is a whole different level of exposure."

Nicole, still hovering nearby, said, "Let's not talk about it anymore today."

Hitch stood. "I'm sorry to be so abrupt, but I need to do some legal research. Thank you for having me over." She waved and walked out.

Conner turned to Kaylee. "If the jury convicts him in Hitch's current case, you'll get some justice."

Nicole sat back down and started planning the menu for their picnic. "I'll make deviled eggs and Greek salad, your favorites."

Kaylee laughed, a shallow sound. "I'm all right, Nico. It feels good to get stuff out in the open."

Conner decided there would never be a better time. The subject concerned them all. "Kaylee, I'm sorry, but I read a page of your journal."

Her eyes went wide.

"I was worried about you and desperate to find you," Conner explained. "I suspected you were with your girlfriend, but no one seemed to know her name. So I looked for it, in a respectful way."

Kaylee was quiet for a long moment. "What page did you read?"

"The worst day of your life."

Tears filled her eyes. "I'm glad you know."

"Know what?" Nicole bit her lip with worry.

"Kaylee witnessed our parents' deaths," Conner said, before she could stop him. "And she feels guilty about what happened. We need to help her understand that it's not her fault."

Nicole's hand flew to her mouth, and tears welled in Gina's eyes.

"But I heard what Dad said about me," Kaylee whispered. "Right before he killed her."

The day replayed in Kaylee's mind, as it had so many times. But this time, she shared the memory out loud, tears rolling down her face. "I was in Mom's closet, trying on hats and scarves for one of those crazy plays I used to perform."

Kaylee heard her parents come into the bedroom and held as still as she could. Maybe they wouldn't stay long or even know she was there. Mom wouldn't be mad, but Dad didn't like kids in his bedroom.

"It's starting again, Ezra." Her mother's tone was both stern and sad, like when Kaylee misbehaved. "You have to get back on your medication."

"I'm fine, dammit. I'm just stressed." Her dad slammed something down. "I work my butt off all day at a job I hate, then I come home to a house full of noisy teenagers. Not to mention the damn birds."

"Lower your voice, please. I don't want the kids to hear you."

"They're all outside. Finally! If I have to listen to that sappy movie song one more time, I'll snap."

Kaylee curled into a ball in the corner. Dad was having another *hard time*, and it was her fault. She would never play her favorite song again. She wished she could promise him that to make him feel better, but she was too scared to interrupt them.

"Either take the medication or go somewhere else. I can't have you around the kids when you're like this."

Oh no. Her mother was using her *last warning* voice.

"Go somewhere else? This is my house, paid for with my money," Dad shouted. "Maybe you should take the kids and go."

For a minute, they were quiet, and Kaylee wondered if their fight was over. She inched toward the closet door and peeked out. Nope. They were standing there, staring at each other, so mad she could see it in the air.

"We were fine with just three," her dad shouted. "Why did you have to have one more? You knew I didn't want another kid. Hell, I was fine with two. A girl and a boy. But you can't seem to manage …"

Kaylee didn't hear the rest of what he said. *She was the problem! The "one more."* Dad was wonderful most of the time, and now she understood why he had these bad moments. She would run away, so he could be less stressed, and the rest of the family could be happy.

"Don't you dare blame me! You're the one who won't get a vasectomy!"

Kaylee had never heard her mother so upset. And Dad was furious too. He was pulling stuff out of a drawer and throwing it everywhere. What was he looking for?

And then she knew. *His gun.* She'd heard Conner talking about it years ago, but Kaylee had never seen it or wanted to.

Dad pointed the ugly black weapon at Mom. "Round up the kids and get out."

His voice was so cold, Kaylee shivered. *Please don't hurt her.*

"No."

"We can't live like this anymore. Something has to give."

"You need to give!"

"I said get out!" Dad stepped toward Mom.

Her mother didn't move.

"Never mind. You're too stupid and stubborn." He let out a strange laugh. "And I'm apparently crazy. The kids will be better off without both of us."

A deafening sound burst into Kaylee's ears. She covered them with her hands, but it didn't help. More shots rang out. Then her parents were on the floor, bleeding.

Conner wrapped his arms around Kaylee. "I'm so sorry you saw all that. And heard Dad say those things. He wasn't in his right mind that day."

Nicole reached for Kaylee's hands. "And none of it was your fault. Dad was off his meds. But he loved you most of all. He told me that on your fifth birthday."

Conner glanced at his older sister. "That must have been painful."

Nicole shrugged. "He was nuts."

Gina giggled. Which got Conner going too. Soon they were all laughing.

CHAPTER 57

Wednesday afternoon

At her desk, Hitch tried to distract herself by reading through the notes she'd created for the case against Ramsden. But she couldn't keep her mind on it. Her phone pinged with a text from the court clerk. The verdict was finally in for the Evans trial.

She grabbed the case file and headed over. On the way, she played the trial over in her head. She hadn't been this nervous about a verdict in a long time. In her experience, the longer juries took, the more likely they would side with the defense. She had hoped this one would take only a few hours, but it had been three days. The only real issue was consent. Since the deliberation had taken so long, that meant they had fought over who to believe. Hitch wondered how anyone could believe Evans after seeing how aroused he'd been on the witness stand as he talked about Heather struggling. The man was sick. And his treatment of Kaylee when she was a minor …

Hitch walked into the courtroom and took a seat at the counsel table. A few minutes later, Arroyo arrived, then the bailiff brought in the defendant. Next the jury filed in, taking their seats in the same exact spots. When everyone had settled into place, Judge Barenski entered, made a few preliminary remarks, then asked the foreman to stand. A fifty-something woman dressed in business attire stood. *A good sign for the prosecution,* Hitch thought, *to have a woman leader in a rape case.* The jury tended to select a foreperson who reflected the consensus of the group. Although sometimes, they just picked a pushy person who made themselves known. As for the woman's business attire, Hitch didn't know what to think. She remembered from *voir dire* that the foreperson had an executive position in a nationwide window company. Hopefully, she wasn't too businesslike, too black-and-white. That might make it hard for her to understand the complexities of consent—or maybe not. *Stop!* Hitch told herself. *Just wait for the decision.*

"Do you have a verdict?" the judge asked.

"Yes, Your Honor," the foreperson said.

"Please hand it to the bailiff."

The bailiff took the sheet of paper and carried it over to the judge, who read it to himself, without any change of expression. Then he handed it back to the bailiff, who gave it back to the foreperson.

Hitch tensed with anxiety.

"Please read the verdict."

"On Count 1, California Penal Code Section 487, Petty Theft, we find the defendant, Jason Evans, Not Guilty."

Hitch's face flushed with heat and her blood pressure rose. If they found him not guilty of the theft—when he had the laptop in his possession—how could they convict him on the burglary or rape charges? They believed Evans had been there with permission. And if he had permission, they must believe the sex was consensual too. *She had failed Heather. This guy was going to walk.*

"On Count 2, California Penal Code Section 459, Burglary, we find the defendant, Jason Evans, Guilty."

What? Hitch was confused. How could they think he didn't steal the laptop, yet believe he entered the house with the intent to commit a felony? *Unless the felony was the rape.* She held her breath as she listened to the last count.

"On Count 3, California Penal Code Section 261, Rape, we find the defendant, Jason Evans, Guilty."

Relief washed over Hitch, and Heather grabbed her hand and squeezed.

"The defendant is remanded into custody until sentencing," Judge Barenski said. He set a date for the sentencing hearing and dismissed the jury. "This trial is adjourned."

Hitch was shocked, but elated. She couldn't understand how they came to that verdict. As she stood, Heather hugged her and thanked her, then hurried out with a friend. Hitch took her time gathering up her files and realized everyone had left the courtroom except the bailiff.

On her way out, she stopped to talk. "I don't get it."

"You mean, how they let him off on the theft and convicted him of everything else?"

"It doesn't make sense."

"Yet it does. Remember, how they asked to have the officer's testimony read back to them? The one who found Heather's computer?"

"Yes."

"Jurors don't pay attention to me when I'm around, so I hear a lot of things I probably shouldn't. And I heard a couple of them talking. They believed Heather, and they believed the informant."

Hitch shuddered a little. She still wasn't convinced Palmer had told the truth, and if the whole Ramsden scheme was exposed, this case could be overturned as well.

"You okay?" the bailiff asked.

"Just a little overwhelmed."

He stepped closer and lowered his voice. "They also noticed the defendant's physical reaction when he testified and thought it was disgusting. They really wanted to convict him. But a few of the jurors thought that since he paid for it as he left, in his mind, it had been a consensual act of prostitution."

"So what convinced them otherwise?"

"His statement to the police that he bought the computer from Heather."

That testimony had seemed so inconsequential. "They decided he was paying for the computer when he threw down the money and not the sex?"

"Exactly."

So unexpected. "Evans seemed concerned about not being pegged as a thief, but his sexual perversions were okay." Hitch shook her head. "People are crazy."

"They sure are."

CHAPTER 58

Conner pulled into the restaurant's back lot, parked, and glanced at himself in the rearview mirror. He'd worn his only button-up shirt and a new pair of black work pants, the dressiest he'd been since renting a tux for prom night years ago. Hitch had called and offered to buy him dinner—to celebrate her victory and update him about Ramsden's scheme—and he wanted to look good. Actually he wanted to look more adult, like someone she could take seriously.

About what? He shook his head as he hurried inside. Hitch was way out of his league, and he would probably never see her again after this. In theory, that was a good thing. She was a prosecutor, someone who typically only showed up to cause him trouble.

She was already seated at a table near the side windows—and looking lovely in a light-blue sundress. He sat down across from her and said, "You look fabulous. That color suits you." He hoped it was still politically correct to compliment a woman.

"Thanks." She gave him a quick smile. "I already ordered a drink and an appetizer. The food here is great, but slow. And I don't want to …" She trailed off.

What? Spend all evening with him? Conner's mood plummeted. "As long as you didn't order calamari." He forced a smile.

"Onion rings. It's one of a few places that still serves them."

"My favorite."

A minute later, a food server set down a margarita and a basket of onion rings. Conner ordered a beer, and the young waitress asked, "Have you two decided on dinner?"

"Jalapeño burger," they said in unison.

"Awww. So cute." The food server glanced back and forth between them. "Did you guys meet on Match.com?"

Conner grinned, and Hitch blushed. "We're just friends," she said quickly.

At least she considered him a friend. When the server had walked away, Conner asked, "What's the update?"

"I have a couple. The first is that GRZ Properties is owned by Gorman, Ramsden, and Zimmers. And when Kaylee is up for it, I want to find out which one of the landlords was giving her free rent in exchange for sex with a minor."

Conner shook his head. "She won't want to testify about that either."

"But I need to know so our office can investigate. There might be other crimes."

"I'll ask her. What else?"

"You're off the hook for Troy Burton's murder."

"More great news for me." He would never ask her about the donated money, knowing it would make her uncomfortable.

Hitch leaned in and lowered her voice. "A PI named Oscar Kolinder has been arrested. He worked for Ramsden, and Fisher says Ramsden ordered the hit on Burton."

"No surprise." Conner took a bite of an onion ring. "I would never wish anyone dead, but the world is surely a better place without Martin Ramsden."

"Agreed. He corrupted Fisher too."

Hitch filled him in on the details of both murders, then Conner told her about Leahy's plan to get his conviction overturned. "Thanks for believing in me. And for helping find Kaylee."

"You helped me too. Without your effort to bring in Darius Williams, I might never have known who Ramsden was working with."

"We make a good team."

A half smile this time. "I wasn't optimistic in the beginning, but I enjoyed working with you."

A wild thought struck him, and it popped out of his mouth before he could stop it. "Maybe we should start our own investigative business."

Something sparked in Hitch's expression, but then she rolled her eyes and shook her head. "Don't get carried away."

About the Authors

L.J. Sellers and Teresa Burrell met at a mystery convention long ago and have remained great friends. Combined, they have 41 highly rated novels with 15 International Readers Favorite Awards, a UP Award, and a San Diego Best Mystery Award.

L.J. writes the Detective Jackson mysteries, and Teresa has authored twelve books in The Advocate series. In addition, Teresa is known for her work as a legal advocate for children, while L.J. writes comedy scripts and loves to zipline.

Dear Reader,

Would you like a free short story about one of the characters in Teresa Burrell's Advocate Series? If so, please visit teresaburrell.com and sign up for her mailing list. L.J. also offers a free short story when you sign up for her mailing list (ljsellers.com).

What did you think of NO CONSENT? We'd love to hear from you. Please email us at ConnerandHitch@gmail.com.

Thank you,

L.J. Sellers
Teresa Burrell

Novels by L.J. Sellers

Detective Jackson Mysteries

The Sex Club

Secrets to Die For

Thrilled to Death

Passions of the Dead

Dying for Justice

Liars, Cheaters & Thieves

Rules of Crime

Crimes of Memory

Deadly Bonds

Wrongful Death

Death Deserved

A Bitter Dying

A Crime of Hate

The Black Pill

Agent Dallas Thrillers

The Trigger

The Target

The Trap

Standalone Thrillers

Guilt Game

The Gender Experiment

Point of Control

The Baby Thief

The Gauntlet Assassin

The Lethal Effect

Novels by Teresa Burrell

The Advocate Series

The Advocate

The Advocate's Betrayal

The Advocate's Conviction

The Advocate's Dilemma

The Advocate's Ex Parte

The Advocate's Felony

The Advocate's Geocache

The Advocate's Homicides

The Advocate's Illusion

The Advocate's Justice

The Advocate's Killer

The Advocate's Labyrinth

The Tuper Mystery Series

The Advocate's Felony

(Book 6 of The Advocate Series)

Mason's Missing

Finding Frankie

Recovering Rita